The RACE

A Novel of Grit, Tactics, and the Tour de France

Also by this author:

The Pendulum's Path

For more information please visit www.DaveShields.com or write to author@DaveShields.com.

The RACE

A Novel of Grit, Tactics, and the Tour de France

by

Dave Shields

Three Story Press
Salt Lake City
2004

Copyright © 2004 by Dave Shields
Cover photo by Phil O'Connor
Author photo by Steve Horton
Cover design by Lightbourne

Library of Congress Number: 2004100328
ISBN #:   0-9748492-0-0

This is a work of fiction. Names, characters, places, and incidents are either products of the author's imagination or are used fictitiously.

Published by **Three Story Press**
5565 Merlyn Circle
Salt Lake City, UT 84117

Manufactured in the United States of America

To the incredible athletes who inspired this story ...

Prologue

Ben's pulse stabilized as he crested Boulder Mountain Pass, one of the most elevated outposts in this region of the southern Utah desert. The nearest human might be ten miles away. He quit pedaling his well-tuned Schwinn road bicycle as it gathered momentum along the asphalt strip that, sixty-five miles distant, would return him to Hanksville. He'd get home before noon. That ought to prove to Dad he had the maturity to take a trip like this, fourteen or not.

He removed his hands from the handlebars and intertwined his fingers behind his head, savoring the serenity of the high alpine setting. Looking skyward he inhaled a lung full of sweet November air. High above a pair of Golden Eagles soared in lazy circles.

Movement in the meadow to his left caught his eye. A mule deer raised its head and stared back, its giant rack spread heavenward. How had such a buck survived the recent hunt? The absence of early snow had surely helped. Frozen dirt, no tracks.

Ben returned his grip to the handlebars and his attention to cycling as the downhill grade increased. He shifted into his highest gear, navigating faster and faster through pine and aspen filled glades. Through cleated pedals and cinched toe straps he transferred maximum power to the wheels.

The road bent right, then a long, steep straightaway opened ahead. The moment he'd anticipated had finally arrived.

Already screaming down the hillside, he steeled himself to attempt the ultra high-speed aerodynamic posture he'd seen in his well-worn copy of *La Bicicletta Magazine*. He couldn't read much Italian, but the photos thrilled him. His favorite shot was on page thirty-four: a guy named Franco Chioccioli careening around a bend on the Col de la Croix de Fer during last year's Tour de France.

The background blurred, nothing but streaks.

Ben eased his hands to a position side by side against the stem. The minor front-wheel vibrations shuddered up his arms, magnified a hundredfold. Carefully he leaned his head forward and down until his cheeks touched the backs of his hands, just like Chioccioli in the picture.

His body sliced through the air like a wing. He felt lift, a diminished sense of the road. The bike seemed to discover a new gear as the orange dashed line on the pavement strobed by.

He lifted his gaze. Just ahead, folds in the asphalt revealed where a falling boulder must have damaged the pavement. Fear shot through him. In this posture the brakes were impossibly out of reach, and he couldn't steer. His muscles clenched. Dad's warning rang in his ears: "Just be careful, Benjamin."

He hit the bumps square on. The front wheel ricocheted left, right, and then hard left. He wrestled the handlebars, but holding so near the fulcrum he overcorrected. The bike twisted, forcing him to jerk the handlebars in the opposite direction. Terrain whizzed by faster and faster as the wobble increased.

Suddenly, the front wheel torqued perpendicular to the road and skidded sideways. The rear end of the bike catapulted over the handlebars. Ben launched, still fastened to the machine via cleated pedals and cinched toe straps.

He splayed his hands in front of him to break the fall. His cycling gloves shredded and his palms ripped open on impact. Bicycle and rider skipped off crushed-rock asphalt, shot toward the edge of the road, and skittered over the embankment.

Now he accelerated down the icy hillside. Branches, rocks, and thorns ripped his clothing and snagged his flesh as he sailed by. This couldn't be happening. Noise screamed in his ears—fingers on blackboards, gravel shaken in a shoebox, a radio squelching at maximum volume.

The silence that followed was worse than the noise. It was as if his world didn't exist anymore. No bicycle shops, no magazines, no red-faced dads.

He tasted coppery blood. Not dead.

He lay silently, wedged among the low-lying boughs of a pine tree. Thank God he hadn't slammed into the trunk.

Dad would be furious. He'd say, "I told you so, Benjamin. Nothing good can come of all this damn bicycle riding."

Ben swiveled to check his bike, then heard a crack as the branches gave way. He crashed to the ground.

He groaned. Breath came in torturous gasps. His left foot was still connected to its pedal. He reached out and grasped the toe cage release strap. It came free, but the cleat bar still held his foot in an awkward position. He contorted his leg to remove it. The motion triggered a pang up the left side of his body. As the leg fell limp he grasped his knee.

Then he stared at his beloved Schwinn. The wheels resembled battered garbage can lids. The handlebars were cocked sideways. The front forks bent at a right angle. Even the frame looked bowed.

He reached for the machine. Maybe he could twist it back into shape. Pain seared his spine.

He lay back and fought for calm. Coach Bill had taught Ben breathing exercises for composure before races. Now was a good time for that. He lay motionless on the forest floor … inhaling … exhaling … gradually accepting reality. The bike was a total loss. His body was not. Best to concentrate on saving what could be saved.

Stinging abrasions oozed blood, but he wasn't going to bleed to death. On the other hand, if he didn't find a way to get help, exposure might kill him. How long until someone sent a search party? Probably too long.

He held down panicked thoughts and tried to think clearly.

'It is what it is.' That's what Coach Bill would say. 'Now deal with it.'

A stressed diesel engine's throaty howl broke the silence. Clattering gears, then an even deeper pitch.

"Hey!" Ben called, but a stabbing gut pain stopped him. He grabbed his side and watched helplessly as the red cab of the semi chugged past, the long-haul driver oblivious to his plight.

The road seemed inconceivably distant—at least fifty yards up the steep hillside.

The left knee throbbed to his heartbeat, a hollow sensation. He looked down, noticing his left hand inadvertently covering the joint. He moved his fingers aside.

Beneath the shredded Lycra of his ankle-length cycling tights, a vee-shaped flap of skin dropped open. The kneecap gleamed white beside red muscle tissue and pink flesh. The knee resembled the cut-away anatomy drawing in his science textbook, except sprinkled with pine needles, bits of dirt, and shards of rock.

Ben stared at the wound. This couldn't be his leg. Something was wrong. He didn't feel the sort of pain a gash like that should produce. He closed the skin flap and re-covered the knee with his hand.

He exhaled. One thing for sure. He must get to the road. But, the knee. Was that really his knee?

He removed his hand and looked at the joint again. Shouldn't there be blood everywhere? This wound only oozed slightly, a dimestore special effect, just a puddle of crimson pooling where the flap hinged open.

But the exposed kneecap was in his leg. He could see that. Jersey, cycling tights, biking shoe. All his. Yep. That had to be his knee.

He lay back and stared at a passing cloud. It looked like a duck. A smaller duck followed. Then an even smaller one. The last one could have fit inside the beak of the mommy duck.

Ben laughed, accidentally causing his toes to wiggle.

Interesting. He could feel both feet moving in the tight leather cycling shoes. That meant he wasn't paralyzed.

He thought about the road again.

Ben writhed to a seated position just as a wave of exhaustion broke over him. He shook it off. Road.

He worked the tights higher on his left leg, gathering material at the knee. Then he used his thumbs to position the skin flap over the wound. He eased his makeshift pressure bandage over the joint. The spandex squeezed everything together. At the very least it would force the gash shut, probably prevent blood loss as well.

Now, the hard part. He drew a deep breath, then pivoted his

legs beneath him. Nerve impulses raced to his brain from every extremity.

He exhaled, long and loud.

How weird that the knee was the only body part that didn't really hurt—just a desensitized ache. Standing, though, was out of the question. He would claw his way along the ground.

He grasped a clump of dead grass and hauled himself forward. The movement triggered another multi-directional drag race for nerve impulses. Electrical signals collided in his brain, a demolition derby for neurons.

Ben clenched his teeth. Getting it over with was preferable to drawing it out. He drew his good leg up and pushed forward again, and again.

Soon his fingers became numb from scratching into the icy ground. He blew warm air into his fists but avoided glancing at the wounded palms. After a moment he resumed the climb. Pushing ... pulling ... inching forward.

Nearly an hour later after two more warming stops, he dragged himself onto the asphalt shoulder of the road. He lay there, thirsty and panting. Why hadn't he grabbed his water bottle? There it sat, still wedged in its cage on the ruined bicycle. Then his vision narrowed and blackened.

* * *

A metallic whine interrupted Ben's fantasy of cycling in the Tour de France. He fought to remain asleep. He tried to continue the journey, but reality had already intruded. The dream couldn't be retrieved.

Reluctantly, he opened his eyes. A rusty blue Datsun sports car bore down on him from uphill. Ben raised his left arm, but the car sped by.

He dropped his hand weakly as silence returned to the forest. They hadn't seen him.

Then, from below, came a high-pitched sound like a wind up toy. He wrenched his neck to look.

Here came the Datsun, rear end first. It stopped several yards away. As a man climbed from the driver's seat a woman leaned out the passenger side window.

"See there, Floyd! I told you I saw something!"

Ben cried. He would live to bike this road again.

Chapter One

Ben Barnes adjusted his position on his Decathlon racing bicycle as he clung to the open window of the Team Banque Fédérale Peugeot station wagon. Ten years had passed since the accident everyone had assumed would end his cycling dreams. Now here he was in the midst of the moment he'd designed his entire life around. Automobile and cyclist jounced through eastern France at forty-five kilometers an hour. The car had so many bicycles on its roof, it looked capable of travel if flipped over.

This year's Tour de France had already covered nearly 1000 miles in just eight and a half days of racing. After the cyclists completed the current stage, there were nearly 1400 miles and twelve more stages to go.

The route eased over a gentle ridgeline, and a fertile valley opened beyond. A white marble chateau stood on a central knoll, presiding over a fairytale scene. Hedgerows delineated rhombuses, rectangles, and other geometric splotches of patchwork farmland, some golden with sun-dried hay, others green with ripening corn. Quaint farmhouses were scattered about like garnish on a gourmet meal.

Pierre, the Team Directeur Sportif, steered the car with his right hand while he tucked a final water bottle into Ben's back pocket. Counting those in his rack and the ones stuffed down his jersey Ben carried nine, plus a handful of energy bars and gels.

As a domestique, a team grunt, refreshing the squad on sweltering days like this was a constant battle. Hopefully he carried enough for a moment of recovery before dropping back to the team car to repeat the process.

Ben glanced back toward Fritz, the wiry little mechanic who was leaning out of the car's rear window adjusting Ben's rear derailleur.

"*Voila!*" Fritz cried, his right thumb raised. The Frenchman's jet-black moustache wiggled in the wind as he shimmied back into the car.

Pierre reached toward Ben's right cheek. He ripped away a lock of hair that had become embedded in the freshly scabbed road rash, the result of the minor crash that had necessitated the derailleur work.

Ben flinched.

"*Vous devez le maintenir proprement,*" Le Directeur Sportif said.

Ben no longer needed to mentally translate the words to English and back to respond. "My wound is clean."

"With hair in it?" The ever-present Gitane cigarette dangled from the left corner of Pierre's mouth. The glowing tip looked ready to ignite his goatee. "You should cut off those long, blonde locks. They aren't making you any faster."

"Bridgette loves my hair," Ben said.

"Oy. My niece? She's not making you faster, either. Get rid of her, too."

Ben looked away. He wished Bridgette could be here today. This weekend she would visit the race at the Riviera.

"I'm serious," Pierre added.

"You don't run my life off the road."

Pierre scowled. "*Pardon?* You should beg me to. You're a replaceable commodity, Benjamin, a domestique, and not even among the best of those."

"That's not true and you know it."

"You should watch your tongue. Once your potential appeared great, but you're nothing now. If you don't want your career extinguished entirely, you had best play by my rules because at this point, 'ordinary' would be a step up. Believe me, Benjamin, if you truly want …"

Ben gritted his teeth as Pierre's rant continued. The words hurt because they contained truth. He wasn't ordinary, but neither had he fulfilled his capability. He had lost something along the way—some edge, some intangible. Maybe it had been jarred loose during grueling training rides over rain-soaked Belgian cobbles. Perhaps it had been left behind while navigating team politics. Possibly he had misplaced it in an effort to fit into a foreign culture. Whatever it was and wherever it had disappeared, he no longer expected to get it back.

Pierre ranted on. "… miserable. Now haul your butt back up front and get that food and water to the men who earn your paycheck or I will …"

It had become obvious that Banque Fédérale had included Ben, the lone foreigner on their Tour roster, as a sacrificial lamb. Assign all the grunt work to just one guy in the first week of the race, and the rest of the team will enter the second week nice and fresh. Who cared if an inconsequential team member falls by the wayside somewhere along course? Maybe someone at Banque Fédérale meant it as a way to get back at him. That was possible, though publicly everyone claimed forgiveness.

Ben couldn't worry about it now. The important thing was his position on this squad put him in the greatest bicycle race in the world, the journey he'd dreamed of for a decade. He'd gladly accept a double workload for the experience. Still, did that oblige him to listen to these lectures?

Pierre's bald round head had reddened with rage. Between quick glances at the road ahead Le Directeur glared at Ben, as if impatient for an answer.

Ben tried to guess what was expected of him. He recalled 'Bridgette' as the last word that had crossed Le Directeur's lips.

"We're in love," Ben said.

Pierre's face turned a deeper shade of crimson.

Ben glanced at Fritz. The mechanic's left arm dangled out the window and he flipped his hand forward, shooing his American friend up-road.

Ben nodded, let go of the vehicle, and started pedaling on his own. He quickly lost ground having forgotten he'd shifted to his largest rear cog to allow the mechanic to do his work.

Pierre laughed hysterically.

Ben clicked to a higher gear. The pedal resistance increased. Soon he was abreast of the team car again.

"Hey Fritzy! Calibration's perfect," Ben yelled.

"But, of course," the mechanic answered.

"*Il faut bosser!* Enough chit chat," Pierre warned. "Save your breath and get back to work."

Ben smiled, touched a finger to his helmet, and then accelerated. "*Salut.*"

Clear of the tobacco-filled car, the scent of fresh cut hay filled his nostrils. Round golden bales, taller than a man, sat at regular intervals drying in a nearby field. On the opposite side of the road green vines climbed the trellises of a small vineyard. Ben shoved thoughts of wine and leisure from his mind. As gruff as Pierre's delivery could be, he was right to emphasize the task ahead.

Ben stood on his pedals. The bicycle leaped forward like an anxious stallion. Damn, this was a responsive machine—hi-tech in the extreme. The frame was incredibly stiff while the components were light. The combination resulted in such an immediate and efficient transfer of energy to the wheels it often stunned him. At the same time, that rigidity resulted in a bone-jarring ride when the terrain was uneven. Ben felt even the tiniest bump in the road.

Wind whipped his hair. Something about rising from the saddle to accelerate always felt liberating. The fluid rhythm of lifting up on the pedals while pulling down on the handlebars made him one with his machine, something far beyond the metallic union of his cleats and pedals. The bicycle became an extension of his body. He felt incredibly strong, despite all the extra weight he carried at this moment. In fact, he'd never been so fit, at least from a physical standpoint.

He'd come to Europe dreaming of taking international cycling by storm, the same way he had with racing in The States. It sure hadn't turned out that way.

In his first European race, his over-aggressive lead-out in the final sprint cost his teammate's victory. The director scolded him and cautioned him to ride within the team concept, or not to ride at all.

Ben continued making similar mistakes, preferring tactics based on gut instinct to those dictated by the men in charge. In his early days on the circuit, no matter how much he admired the tactical complications borne of the discipline of road cycling, he couldn't muster the patience to wait for his adversaries to lay their cards on the table before he played his.

What a different rider he'd become. Getting thrown off his team had really opened his eyes. Nowadays, after a year's suspension that knocked him out of European racing, and another year as low man on the totem pole for Banque Fédérale, he could hardly imagine what it would feel like to behave so independently, so selfishly. He'd been broken, and in a strange way he was proud of that.

Doing a domestique's job right demanded that he leave the thinking to others—following orders automatically. No team could function at its highest level unless every member both excelled at his particular job and stayed out of the way of the other members who were doing theirs. This was true of everyone from the owner to the soigneurs, the omnipresent team aids who could be counted on to provide anything from a breath mint to a full-body massage. Strategy, as much as he loved thinking about it, was not Ben's job. He'd learned to keep his tactical ideas to himself.

It was hard to back down when Pierre attacked, but Ben now took great pride in his role. Those close to him, even Pierre, regardless of what he said, knew Ben did his job right. So what if he still second-guessed his superiors? As long as he didn't share those thoughts, no one would be the wiser.

"*Ich habe einen flachen Gummireifen!*"

Ben strained to pick up pieces of conversation as he fought to pass the rival team's cars.

"*Wir erhalten Ihnen Reserven.*"

Something about a flat tire. As usual, the chatter was partly undecipherable, partly unimportant. Still, the chance of hearing something that might benefit Banque Fédérale always existed so he'd keep his ears cocked.

Splotchy shadow on the pavement ahead grabbed his attention. He wove through a messy stretch of potholes.

These roads.

He smiled at his good fortune at getting through smoothly only a fraction of an instant before his rear wheel slipped into the last divot and sent a jolt through the bike frame. His teeth clacked together, clipping his tongue.

"Damn!"

An automobile behind him beeped its singsong horn. It trilled its way up to a high note, then back down. Why a driver paid to follow bicycles would harass athletes for reacting to road conditions he couldn't imagine.

The horn trilled again. The little tune must have been some engineer's effort to soften the impact of the nearly constant use that came when spectators clogged the course or finishing chutes neared, but it only put Ben on edge, more anxious than ever to rejoin the cyclists ahead.

Increasing his effort, he clawed his way through the remainder of the vehicular caravan. One by one he overtook the colorful assemblage of team cars, officials' motorcycles, and press vehicles. Still, at close to maximum effort, he barely made headway in relation to the moving mass. He bore down and powered forward.

A motorcycle veered in front of him. He swerved, feeling serious and tense.

To the left he glimpsed local villagers in grotesque papier-mâché masks dancing on the back of a flat bed lorry. Behind them, mounted to the cab of the truck, a sign proclaimed, "*Bienvenue au Tour de France.*"

Ben blew out air in a burst, an inadvertent quasi-chuckle. The party at the roadside reminded him of the immensity of this exploit, the world's largest annual sporting event by nearly any measure, and the circus atmosphere that surrounded it.

He pushed hard for a few more revolutions and caught the peloton, the main platoon of riders.

Almost immediately the pack of cyclists enveloped him. Swaths of color, jerseys covered with logos and sponsor names, surged forward and back. Of those losing ground, some were headed for a rendezvous with their team cars; others were struggling to avoid being shelled off the back, dropped at the side of the road like the spent part of a nut and left to struggle to the finish alone.

Ben moved to a more upright, less aerodynamic posture, and poised his fingers over the brakes. In the heart of the peloton wind resistance became minimal. At times he even felt a breeze at his back. Within the pack Ben experienced one-third less resistance than when he plowed through the air on his own. This is how it must feel to be one starling in a massive flock—independent, yet defined by the actions of a bigger whole.

Pedaling was different within the group, not the constant grind characteristic of a lone cyclist. He turned the cranks fast and furious one moment, then tapped the brakes the next. Often he glided for extended periods, cautiously eyeing the gap between his front tire and the rear wheel of the man ahead.

The noises outside this group all but disappeared, lost in the swirling whitewater of the massive pack. Now, three main sounds, the percussion of lubricated metal on metal, the bass riff of nearly 400 rubber tires on asphalt, and the rhythm of half that many men conversing in competing languages gave the peloton a unique musical quality.

The odor of sweat hit hard as he navigated through the competing mass. The sweet crops surrounding the road may as well not exist for how completely inaccessible they were to every sense but sight. The pace had been high all day, and the athletes were at their limit. In the intense heat their bodies retained moisture less effectively than a potted plant swaying in a stiff breeze.

While only one in nineteen riders wore the same Banque Fédérale purple and green as Ben, he felt close to every one of them. Well, almost every one. Within this pack of 168 remaining riders lurked Kyle Smith, his greatest enemy. They'd avoided one another so far. Hopefully they would continue to do so.

Tour veterans said the kinship Ben now felt paled in comparison to what he'd experience if he survived through the Alps and the Pyrenees, then crossed the finish line in Paris. Ben bought that. Some years, so epic was the journey, less than half the riders made it to the end. Crossing that line in sight of the Eiffel Tower and Arc de Triomphe must be almost otherworldly. Abandoning the race somewhere between here and there would devastate him.

A wave of outstretched right arms accompanied by yells of "*A droite*" rippled down the peloton, cyclists signaling those who followed that the route would soon take a sharp turn.

The body of riders drifted to the left hand shoulder of the road, giving themselves the maximum radius possible to complete the turn. Then bicycles dove toward the corner, one after another.

Two cyclists ahead touched, handlebar to handlebar, pedal to pedal.

"Hold your line!"

"*¡No puedo! ¡Potholes!*"

Ben touched his brakes and drifted wide, hoping he could avoid running over bodies and bicycles ahead of him if riders went down.

The bikes separated. The sigh of relief that metal components hadn't intermeshed swished through the rear of the pack. Such mistakes could cause lightning-fast chain reactions. That's why the back end of the peloton was the most dangerous position.

Ben and the riders near him sprinted to make up the gap that had suddenly formed between riders. A moment later, too intent on what might come next, the athletes had forgotten the exchange entirely.

"*Wo ist meine Mannschaft Führer?*"

"Out of my way!"

"*Agua!*"

No one man talked much, and there were long periods where none talked at all. In this game, breath was too precious to waste on unnecessary words. Still, there were times it became a cacophony of human voices, a United Nations debate on skinny tires, minus the decorum. A congregation unlike any other, and one that Ben loved. Here in the main body of riders, wheel-to-wheel with the world's strongest cyclists, he felt above all else a sense of brotherhood and common purpose.

Ben made his way toward his team. For the last hour they'd been working hard at the front of the peloton, driving the pace. Ben continued to overtake riders, both left and right.

The route became trickier as it rushed into the village of Lagnieu. Enthusiastic cheers echoed down the narrow stucco corridors.

Even once Ben caught sight of his teammates at the front of the peloton, he had a hard job to actually catch up. Banque Fédérale rode in a single file line protecting Thierry Depardieu's "maillot jaune," the yellow jersey that designated him as the current overall race leader, the rider with the fastest cumulative time through the first eight stages of the Tour.

The General Classification, or GC, was the scoreboard for the Tour de France. The fastest rider and his cumulative time, currently Thierry Depardieu at 39:27.22, were listed at the top. Almost forty hours pedaling in just eight days. In the next column it showed he was zero seconds behind the lead.

For trailing riders, GC listed only their names and how far out of the lead they stood. Second place was Gunter von Reinholdt, twenty-nine seconds back. Kyle Smith was third, off the pace by one minute and twenty-three seconds. And so on down the list. Ben held a respectable thirty-third position, five minutes and forty-three seconds behind Thierry.

Ben worked to catch his team, but the pace kept increasing. Cyclists surged up either side of the road, testing whether or not they could escape off the front. Usually a short stint in the wind convinced them the effort wasn't worth it, and they were reabsorbed by the group. As a result, the leading edge of the peloton resembled flash floodwaters filling a dry river basin, surging here, slowing to fill a depression there, tumbling rapidly over boulders in another area.

Banque Fédérale meant to keep Thierry's lead safe by neutralizing all these attacks. Team members had to keep the pace high enough to prevent anyone from surging off the front, but they didn't want to go any faster than they must and stress the team unnecessarily. Tactically, Banque Fédérale found itself in a lousy position. They were working to defend the jersey while their most dangerous competitors bided time in the pack.

The Alps, already evidenced by the growing hills and cliffs on either side of the Rhône River valley through which they traveled, were only a day ahead now. Those enormous obstacles haunted every rider's thoughts.

Tomorrow's race, this year's first mountain stage, would ascend four peaks along a 240-kilometer ribbon of road—150 miles of treacherous terrain. The final three pinnacles in tomorrow's contest were so steep and long they exceeded professional cycling's classification system. Such climbs were referred to as "*hors' de catégorie*," out of category.

Before ascending one of these mountains in race conditions Ben had thought such a designation sounded a bit extreme—almost like calling the mountain unclimbable. Having since experienced such rides, he now considered the name apt. More than once while en route on such a climb, he'd cursed the road builders and questioned their sanity.

Tomorrow's torture culminated on the legendary Alpe d' Huez, *les lieux sacrés'*, a sacred place with mythical status. The impending trek had even the strongest climbing specialists whispering with trepidation. According to some, Stage Ten would be the most demanding single stage ever included in The Tour.

Any race historian could disprove that. In the early years riders pedaled primitive bikes over dirt cart paths meandering through these same hills. Worse yet, they weren't allowed to accept any assistance at all. Unlike today when a cyclist could retreat to the team car for a repair on the fly. A rider was once disqualified for allowing a blacksmith to work the bellows as he welded his own shattered front fork following a particularly harrowing descent. Still, tomorrow would be a severe test.

Ben pulled alongside purple and green clad riders and began handing out bottles. "*De l' eau.*"

Thierry Depardieu, his yellow jersey practically emanating heat as if powered by the sun, moved beside him. Ben looked over at the team leader. The maillot jaune fit the guy like no one else. In any other color Thierry looked uncomfortable, while in yellow he exuded charisma.

In comparison, the pretenders who'd worn the leader's jersey for the first few stages had appeared almost apologetic, as if they knew as long as King Thierry reigned over the peloton the maillot jaune was only borrowed.

"*Merci,*" said Thierry as he slid a plastic bottle into his water cage. His close-cropped prematurely graying hair and rugged countenance spoke of someone who wasn't obsessed with appearance. A scar extended from his upper lip to just below his left eye.

Thierry held out his hand. For a moment, Ben interpreted it as a gesture of acceptance. He nearly slapped it, but then realized Thierry wanted food. Ben handed him an energy bar and a gel.

This Tour de France was the first event where Thierry and Ben had ever participated as teammates. That probably meant little to the team leader, but it meant everything to Ben. He could hardly believe he now rode side by side with his hero in the greatest race on earth. Until now Banque Fédérale leadership had always assigned them different races. Though they'd had brief conversations, Ben wondered whether they'd ever get the chance to really clear the air.

Thierry dropped the bar into his jersey's back pocket, then ripped the gel open with his teeth. He squirted the gooey contents into his mouth, grabbed his water bottle backhanded and flicked it forward so that it rolled over the backside of his fingers and settled pointing into his mouth.

Thierry winked, and only then did Ben realize he'd been gaping at the yellow clad rider. He tried to dismiss his awe by turning his expression into a friendly smile.

Movement on the left hand side of the road caught Ben's eye.

"*Escapada!*"

"*Comece sua roda.*"

"*Allez!*"

"*Cójalo!*"

"Go Mate! Go!"

"*Interferiscalo!*"

Riders yelled out in a half-dozen more languages. A cyclist in a red Megatronics jersey streaked up the road. Ben focused on the number 31. Even without the jersey number, the curly black hair sticking out from under the helmet gave him away. Kyle Smith!

Ben's blood boiled.

The yelling continued as a flurry of bright jerseys scrambled toward Kyle's rear wheel, each man wanting to take advantage of the attack by tucking into the lead rider's draft and gaining distance on the field while still expending as little effort as possible.

In seconds, the opportunity to join the breakaway evaporated. Banque Fédérale was one of the teams that didn't react quickly enough.

Ben, his jersey still partly weighed down with water bottles, watched the half dozen riders disappear around a bend in the road fifty meters ahead. He looked at Thierry. "Don't we need representation?"

His team leader turned to him with a relaxed expression. "Let them go. Gunter is still in the peloton."

Ben didn't need Thierry to explain his thinking. Gunter von Reinholdt was widely regarded as Thierry's primary challenger in this race. If Thierry spent unnecessary energy chasing down lesser rivals like Kyle, Gunter would make him pay for it later.

Besides, with well over half of today's stage behind them, the sprinters' teams might feel they had enough at stake to take over the task of leading the pack. By hanging back, Thierry hoped to force them to assume the work of driving the peloton. Thierry would prefer to let his competitors lead the chase down the final stretch, saving his team's energy for tomorrow.

Ben respected the team leader's cool way of looking at things. Still, gut instinct said Banque Fédérale would be better off with a member in the break. Kyle needed to gain only a minute and twenty-three seconds to steal the maillot jaune.

The team radio crackled to life. "Benjamin, can you bridge up and cover that group?"

All nine team members wore one of the communication devices. They each carried a tiny receiver in a jersey pocket. A wire ran through a hole in the jersey, up the chest and neck, and into the ear. A microphone pickup was attached to the wire at mouth level and a transmission button was attached beneath the jersey at chest level.

The request caught Ben off-guard. Not only was it a surprise to be tabbed by Pierre for a tactical role, but hadn't he just struggled forward with the water to keep his teammates fresh for an occasion like this? His throat caught. He squeezed the transmission button. "*Moi?*"

"Television is on the breakaway now. They look strong. Seven men, no two from the same team. None dangerous to our lead except Kyle Smith. He's down a minute and three quarters in the GC. If he gains he might become a problem. Now Benjamin, answer me. Do you have the strength?"

"I do." What irony. He'd been carefully avoiding that phrase in his personal life.

Ben decided this occasion was worth wasting precious breath, just to be clear on his task. "You're betting Kyle won't want to pull me to a stage win in his effort to grab the maillot jaune, right?"

"Don't overcomplicate. I handle strategy, you ride. When you get there simply force him to drag you. Are we clear? Never take a turn at the front. We'll see how he likes that."

"I know how to make a nuisance of myself."

"How… American of you," came Pierre's crackling reply.

Ben wished he could take his words back.

Thierry rolled his eyes. "Don't worry about him. Just go! If you catch that group and sit on until the sprint, you just might win the stage. I'm pulling for you."

The thought energized Ben further. He handed off supplies to his teammates Albert and Rikard as quickly as possible.

"Benjamin," Le Directeur's voice broke in again, "If you strand yourself in no man's land I'll be extremely put out. *Comprenez?*"

"*Oui.*"

Thierry smiled. "Go!"

Ben nodded. Adrenaline surged into his veins. At last, an opportunity to fight!

Chapter Two

Two quick clicks of the shift lever and Ben was in high gear. The pedal resistance increased. He leaned forward, out of the saddle, and rocked the bicycle side to side, pumping down with one leg while lifting with the other. The bike leaped from the pack. Ben's thigh and calf muscles caught fire as he went anaerobic, passing the point where fresh oxygen can no longer be delivered to the muscles quickly enough to maintain long-term effort. He dug deeper, ignoring the pain, and opened a gap.

He glanced back. Three chase cyclists from three different teams clawed their way forward. He slowed to let them move into his draft. The four of them fell into paceline like a practiced squad, working as one to slice through the resistant air. As lead man, he initially took the brunt of the wind. When he tired he moved aside and drifted toward the rear.

As the members of his breakaway group slowly passed him, Ben inspected them. He felt a wave of satisfaction at the small group's random, but fortunate, makeup. These were all riders with solid reputations. Their contorted expressions as they fought forward spoke of obvious desire.

Once behind the last man, Ben eased into the wind shadow. Now he could relax a bit as he worked his way back up the line. Each time he pulled into the lead position he pushed harder, increasing the speed. Using this cyclical pattern to attack the wind in an organized fashion the breakaway group accelerated to and maintained speeds a lone rider couldn't possibly match. Ben's cyclometer, the small computer readout mounted in the center of his handlebars, read fifty-two kilometers per hour.

Of the three other breakaway members, he knew the Italian, Luigi Figanaro, best. Ben liked him a lot, but what would Luigi gain in a move like this? Ben raised an eyebrow.

"I smell," Luigi said, tapping his monstrous nose, "trouble ahead." He chuckled. "I will enjoy to see."

Ben grinned. Some observers looked forward to a reunion between himself and Kyle. The media had certainly played it up and so had many fans. So far, Ben had dodged it. While Kyle strutted like a peacock for fans and media, Ben stayed unobtrusive, nose to the grindstone. But Luigi was right. Pushed together in a small group, there'd be trouble ahead. Given Ben's assigned task, this could get messy.

"Control your focus." The words of Ben's long time mentor, Coach Bill, played in his mind. "In any bicycle race there are three key mental states. Sometimes you need to pay riveted attention to what's going on around you. Other times you should allow your thoughts to wander to rest your mind. And once in a while you must focus on the past to increase motivation. Master your mind. Knowing what to do when is the mark of a champion."

Ben had long ago learned that working his way up the tail end of a rotating paceline created a good interval for contemplation. Now was the time to remind himself why Kyle Smith was a man he must thwart.

* * *

Ben first met Kyle three years earlier. In the Oregon native's gleaming green eyes, Ben immediately sensed the desire he coveted in teammates and feared in rivals.

"So you're the new guy? Welcome aboard," Ben said, extending his hand.

"Not much newer than you." Kyle ignored both the greeting and the handshake. He spoke in an unexpectedly deep voice, almost a rumble. The cadence had an unhurried quality. "You've been professional less than a year, right?"

"Yep, but I came up through Megatronics amateur ranks for two years before that, so I already knew the guys. It's much more intense as a pro, though. You'll put in over 20,000 miles in the next twelve months, race a hundred times, and spend 330 plus days in the saddle." He blew out a long stream of air. "If you're anything like me, a couple of months down the road you'll look back on your first day in the business and you won't believe the change."

"Is that right?"

"Yeah. Mentally, physically, emotionally, even spiritually. I can't think of an area where I haven't improved."

Kyle looked him over skeptically. "Sounds like sissy stuff."

"Suit yourself," Ben said, dropping onto the waiting room couch. No need to argue. Kyle was sure to think differently as he dragged himself up hills on their training rides. Ben picked up a magazine and leafed through it.

"If I need your advice I'll ask for it," Kyle added.

"And I won't withhold it just because you're too proud to let someone show you the ropes on your first day."

Kyle's brow creased. "Ropes? I'm here to ride a bike."

Ben laughed. "Aren't we all?" Nice sense of humor.

"Maybe you should tell me about these ropes." Kyle forced a chuckle.

A door opened and a pretty clinician with shimmering auburn hair stepped into the lobby. "*Bonjour,* gentlemen."

Ben stood. Both men turned to face her.

The shapely young woman smiled, her blue eyes sparkling.

Kyle stepped forward. He lifted her suntanned hand and pressed his lips to it. "I'm Kyle Smith. What's your name?"

The nurse blushed. "I'm Bridgette. The director warned me you were a ladies' man. Apparently it's true."

"There's much more to hear," Kyle said.

"Maybe some other time. I prefer the strong, silent type." She stepped toward Ben. "*Salut Minet.*" Then she kissed him on the lips.

Kyle's face reddened in humiliation … or anger.

Ben wished she hadn't kissed him in front of Kyle, but maybe it was her way of making sure he understood she was off the market.

"Are you boys ready for your VO2 tests?" she asked, speaking of the test that measured an individual's ability to consume oxygen. Athletes able to deliver higher quantities to their muscle tissue where it could be used to burn fuel had obvious advantages over those with lower capacities.

Ben slapped his new teammate on the shoulder. "We're headed for the ropes. Try not to hang yourself."

The three stepped into the next room, and both men climbed aboard stationary bicycles. They began a gradual warm-up, pedaling with low resistance as they adjusted the straps on their oxygen masks. Bridgette busied herself typing data into two computers and readying two testing stations. She prepared everything with competent efficiency.

Ben's VO2 Max readings had always been off the charts, at least when compared to the general population, but no matter how hard he trained, among professional cyclists he was just another data point in the middle of the range. What sort of a score would Kyle register? He hoped to beat it.

The men pulled on their oxygen masks. Bridgette started the test. Soon both cyclists were riding too hard to pay much attention to one another. Sweat streamed off them as they raced one another on bicycles that wouldn't move.

After thirty minutes of hard exercise the test ended.

Gasping for breath, Ben removed his oxygen mask and leaned toward Bridgette. "How'd I do?"

She shook her head. "Not as good as your friend, here. I've never seen a higher score."

Kyle smiled. "Do I know how to wow the ladies, or what?"

The Oregonian's test result was already legendary by the time the team convened for their evening meeting. The twenty Megatronics cyclists sat expectantly as the director scribbled a list of names on the chalkboard. Both Ben's and Kyle's were among them. "These are the men we're sending to the U.S. Professional Cycling Championships next week. The leader is …," he circled Ben's name, "… you, Barnes. Ready for your big break?"

Ben nodded, almost dazed. He fought to concentrate on details as the chosen teammates crowded around. The director described the plan for the coming race.

Ben watched his dream materialize before his eyes. Every feint and jab Megatronics would attempt was designed to put him in position to claim victory.

"Kyle, you built a reputation as a winner in the amateur ranks. May as well throw you right into the fire now that you're a pro. You'll be Ben's right hand man. Can you handle that?" the director asked.

"Absolutely," Kyle answered.

"Very well," the director said. "Just so we're clear, I expect you to do everything in your power to protect Ben for the first ninety-five percent of the race. That includes keeping him in your slipstream when our team is forced to take the lead, chasing down breaks when rivals attack, even getting Ben water and food if necessary. In short, delivering Barnes to the end of the race in as fresh a condition as possible. I want you completely spent with five kilometers to go. Understood?"

"I already said so, didn't I?"

* * *

Just as he'd hoped, recalling how Kyle had set him up sharpened Ben's motivation to hunt his rival down today. He broke into clear air at the front of the paceline and bore down. The other cyclists responded, grateful to hand him as much of the workload as possible.

Beside the road thousands of giant sunflowers, their heads turned in obedience toward their namesake in the sky, highlighted the land's bounty. The crop glowed with surreal energy. In the next field a shining stallion reared, then sprinted alongside the competitors. Farther on, beside a tiny cottage a pair of drab olive workpants danced on the clothesline, gyrating in a way their owner probably never dreamed of. His plaid shirt applauded enthusiastically while a couple of his wife's ample brassieres jiggled and laughed.

Ben broke off the front of the paceline, purposely drifting into his private thoughts as he fell back for another rest.

* * *

The day after the Megatronics director announced the cyclists who would compete in the U.S. Championships, the chosen men flew stateside to Philadelphia. Ben was primed for the opportunity.

From the moment the starting gun sounded, the attacks began. Despite his promises, Kyle didn't cover any of them; he didn't even make an effort. Ben urged his teammate on, but it was no use. Kyle was lethargic. He complained of stomach pains. Ben worked much harder than he'd have liked while Kyle tagged along for a free ride.

Still, as the race neared its conclusion things fell into place. Fifteen kilometers from the finish Ben sensed victory. He'd been forcing a high pace, and at the base of the famous Manayunk Wall his group reestablished contact with the race leaders.

As a result, other than Ben's exhaustion, Megatronics was in the position they'd hoped for in their tactical meeting. Kyle and Ben were the only set of teammates in a group of half a dozen riders at the head of the race. The winner would certainly come from this small party. It was time for Ben to take over. All he had to do was dig a tiny bit deeper.

That's when he felt the first little tickle, a minor involuntary contraction, deep inside his gastrocnemius muscle. He hesitated, waiting for the feeling to pass before attacking. But it was almost as if thinking about the sensation caused the spasm to expand. He tried to focus his mind on something else.

Kyle peeled off the front of the pace line. Ben confronted the wind, immediately noticing a discarded water bottle only feet ahead. Why hadn't Kyle pointed it out? His body position had hidden it from Ben until the last second. Even rivals warn trailing riders of hazards.

Ben swerved, but his front wheel still clipped the water bottle. The container rolled forward under the bicycle's weight, then flattened and slid sideways. Ben's front wheel slid with it, shifting out of position.

He fought for control of the bike. Suddenly, like a flame touching petroleum, the cramp consumed his entire muscle. The calf contracted so completely and painfully it caused him to lose balance. He hit the pavement face first. The left side of his body from cheek to thigh ground against the rough asphalt as he slid to a stop.

"Are you kidding me?" Kyle laughed as he and the other cyclists flew past.

Lying on his side, spitting bits of gravel, Ben reached for his leg. He had to relieve the agony. He tried massage. The muscle felt hard as bone. He lay for a moment, kneading his calf while he watched the race lead disappear up the road. His dreams, like dandelion spores scattering in a gale, sped irretrievably over the hill.

With gargantuan effort Ben struggled to his feet. He remounted his bike and started to pedal, looking over his shoulder to verify the peloton still wasn't within sight. He made steady revolutions, resigned that he'd now finish no better than sixth. If he didn't move quickly his end result might be much worse than that.

The burning from the road rash hadn't yet begun to register in his nervous system. So far he felt only the strangely comfortable sensation of blood rising to the surface. Adrenaline might delay the pain for several hours, but then he'd become extremely sore and stiff. It would be hard to move at all once the whole area scabbed up. After that, the slightest gesture could result in painful cracking and bleeding. His training would be set way back.

Ten minutes later he limped across the line, taking solace that somehow he'd held on to sixth. A glance at the leader board told him Kyle had found the reserves to win. He wished his teammate had been able to perform so well during the course of the race, but that was how cycling sometimes went.

Ben pedaled beside Kyle and listened in on his teammates conversation with the press.

"No doubt you're thrilled you'll be wearing the red, white and blue national jersey for the next year," a reporter said. "You were clearly the strongest rider in the last mile. How did you find the reserves to win?"

"I'd ridden all day, supporting my teammate Ben Barnes, but when he made a mistake I knew I'd have to do something special to save the day. Honestly, I don't know how I did it. There are times when desire overrides all else. This was one of them."

The reporter turned toward her cameraman, "So there you have it. Kyle Smith, an undeniably charismatic young man captures the U.S. Professional Cycling Championship in his very first race as a pro. Incredible!"

As Kyle turned from the camera he and Ben made eye contact.

Ben reigned in his negative feelings. He was charged up and might see things differently when he cooled down. "Congrats, man."

Kyle ignored him, looking toward another reporter and beginning a new interview.

Ben dismounted his bike and shuffled toward the team trailer. Once there he overheard his team director and their lead mechanic talking inside the vehicle. "Looks like we've found our team leader," said the mechanic.

"Yeah. The kid's got the whole package, hasn't he. Including killer instinct. I don't know exactly what happened out there, but what I do know is Smith found a way to win and that's what matters to me. He fought his way to the top of the food chain and closed the deal. He's a carnivore, and carnivores always win. It's going to be exciting to mold his career."

A fist to the gut wouldn't have stolen Ben's wind any more effectively.

* * *

Anger at the memory fueled Ben. As he pedaled through for his turn at the front of the line, he found himself heading directly for an ancient cemetery. Its walls seemed barely able to contain the thousands of tombstones leaning this way and that. The route bent right. On the opposite side of the road, a narrow chapel balanced atop a forty-foot cliff. Farther on brilliant pink, orange, and green shutters set off beige and gray stucco walls. The splashes of lively color gave the town a vibrant feel.

Ben lifted the pace. The quicker his group could reach the breakaway ahead, the sooner he could rest. He glanced under his arm and saw the other three riders accelerate to hold his wheel. Ben looked forward to seeing Kyle's expression when they met up. He doubted he'd be greeted with his ex-teammate's famous smile.

* * *

Kyle stepped onto the set of The Tonight Show within a week of his U.S. Pro Championship. Ben watched, sitting on the bed in a budget hotel room.

Jay Leno grinned at Kyle. "You won the United States of America Road Cycling Championship in your very first race as a pro. How good did that feel?"

"I laid it all on the road and ended up with a great result. It wouldn't have happened if some of my teammates and competitors hadn't faltered under pressure. You learn a lot about yourself in the heat of battle. I guess I learned what I've always known deep down. I have what it takes to win."

"Well said, and I don't know who could argue with that. To top it off, you've got the look."

Kyle furrowed his brow. "The look?"

"You don't have to be modest. I'm sure our audience agrees; you look a lot more like a movie star than a bicycle rider. The girl's go ga-ga for you, right?"

The female portion of the crowd screeched.

"Even more so once they get to know me. Girls drive me to do greater things, if you know what I mean." Kyle flashed his confident smile.

Ben switched off the set in disgust.

Three months later, with four more pro victories under his belt, that same smile graced the pages of *People Magazine* when Kyle was named one of the "beautiful people." The thought made Ben burn.

Few seemed to notice the price Ben paid for Kyle's success. Meanwhile, Kyle continued slopping a bottomless trough of insinuation and accusation on Ben.

At first, Ben saw the whole circus act as a misguided attempt to drive him from the team. He tried to explain to his teammate that there was room for both of them, no need for a coup, and that during the course of the European racing circuit they stood to benefit from one another's strengths.

In retrospect, Ben realized Kyle had set him up from the first, always planning to steal the U.S. Pro Championship race at the line, always looking for a way to supplant him as team leader. He hadn't been having a bad day as he'd purported. He'd been saving his strength. Everything made perfect sense once Ben understood the character of the man he'd been dealing with.

It didn't take long until everyone within the cycling community had learned Kyle lacked class. For team ownership, though, camouflaging pig tracks was a small price to pay for winning and the loads of positive publicity that came along with it. They cranked up their PR machine full bore, selling their star as the all-American boy. The public bought the image. In fact, they couldn't get enough of him.

* * *

Ben pulled into the chase group lead, head down, legs churning. He had to angle his eyes steeply up to glimpse the horizon. Kyle still wasn't in sight, but they must be closing the gap. Ben couldn't imagine any cyclists covering this terrain any faster than his group was now. They were flying.

A group of a half dozen roadside spectators cheered wildly at the chase group's approach, obviously excited their particular vantage point had turned out to be the location for a flurry of aggressive tactics.

Ben couldn't unlock his gaze from the least active member of the clan, an old, wrinkled farmer with penetrating eyes. The aged man sat in a lawn chair, a glass of red wine raised above his head. The family jumped and screamed while the patriarch, perched in the center, spoke. His aged lips crumpled into a frown, and so did everyone else's. Ben passed close enough to have toasted the wine glass with his water bottle just as the family's cheers turned to derogatory whistles and boos.

"They love to hate you, Ben from America, do they not?" asked Luigi.

Ben nodded. Yet another group of partisans who couldn't forgive him for his involvement two years before in the accident that had killed Nicolas Depardieu, Thierry's younger brother.

Chapter Three

As Ben peeled out of lead position and drifted back for another rest, the chain of events that had led to the tragedy scrolled through his mind. He wasn't anxious to revisit such negative experiences, but then a thought occurred to him. Whatever that missing edge Pierre had alluded to was, he'd had it before the downward spiral leading to the disaster with Nicolas. Maybe he could get it back.

* * *

As the season following the sabotage at the U.S. Championships began, Kyle sat firmly entrenched as the team leader. To Ben's dismay he still seemed to enjoy throwing venom Ben's way.

Because of Kyle's popularity with ownership, teammates and staff understood that crossing the leader might mean career suicide. No one would join Ben's fight. In fact, since Ben would rather keep his dignity than defend his reputation, no one even heard his side of the story. He'd joined the team to race bikes while Kyle came to gain fame. Where those goals conflicted, the man willing to fling muck apparently had the advantage.

The evening before Paris-Roubaix, one of the most prestigious one-day classics, Ben waited for Bridgette at the little café across the river from the team hotel. Whenever he was near Paris, they got together. For weeks, he'd looked forward to a romantic stroll through the beautiful gardens of the Chateau de Compiégne. Instead, he stood there shuffling his feet. Curfew would come all too soon. Where was she?

Bridgette was always punctual, and he became worried. He

returned to the hotel, checked in with the team director, and then went to his room and called her apartment. He left a message then hung up, feeling depressed and jilted.

Prior to the race start he searched the crowd for her beautiful face, but he never saw her. When the starter's flag waved he reluctantly mounted his bicycle and rode through the streets of Compiégne toward the treacherous cobbles leading to Roubaix with the rest of the peloton, still searching the spectators for a sign of his girlfriend. As the route swept through a narrow alley Ben was briefly side-by-side with Kyle.

"Bridgette was F I N E last night. Now I know why you're so crazy about her."

Ben balled his fist and cocked his arm. He flexed menacingly at Kyle.

Kyle swerved, panic in his eyes. His bicycle lost traction. He hit the ground hard. Seven trailing cyclists crashed in a heap over his body. Ben looked back to see an eighth man cart-wheeling up the road like a rag doll.

The riders behind the accident skidded to a standstill, the narrow road completely clogged by strewn bodies and machines. Crashes were common in this race, so although pandemonium ruled as men scrambled to remount their bikes and catch up with the peloton, in another sense it was business as usual.

Ben's relationship with Kyle was another matter. He pulled off the road and sprang from his bicycle. Kyle's objectives were more far reaching than he had ever guessed. His so called teammate meant to steal his girl, and apparently he'd been successful. Ben strode back to the scene of the accident anxious to punch Kyle for real this time.

The team leader had just regained his feet. He turned toward Ben. Renewed fear saturated his expression.

"Are you crazy? Look what you've done," Kyle screamed.

Riders clambered through the carnage to resume the chase. Mechanics switched out bikes. Kyle's twisted and useless front wheel was among the casualties.

Someone groaned—a cyclist writhing in pain, his collarbone sticking through skin and jersey. The gruesome scene drove sense back into Ben. He'd caused this innocent man's suffering.

Ben turned to Kyle. "Use my bike, you loser."

Kyle gave him a wide berth, facing his teammate as he moved toward the offered vehicle. He climbed on, spat blood, and then headed down the road swearing and scowling.

The injured man groaned again. Ben hurried to him. It was Nicolas Depardieu, the younger brother of Thierry Depardieu, cycling's current dominant athlete. Nicolas' body convulsed.

"No, don't do this!" Ben dropped to his knees and tried to steady the injured man.

Nicolas spat blood. A pool of crimson liquid grew like a halo behind the Frenchman's head. Nicolas' eyes rolled back.

"No! No! Please! You're going to be okay!"

Unseen hands dragged Ben backward. He found himself propped against a weathered brick wall. A team of medics surrounded the groaning Frenchman.

"Sorry," Ben cried. "It's all my fault."

The paramedics inserted an airway down Nicolas' throat, slid a backboard beneath his body, hung IV's and plasma on a rack above him. Ben watched helplessly. He knew long before anyone told him that Nicolas would not survive.

Even after the stretcher was loaded and the ambulance screamed away, sirens blaring, Ben couldn't regain his feet. He looked around at the devastation, crying and talking to himself.

The next morning his admission of guilt: "It's all my fault!" headlined a major newspaper. Similar quotes found play in every European media outlet. One spectator likely got rich off a snapshot showing Ben with his arm cocked, his fist clenched, and a crazed look in his eyes. Kyle, seen from behind, appeared to be the imminent recipient of a madman's wrath. The photo showed up everywhere.

Kyle's story matched the evidence. "I was the innocent victim of a brutal attack," he claimed. "Barnes blindsided me with a fist to the head."

It didn't matter that the punch left no mark or that none of the trailing riders recalled seeing any physical contact between the two Megatronics teammates. There was no video footage to conclusively settle the issue, but that didn't matter either. Minds were made up. After all, there was that chilling tape of Ben rocking back and forth against a worn brick wall, blaming himself for everything. Who hadn't seen that a hundred times?

The sports governing body, Union Cycliste Internationale, handed Ben a one-year suspension. A day later Megatronics trumped that by delivering his walking papers. The move earned the company much goodwill with the French press, and to ice the cake, the tabloids did everything possible to make sure Ben's name remained permanently linked to the death of overnight folk hero, Nicolas Depardieu. Nicolas, the national treasure stolen before his prime by poor American sportsmanship. Nicolas, the younger and even more promising brother of cycling's most dominant athlete in a generation. Nicolas, a man whose legend was the antithesis of everything Ben Barnes appeared to be.

* * *

Wind slapped Ben in the face as the rider ahead pulled off the paceline and turned the breakaway over to him. Thank God Kyle's implication of seducing Bridgette had been yet another example of his fondness for fudging facts. Truth was, the two had been together … along with the team director. They'd been making wind tunnel adjustments to the team leader's new time-trial bike. None had slept in an unexpected bed. Bridgette had been enlisted to deliver the state of the art machine to the town where it would be used two days later.

Ben glanced at his jersey—the same purple and green Nicolas died in, the same colors Thierry had worn his entire career. Of all the squads for Ben to end up riding with, Banque Fédérale had to be the least likely. But it was an opportunity to repay his debt to the Depardieu brothers. He dug deep, elevating the pace yet again.

Chapter Four

The chase group streamed through a small village. They rode in the narrow gutters to avoid the cobbled street. They still hadn't caught a glimpse of the cyclists up the road, but the position of a hovering television helicopter told them they were closing in.

Large numbers of fans crowded about the city square.

"Murderer!" yelled a pretty girl.

The story of the accident and Nicholas' death had received lots of play when Ben was announced as a participant in this year's race. Now that he was in a breakaway instead of an anonymous member of the peloton some fans seemed anxious to unleash anger.

He wished he was blameless, but that wasn't the case. A familiar wave of grief and shame overcame him. Nicholas lay in his grave while Ben competed in this great race. Life could be so unfair.

"Boo!" screamed a young boy.

A man shook a makeshift sign that said "Yankee go home!" He tried to reach out and touch Ben with it as the cyclists flew by.

For the other three breakaway members, the venomous words seemed to energize their cause. Ben lost ground.

"Get your head straight!" Luigi yelled.

Ben gritted his teeth and dug deep to keep up. He shut out everything external and refocused on the task. Soon he'd rejoined the break.

The chase group pushed with superhuman effort for ten kilometers before Ben caught his first sight of the lead cyclists on a long straightaway. The brief visual of their quarry whetted the four riders appetites, and their speed surged again.

Ben now salivated at the thought of a reunion with Kyle. Coach Bill's trick of reaching into the past had worked. The vivid memories were like a secret weapon, providing the motivation to push harder than he ever could have without them. He lifted the speed each time through and took longer pulls than the others at the front of the paceline.

What a beautiful opportunity. If he joined the lead break and stayed on Kyle's wheel as instructed, limiting his rivals' gains and simultaneously conserving energy for the final surge, he'd surely have the strongest finishing sprint. Even Pierre would have to take pride in such a result.

Mere minutes before, Ben's future had seemed so bleak. Now the setup was perfect for a stage victory. Not since Kyle had sabotaged him at the U.S. Cycling Championships had a win seemed a more realistic possibility. Such a result might alter his career.

As they approached their target, Ben considered his strategy for limiting Kyle's gains. Hate seethed from deep within. Ben had been forced to confront the dark side of human nature since the day Kyle duped him. He wouldn't stoop to the tactics of his despised rival, but he must understand what Kyle was capable of. To Kyle, bending the rules and deceiving those who trusted him were part and parcel to the game. It would be so satisfying to make him pay. The time had come.

A motorcycle moved alongside. The driver stared intently at the road ahead, while behind him a cameraman focused his lens directly on Ben.

Ben maintained as placid a look as possible. He recalled joking around with Bridgette, showing her the expression he'd wear when he became a focal point of a race.

"Thank God you'll never get to use it." Her teeth glimmered behind shining red lips.

"What are you talking about?" Ben asked.

"Banque Fédérale will never give you a chance to show off. We both know that's not why they signed you. Besides, it's a silly expression. It makes you look boring."

Ben punched her playfully in the shoulder. "It isn't a bored look, it's calm. And the time will come to use it. I guarantee."

Now it had.

He wondered what Bridgette, probably watching televised race coverage from her Paris flat, thought of his expression now. She certainly wouldn't be bored. He pictured her dancing on the couch, screaming at the top of her lungs. He had to fight the urge to wink at her. God, she was fun to play with.

When the camera moved away he gritted his teeth and picked up the pace another notch. This race, the Tour de France, was the one real chance for people in the States to see what he did for a living. The faces of friends and acquaintances who might have caught a glimpse came to mind. How were they reacting?

All the training, all the difficulties of living in Europe, all the obscure races in lousy weather, everything he put up with was worth it at this moment because of the unexpected opportunity to play a role in a single stage of this great journey. This was the stuff he had dreamed about.

He drove on, legs aching. Ben felt satisfaction at his accomplishment. The feeling made him want more. The thought of what might be excited him.

His fellow riders remained silent, but as he dropped back, he saw gritty determination in their eyes.

When he pulled through for his turn at the lead again, he pushed even harder, increasing the speed another two K. The gap to the breakaway group narrowed. Ben dropped back for another rest.

Luigi smiled at him with a devilish grin. "Don't burn everything here, *il mio amico*."

They jammed along at fifty-seven klicks an hour even as the road climbed the cliff to get around a narrow river cut. To their right ferns, bushes, and grasses sucked life out of a rock wall. On the left a tangled briar of pines, birches, and vines created a barrier nearly as dense. The river, increasingly far below, could only be glimpsed periodically as they sped through the slot canyon of greenery.

Despite the physical pain, Ben felt hard-wired to a limitless energy supply, excess voltage pouring off his body. As if his compatriots could draw electricity from the air, the pace stepped up yet another notch.

After three more kilometers of all-out riding the lead group was within striking distance. At the same point a new slot canyon, this one formed by the stucco walls of Champ Angeaux, replaced the first.

Ben went anaerobic for the final push, an all or nothing gambit to bridge the remaining gap. His muscles screamed for mercy as the interval to the riders ahead collapsed. Finally his legs gave out, the lactic acid buildup too extreme. But in that same moment the draft of the trailing rider on the lead break sucked him forward, like being pulled into a mother's arms.

He rose from his handlebar drops, sitting erect and sucking air. His pounding heart shook every extremity. Years of experience had put him in tune with his body. Even without timing his pulse he knew the rate was around 200 beats per minute. As it subsided, he drew satisfaction from his rapid recovery.

One by one, the three members of his chase team moved alongside, the first slapping Ben's back, the second reaching over and laying a hand on Ben's, and then Luigi.

"*Fabulisimo!* My best chase ever."

Ben smiled, having recovered significantly in the short respite. "Here goes. Watch my back?" He nodded toward Kyle, signaling his intent.

"*Naturalment.*"

Ben picked up the pace for a couple of pedal revolutions and then eased again as he approached the man in the red Megatronics jersey.

Chapter Five

Kyle spat over his shoulder as if he had no idea someone might be there. He knew. Ben's shadow preceded him up the road, plus Kyle's directeur sportif would have long ago told him over team radio who had bridged up.

"Missed me," Ben said.

"No. I'll never miss you."

"Very clever. Or was that another of your accidental jokes?"

Kyle grunted. "Banque Fédérale's weaker than I thought if the best they can send is you. I'll dirty this road with your carcass. Bridgette will see she chose the wrong man."

"Sometimes she screams your name."

Kyle glanced into Ben's eyes, an uncontrolled, hopeful expression.

"Nightmares," Ben said.

"I don't believe it."

"Believe it. By the way, found the ropes yet?"

"Huh?"

It seemed unfair a guy like Kyle would have such potential. His stratospheric VO2 Max scores proved if he'd put in anything approaching the effort of the other riders he'd dominate. Fortunately, he cut corners in training.

"So let's go, Ben. Mano-a-mano," Kyle taunted.

"No can do. My orders are to sit on your wheel and drive you crazy. I can show what I've got once in sight of the finish line. Can you wait?"

Kyle's tangled expression slowly transformed into comprehension. "You think I'm gonna tow you to glory?"

"Think of it. Sports Center highlights of me crossing the finish line with arms raised victorious, followed by you pulling on a yellow t-shirt. Which one means more to an American audience?"

Kyle steered off his line, leaning momentarily into Ben.

Ben held his ground.

"I ought to punch your lights out," Kyle said.

Luigi spoke up from behind. "Ahh, this big nose. It never fails."

Kyle turned. "What are you talking about, Pizza Eater?"

Luigi deftly maneuvered his front tire to touch Kyle's rear one.

Kyle's bike shimmied. He tightened his grip on the handlebars. "Watch it!"

"If I put you down I would be the hero of the peloton," Luigi said.

Kyle snarled. He glanced at Ben, then riveted his eyes on the road ahead. "What is this? You can't handle things alone so you brought along your Mafia buddy to quack me? Get out of my moment, Barnes."

"Nope," Ben said. "Here's your choice. Forget about the overall lead today, or drag me to a stage win in the process."

Kyle's deep voice somehow reached a whine. "I deserve the yellow jersey."

"Wrong. Thierry will limit your gains and wear yellow tonight. You can take pride in my win, though."

Ben knew Kyle would give nearly anything for the maillot jaune, but did that include handing his enemy such an enormous prize?

Kyle looked angry enough to chew through his handlebars. He spoke into his radio. "What's our gap?"

Though Ben couldn't hear the conversation he knew the answer—around a minute and a half. If the peloton became motivated, 'très irrité' as the French liked to say, they could usually take back a minute every ten kilometers. Using that calculation, neither the time gain Kyle coveted, nor the stage victory Ben dreamed of were anything close to assured. Ben's goal, however, was far more likely.

"Shit," Kyle said. "It ain't worth the hassle. I'll save my energy for the mountains." He peeled out of the paceline and quit pedaling.

Ben couldn't hold back a laugh. He hadn't dreamed his words would work so perfectly. Kyle was so impulsive and self-centered, not to mention stupid, that he'd abandoned the group and all the effort it had taken to build a lead. Meanwhile, Ben remained in decent position for the stage victory.

"*Arrivederci*," yelled Luigi, looking back at the retreating Megatronics jersey.

Without the excuse of sitting on Kyle's wheel to protect Thierry, it would be classless for Ben not to do his share of the work. He might find glory in this one race, but he'd be a marked man afterwards. While joining in the work significantly reduced his chances of a win, it didn't eliminate them.

Ben's fellow cyclists admired him every bit as much as certain French fans despised him. To him, the opinion of the former group mattered, while the latter did not. He had no intention of doing anything designed to change either impression. Those who hated him didn't really want the truth, anyway. They just craved the juiciest story. If he ever won the fans over, it would mean they'd accepted him despite his contributing role in the tragedy. He'd never spin the facts to diminish his involvement.

Ben played through his archive of experience in racing toward the line. In cycling a seemingly limitless number of factors could rise up and affect the outcome of the race. A changing breeze could scramble tactics; an overenthusiastic fan might hold a flag too close to a rider's face; a pothole could transform an otherwise perfect line into disaster. Anything could go wrong. Being the strongest man in the pack didn't ensure victory.

His headset buzzed. "Benjamin, I've moved the team car into the gap behind you. Drop back for supplies and instruction."

Ben clenched his fist and whispered, "Yes!" Such a move meant Pierre believed in him. Other team cars had long ago moved forward in support of their riders. Pierre's presence meant Ben was now on equal footing. The ability to easily resupply from a following car would be a huge help. He dropped alongside the Banque Fédérale Peugeot. Pierre handed him a water bottle and an energy bar.

"*Merci*," Ben said.

Pierre handed out another water bottle.

Ben took it, curious. Why should he carry an extra bottle with a support vehicle so accessible? He shrugged and stowed the container.

Pierre handed out two more bottles.

"You can't be serious," Ben said.

"Take them!"

Ben's spirits deflated. He looked away and ground his teeth. How could Pierre ask him to abandon such a hard earned position on the road? This time Le Directeur had really double-crossed him. Without explaining a thing he had relegated Ben to an unfathomable task: purposely fading from a surging breakaway to deliver supplies to his trailing team. All that time gained at such great physical cost, and now he had to throw it away. And why? Just because this damned goatee stroking, bald-headed, xenophobic, Alaskan chimney stack posing as a directeur sportif said so.

He pursed his lips and looked toward Pierre. He frowned as he accepted the containers.

The moment he stowed the bottles in his back pockets, Pierre extended two more. "Why the sorry expression?"

Ben accepted the water but ignored the prod.

"You claim to be a great domestique. If so, you should fill your role without complaint."

"That's what I'm doing."

Pierre grunted. "Not happily."

Ben choked on the insult. He'd accomplished the initial goal of getting Kyle to give up the chase. He'd single-handedly rescued the maillot jaune for Thierry. Now he was about to sacrifice a position earned at gargantuan effort to run a routine errand. Any team member back in the main pack could make this water run in the ordinary way. They ought to be nice and fresh. Yet despite all that, Pierre expected happy expressions?

Ben took the last bottle from Le Directeur. "What are my instructions?"

The Frenchman fingered his goatee. "We'll try to earn a sprint victory for Rikard. That would lift his spirits and encourage him to fight through the Alps. You can help lead him out."

Ben shook his head slightly. The nine remaining members of his former breakaway were going to survive to the finish. That meant even if Rikard did win the bunch sprint to the line, the best he could finish was tenth. Big whoop.

Pierre held out a large handful of energy gels.

Ben crammed the wad down his shirt and faded toward the main peloton.

In the calm void between the fleeing breakaway and the surging peloton Ben's heart rate slowed. Sounds and sights that a moment before had been filtered out by intense concentration now claimed Ben's attention. The mighty Rhône flowed at his left. An unseen finch twittered a tune from deep within the wall of giant pine trees to his right. Her chicks cheeped in response, no doubt clamoring to be first fed. For that instant Ben's concerns seemed trivial, nothing next to the everyday functions of a universe chock full of creatures fighting for survival. Here he was, upset over the way tactics in a game temporarily affected him. Get over it.

Then the peloton consumed him. Neon cyclists poured past on both sides. It felt like tumbling down the gullet of a hungry dragon. Ben shook his head, rattling his brain back into perspective, refocusing on his assigned task.

Banque Fédérale had already allowed sprinter's teams to assume the chase, so Ben didn't begin seeing purple and green jerseys until a quarter of the pack had passed him.

"What are you doing here?" Thierry asked.

Ben handed him a water bottle and a gel. "Obeying orders."

"I'm surprised you couldn't hang with the lead break. I thought you were strong, that you might win." Thierry ripped open the gel and squirted it down.

Ben stared at his team leader. No use explaining. Only a couple of people understood exactly how he'd contributed to his team's success. The story might never get out. When Thierry pulled on the maillot jaune that afternoon, Ben would have to take quiet solace in the fact that from a team perspective, his tactic had worked to perfection. He prayed he'd still have both the strength and will to perform when the sun rose again. He'd left an awful lot of himself on the road today.

Chapter Six

The soigneur's knuckles dug deep into Ben's calf muscle. "Cramping. This is your weakness, no?"

"Yeah. I guess."

"I fix it. Right?"

"So far, so good."

"Must massage deep, plus keep mineral reserves high. You taking the tablets?"

"Of course."

The tablets the soigneur referred to were nothing but mineral supplements, mostly sodium with trace amounts of potassium and magnesium. Because no drugs were involved this was one of the few pills Ben felt comfortable taking. Cyclists were under such scrutiny for drug violations, and so many substances were banned either as performance enhancers or masking agents, that athletes had to be obsessive about what went into their bodies.

In extreme cases some cyclists, men who inflicted pain on themselves of proportions unfathomable to most people, didn't dare take aspirin for a headache for fear of being tagged as a doper.

Ben's tablets had worked wonders in training, but training couldn't simulate an all-out race. He hoped the cramping precautions would work when it counted.

"Remember, the tour will be won off the bike," the soigneur said.

It was good advice. Taking extreme care of the body during the downtime of this three-week ordeal— sleeping, stretching, eating— translated into success on the road. In the bicycle racing world, sleep was said to be the hobby of champions.

Ben yawned.

The door opened and Rikard stepped into the room.

"I thought you had tenth place in that sprint today," Ben said. "Too bad."

Rikard frowned. "My turn. Scram."

Reluctantly, Ben rose from the table and looked at the soigneur. "You have magic fingers. I feel like a new man."

"Good. Stretch next," the soigneur suggested.

Ben nodded. "Will do."

He strode into the narrow hallway of the Beau Riyage Hôtel, running his left hand along the uneven plaster wall. Beneath a Persian carpet runner, ancient floorboards creaked. Why was it so comforting to hear a building express its instability?

At regular intervals, wall mounted vases held singular fragrant red roses. Upon each inhalation the fresh scent triggered ripples of pleasure in his brain, like pebbles hitting pond water.

The massage had infused him, as usual, with a sense of calm control. Not only had the competent hands soothed his aching muscles, but manipulations had somehow eased his mind. He paused to concentrate on his heartbeat, currently about forty-five contractions per minute. Later he'd get it into the mid thirty's by lying down and meditating.

He stretched into a sprinter's crouch. The calf muscle of the trailing leg elongated, compliant and relaxed. After a long moment he moved forward, slowly stretching the opposite leg.

"You are not an excuse maker, are you?" The words were spoken in halting English.

Ben turned to see Thierry striding up the hall behind him. "No. Not my style."

Thierry smiled as he moved alongside Ben. "I know what happened. Asked a couple questions about what went on and got interesting answers."

Ben nodded.

"You showed me much out there. You were right. Because of you, Kyle … um … *cesser*."

"Yes, he quit." Ben rose from his stretching position.

Thierry's sincere effort at English felt like a great compliment. Maybe this would be the chance for the serious talk Ben had long hoped for. Either way, it felt comforting to know someone else understood.

"You read him well."

Ben switched the conversation to French. "*Oui.* He and I go back a long way. I know a bit more about him than I wish I did."

Thierry put an arm around Ben's shoulder. "There's more than that. You outworked everyone and still looked fresh at the line."

Ben shrugged. "My form has come around. The timing is lucky."

"*Chanceux?* You're more than lucky. You're good. Maybe the best rider on our squad."

Ben looked into Thierry's eyes. What was he saying? Could he be trusted?

"Let's take a walk," Thierry said.

From the front side of the hotel came the sounds of celebration, but the park behind was vacant. Ben followed Thierry down two flights of stairs. Rather than turning toward the front door, the team leader cut into the restaurant kitchen.

"Thierry Depardieu! Autograph please?"

Thierry put a finger to his lips. "If you lend me your hat, I'll bring you a signed jersey."

"An autographed jersey! Here. Take the sunglasses, too."

"*Merci.*"

Thierry put on the disguise and headed out the back door. Ben stepped cautiously into the cool evening air of the subalpine village.

Apparently the festivities on the next street over were a roaring success, sucking the park devoid of life for the moment. The two men headed toward the nearby harbor.

Thierry spoke again, "Pierre doesn't like you. He didn't want you on the Tour roster. Up until the last moment he fought to have you removed."

Ben looked directly into Thierry's eyes.

The team leader nodded. "The only reason you're here is because I demanded it. You may as well know that."

Ben nodded. "You pulled the strings? After your brother and all. Why?"

"Only one thing matters. Winning. To do it I need the best.

Period. You're one of them. As for my brother," Thierry sucked in a deep breath as he turned the corner and headed down a concrete and rock pier, "You apologized. Still, I could hate you. Easily." His faced tensed, then relaxed. "But it wouldn't be right. As I told you when we spoke after the accident, it wasn't your fault."

"You were in shock."

"I may have been in shock. Still, I meant what I said."

"Yeah, but …"

"But nothing." Thierry looked stern, but sincere. "The crowd punishes you mercilessly for Nicolas' accident. We cyclists understand many factors contributed."

In the slight breeze mainstays clanged against masts. Each sailboat seemed to have a distinct note. Some crafts looked like the cobwebs alone would hold them to shore.

"It wouldn't have happened if not for me."

Thierry ran a finger along the scar below his eye. "Ours is a dangerous business. Nicolas accepted the risks. I do too."

Ben nodded, then tapped his tongue on the roof of his mouth. There really didn't seem to be any hard feelings. "Well then, I owe you thanks for getting me on the Tour roster."

"It was meant as a favor to me. I already explained that. Now things are becoming even more complicated. Your involvement puts you in a more … tenuous … situation than I think you realize."

Ben regarded the team leader. "My involvement? Tenuous?"

"Let's sit. Our legs deserve a rest." Thierry crouched, then dangled his legs over the sea wall.

Ben followed suit, gazing at the slowly meandering sailing vessels and the castle clinging to the steep opposing shore.

"I'm going to be more blunt than I'd planned. I don't want to put crazy ideas in your head, but neither do I want you to make serious errors out of blind compliance."

"What are you talking about?"

Waves lapped at the boulder breakwater and pier base below them. Underwater moss and grasses swayed in rhythm to the liquid tune.

Hesitantly, Thierry spoke, "This is delicate, but it's likely you haven't seen the last time Le Directeur's tactics aren't best for you."

"I've accepted that. My goal is to serve the team the best I can."

"You shouldn't have been asked to leave that break."

"Asked? I had no choice." Ben shrugged. "*C'est la vie.*"

Thierry shook his head. "You had a shot at the stage win. A victory would have been huge for team morale. Pierre stole the opportunity because he doesn't dare allow you to become a star. The last thing he wants is another American succeeding in The Tour. You've heard the way he goes on about Yankee commercialism. He's not fond of your culture, to say the least."

"He isn't crazy about me dating his niece, either."

Thierry nodded. "That too. Then again, Pierre would never have offered you a contract if not for her."

"True. So, what should I have done?"

Thierry rubbed the right side of his face as if trying to massage a lodged thought free. "Pierre is trying to wear you down early by assigning you all the grunt work. If you're tiring you have nothing to be ashamed of, but I get the opposite impression. You seem stronger every day. Today you even exceeded your performance in the team time trial. Pierre sacrificed team tactics there to do you harm as well."

Team time trials are uniquely formatted races where the nineteen squads start at regular intervals to space themselves on the road. The ability of a team to hide its weaknesses in the peloton disappears. All nine team members drive in a unified effort against the clock, pushing to bring their leader across the line in the fastest time possible.

Through the halfway mark Ben had been riding well. A sudden, "Shhhhh," and loss of control told him he'd flatted. He pulled out of the paceline and squeezed his brakes.

"Faster, everybody," Pierre instructed over the team radio.

"I've got more to give," Ben said.

Usually teams slowed under such circumstances. The twenty seconds lost for a tire change could easily be made up if the retained cyclist was strong. His continuing efforts in the paceline meant longer rests for everyone, and the extra manpower resulted in higher speeds.

"Catch up on your own." Pierre's tone was flat.

Was it meant as an insult? A lone rider had no real prayer of making up distance on a well-oiled group. Nevertheless, Ben wasn't about to talk back. This far into the stage most teams started shedding exhausted domestiques, anyway. At the finish line the first five riders would receive the fifth man's time. Trailing riders received their actual time. As long as the team leader and other cyclists who were meant to perform well in the General Classification were still in a lead group at the finish, the team was not beholden to wait.

Fritz leaped from the support vehicle, new wheel in hand. "If anyone can catch back up, you can!"

Ben had already removed the quick release. A second later Fritz had the bicycle ready to go. The mechanic gave Ben a running shove down the road. He accelerated quickly and drove for his teammates with all he had.

"*Vas-y! Vas-y! Vas-y!*" Fritz yelled from behind.

Ben poured his heart onto the road. Fritz had proven to be a reliable friend. The least Ben could do was reward his confidence with maximum effort.

Presumably, despite his words, Pierre saw things differently. He expected Ben to give up. Normally dropped riders simply limp to the finish alone, spending no more effort than necessary to cross the line ahead of the disqualification time.

After three kilometers of all-out effort, Ben caught the team. It was an accomplishment no one had seemed very impressed with until now.

"I didn't know you saw it that way. I figured it was partly your decision to finish the team time trial without me."

Thierry nodded. "By default, maybe. I guessed you were strong, but I didn't know you were that tough. My mistake."

"Once I caught up I had nothing left."

A double-decker sightseeing boat labeled *Helios* pulled out of port. In an amplified echo the tour guide asked how many passengers expected Thierry to win? A roar rose from the boat.

Ben smiled. "See there? The important thing is how fast we get you to the line, not me."

"If you think Pierre is sacrificing you to help me, then he has you brainwashed."

Ben shrugged. "What's his reason, then?"

Thierry's stare pierced right through him. "He has you walking scared. He likes that. You truly believe that if you don't play by his rules the game might be over."

"That's because it might."

"*Non.*" Thierry emphasized his opinion by slapping Ben's knee. "Not unless you allow it to be."

Ben furrowed his brow.

"You don't see it? You could become a great cyclist. Pierre knows that. That's why he can't bear to see you post a good result. He wants you to fall back in the General Classification. What place are you in now?" Thierry asked.

A freshening breeze lifted the Hobie-Cats onto one pontoon with an unseen hand. The windsurfers and Optimist Dinghies accelerated, too.

"Thirty-third."

"Who could guess with such a workload you could be among the top forty riders in the GC after the first week? But here you are."

Ben nodded. "My biorhythms are peaking at the right time."

"Is that it? Then take advantage. Golden opportunities to win stages, to make a name for yourself, come rarely. When they do you must seize them!" Thierry grasped a handful of air with a fist.

"I have to ride with the team in mind."

"Listen, Ben, I understand why you pulled out today. Let's not rehash it. My philosophy is to look forward, not back. *Carpe diem!* But blindly following Pierre's orders may not be the right strategy next time. Listen to your instincts."

Ben tried to process the words. Thierry seemed honest, but could he be trusted? How many times could Ben cross Pierre without getting booted from the squad, anyway? Probably once.

"Wouldn't you rather I thought of what's best for you?"

"A single stage win transformed my career. One day I pushed

harder than anyone thought I was capable of. I overcame more pain than even I believed I could. It got me noticed, gave me the opportunity to race against the best. That's what I thrive on. You and I both know that only a few men are capable of winning any given tour, right?"

"Of course."

"And it's not merely ability that puts them in such circumstances."

"Sure. They must have the support of a strong team."

"There's something far more important than that." Thierry tapped his forehead with an index finger. "Attitude. Confidence. Sure, it can get political, too, and there can be other unexpected complications, like injury. But if you put the things you can control in place, you might become a force to be reckoned with. If that happened, I'd like to prove I could beat you."

Ben laughed. "You're that competitive?"

Thierry winked. "You watch your backside. If we ever become adversaries I'll—how do you Americans put it—pull out all the stops."

Ben bit his lip. Subjugating personal goals to those of the team had always been difficult. Surprisingly, Thierry's words made it easier. Being recognized for his contribution and value made all the difference.

He'd have thought such praise would have the opposite effect. Did the team leader understand how the words were affecting his domestique? Was it only Ben's imagination, or had Thierry given him the green light to disobey Le Directeur's orders at some future time?

Ben felt a wave of loyalty, and silently renewed his vow to do whatever he could to get Thierry across the line first— this year. The French demanded *politesse* from their heroes. It meant they expected something beyond essential good manners; they required class. Thierry was the embodiment of that sort of champion. The quality of the man made him easy to admire, even to revere. As highly esteemed as Thierry had been in Ben's mind, he had elevated himself yet again as a result of this conversation. Maybe next year they could become rivals. If things played out that way, no competitor could be more worthy of his respect.

Thierry stood, "Let's head back."

"Tomorrow is going to be a difficult day," Ben said, rising.

"Yes, very hard. Will you have the strength to ride with me?"

Ben wasn't sure he understood. "You mean beside you at the front of the pack?"

Thierry nodded.

"I … think so." Was Thierry suggesting Ben supplant Albert as first lieutenant, the leader's right hand man? How would Albert react to such a slight?

"There's that lack of confidence again." Thierry shook his head and walked away.

Ben caught up with a couple of quick steps. "Do you really believe I lack confidence?"

"I know you do."

"Accepting my role has been a challenge. It's required me to become a foot soldier, not a commander. I've accomplished that. You seem to be saying the adjustments I've made for your benefit don't meet with your approval."

"They don't."

Ben looked the other way. In a flurry of squeaks and honks, a small black duck stole food from a bigger mallard. "Yes. I can ride with you."

Thierry's pace didn't slow. "I'm not so certain anymore. You're too determined to think like a domestique."

"I can adapt."

"Ben, you have the skills of a star, but instinct has been beaten out of you. I demand decisive action. I'm not about to surround myself with caution because, do you know what?"

"What?"

"It rubs off … and I don't want any rubbing off on me. There is something holding you back. You seem incapable of giving cycling everything. I suggest you figure out why, because that's what it takes to become a star."

Instinct took over. With a quick pivoting movement Ben

stepped in front of Thierry. The two men collided face to face. "I'll ride with you tomorrow," Ben said.

Thierry stumbled backward a step, then laughed. He slapped Ben across the head. "Maybe there is some fight in there."

Ben glared.

"That lacked caution too. Now, the question is, do you understand the difference between courage and carelessness?"

Ben nodded. "I'm the best choice for your right hand man."

"Is that so?"

"I can back up my word."

The team leader grinned.

"Do I get my chance?"

Thierry nodded. "*Oui*. I'll tell Pierre I want you at my side all day long. That means I don't want you off fetching water or running errands. *Comprends- tu?*"

Inwardly, Ben experienced a tingling sensation. What an opportunity! Outwardly, he did his best to maintain the appearance of composure. "Yes. I understand."

"I hope you do. I'll be very demanding."

"You can count on me."

Reaching the end of the pier, the men walked along the shore beneath a grand column of palomino coated Sycamores. A string of large light bulbs stretched from tree to tree. Red, pink, purple, and white impatiens grew with ferns and decorative grasses in whisky barrel pots.

"Why are you giving me this chance?" Ben asked.

"I'm not giving you anything. The presence of strong teammates will keep my enemies honest."

"Keep them honest?"

"*Oui*. The maillot jaune is both blessing and curse, like tying Superman's cape on a mortal. In the mountains, rivals form alliances and attack relentlessly. They'll hit hard when we're desperate to recover. They want to prove I'm human … that I can fail. You and I both know I am and can."

"You may. I don't."

"Then you are going to learn," Thierry said.

A rowboat passed. The pilot stared lovingly into the eyes of the beautiful girl sitting in the stern.

Ben thought for a moment. "Do you know how rival cyclists see you?"

Thierry didn't speak.

"I've heard competitors say it's comforting to ride in a field led by you."

The team leader shook his head. "No true competitor can ever be comfortable in a race controlled by another team."

"But they are, and now I understand why. Before you took the lead this race was mass confusion from start to finish. One attack after another flew off the front, usually with no real chance for success. Zing! Zing! Zing!" At each exclamation Ben clapped his hands and shot an alternating index finger forward—miniature bicycles zooming into the distance.

"That's the way it always is at the beginning. Legs are fresh and possibilities limitless," Thierry said. "I'm not preventing that now. Exhaustion is."

"No," Ben said. "There's more to it. It was madness. Insanity. The atmosphere changed the moment you put on yellow. I felt it."

"I never have. To me the race becomes many times more intense once I wear the maillot jaune. I feel responsible to control the peloton from that point."

Ben scuffed his shoes along a decorative sequence of inset cobbles. "Maybe that explains it. I'm telling you, there can't be a rider here who doesn't feel the difference. There's still lots of aggressive riding, but it's more tactically sound than before. The field has obvious respect."

"That I believe, but it's an odd sort of respect." They navigated the crowds in front of the Beau Riyage Hotel. As the fans recognized him, Thierry held up a silencing hand. "Thank you so much, but now we must sleep. Can the party be moved?"

In a flurry of strobing flashbulbs, the gathering seemed to agree.

"The fans do more than respect you," Ben said. "They love their champion."

Thierry smiled, but he looked tired. "Every year it gets more difficult to remain champion. The competition knows more and more about my capabilities. They understand my strengths and weaknesses." He opened the big oak door and held it for Ben. "But they don't know your strengths yet. I'll be depending on them."

Ben thought of the number nine he wore on his jersey. Like most teams, Banque Fédérale gave out jersey numbers roughly equivalent to the rider's position on the team. The team leaders numbers were one, eleven, twenty-one, thirty-one and so on. As defending champion Thierry wore number one. So, for a spectator, a single glance at Ben's number nine was all it took to peg him as the lowest ranked member of the defending champion's team. Now he would ride as the first lieutenant to the yellow jersey.

He extended a hand.

Thierry clasped it. "Tomorrow will be a day to remember."

"Yes, it will."

Thierry held onto Ben's hand. "Will you accept another piece of advice?"

"I'd be grateful."

"Let go of your anger toward Kyle. You may not like him, but he's a worthy competitor and that's all that matters. Today you saw firsthand how his feelings toward you warped his judgment. Don't let that happen to you."

Ben tried to respond, but choked on his words. His gut felt inhabited by a nest of excited sparrows. He settled for a nod.

"Don't let me down." Thierry stepped into his room and the door swung shut.

Chapter Seven

Ben stood in the empty hallway. The smart move would be head straight to bed. Get serious rest and ready himself for tomorrow's trial.

He couldn't do that. Not yet. Not with his mind flipping and flopping like a freshly snagged trout just chucked into an ice chest. It was tempting to believe all Thierry said about Pierre and how he was sabotaging Ben even to the team's detriment. It was all there, so easy to see now that Thierry brought it into the light. But going against Pierre? That could easily be career suicide.

What if Thierry's advice was meant to hurt Ben, not help him? Thierry warned Ben to let up on Kyle—advice that sounded in Ben's interest, but maybe ...

With his mind tuned to the dark side of human nature thanks to lessons Kyle had taught, it was possible to imagine Thierry's words as a brilliant strategy designed to get Ben out of his way. By making Ben his right-hand man tomorrow, Thierry ensured the entire team would resent Ben. If Ben then boldly defied Pierre to advance himself in the race as advised, he'd lose the respect of his team. And be thrown off it.

What a way to both eliminate a challenger and take vengeance on the man you held responsible for the death of your younger brother.

Was his imagination running out of control? Ben needed to get his mind straight. He'd like to call Bridgette. A dose of her calming optimism would do him wonders right now, but she wasn't available tonight. She'd still be tied up in the nursing conference that had prevented her from joining the Tour except on weekends. Maybe Fritz would help.

Ben walked the short distance from the hotel to the tricked out semi-trailer that served as the team's bike repair shop. The sides were painted with advertising to make the truck a rolling billboard. Ben opened the door to bright fluorescent lights and the smells of grease, glue, and rubber. The room exuded military-like order. High to his left several dozen bikes were mounted in rigid racks. Platoons of extra wheels hung ready in another upper corner. Gears, hubs, cranksets, deraileurs, and other equipment waited in perfect order in other sections of the shop. Two gleaming workstations contained the latest hi-tech gear. Over half a million dollars worth of bicycle equipment packed into this small space.

Fritz looked up from his work. "*Bonjour,* Ben. What are you doing here?"

"Just missing you, Fritzy. Hoped you'd come tuck me in."

Fritz broke into a wide grin. "*Non,* but maybe this means you're finally ready for a French *bise.*"

"Never. I don't kiss men."

The Frenchman laughed. "You're so uptight. It's not sexual, you know."

Ben chuckled. "Nevertheless ..."

"So, what are you really here for?" Fritz loosened a clamp and deftly spun the bicycle in his repair stand to an inverted position. "I can see there's something."

"You can see?" Ben noticed it was his bicycle the mechanic now serviced.

"Of course. Out with it."

Ben stepped closer and put a hand on his bike's front wheel. He spun it, watching the rim in comparison to the brake calipers on each side. The wheel spun true as Belgian rain in April.

He had attempted straightening his own rims on many occasions. Each time he tightened one spoke to eliminate a wobble it somehow caused a second spoke to become misadjusted. Fritz, in contrast, was an '*artiste.*'

The mechanic ran his hands along the tubing, seemingly sensing things about the bicycle's condition Ben knew he could never comprehend. Then Fritz grabbed the still rapidly spinning front wheel and stopped it. He put a finger on each side of the front forks, leaned his ear close to the assembly, then wiggled the handlebars.

"What are you doing?" Ben asked.

"Since you have nothing to say I figured I would talk with your bike."

Ben believed him. Fritz was one of those rare individuals so in tune with his craft that inanimate objects responded to him.

"What does it have to say?"

"She tells me she feels very good."

Ben smiled. "Yes, she feels great, though all this time I had no idea my bike was female."

Fritz tapped his temple with an index finger. "There is much I know about these things. But I wonder, would you kiss her?"

"Gladly." Ben bent forward and smooched the top tube. "So, you may as well know what's on my mind. How much do you trust Thierry?"

The mechanic looked up. "Same as I trust you, one-hundred percent. He's a good man."

Fritz squirted a tiny bit of lubricant onto his index finger. Banana smell filled the closed space. Fritz worked the odd smelling oil into a spot just below the headset.

"Well, I think I trust him, too … but he said some things I'm not sure about."

"Like?"

"He told me I'm the best rider on the team—even implied I might be better than him." Ben watch Fritz's expression carefully. "And he suggested I should disobey Pierre's orders if I sense opportunity."

Fritz let out a long whistle. "He said that?"

Ben nodded.

"Well. I knew he was honest, but I didn't know he was that honest."

There were many responses Ben had prepared himself for, but this wasn't one of them. His mouth dropped open. "You agree?"

"It's how Thierry proved himself years ago. He broke free of an iron-fisted directeur, and after that no one could hold him back. So I don't think he's trying to trick you if that's your concern."

"It crossed my mind."

Fritz continued running his hands across the bicycle, tightening here, loosening there, tweaking this a bit. "You can't get ahead while under Pierre's thumb. So the question is, do you wait around for a better situation or do you take a chance and see what happens?"

"Which would you do?"

Fritz shook his head. "How can I say? I'm me, not you. I'll always understand more about what is going on with a bike than what is happening in a cyclists head."

"A lot of help you are."

"You have great strength Ben, but champions rely on much more than power. Whether or not you're the best rider on this team, Banque Fédérale has only one great cyclist. You're not him."

Ben stared at Fritz.

Fritz shrugged. "I'm honest, too."

"I know." Ben pursed his lips and nodded slightly.

Fritz spun the bike upright. He released the clamp and removed the bicycle, balancing it beneath the top tube on one finger. "She is perfect."

"If you were me, determined to earn Pierre's respect, what would you do?"

The mechanic laughed. "Renounce my American citizenship."

Ben scowled.

"Or I might cut my hair."

Ben froze. He ran a hand through his blonde locks. Pierre had told him to cut his hair today, hadn't he? What better way for Ben to prove his willingness to do anything asked of him than to follow an order Pierre had no right to give? Losing his hair would be painful, but if he gained the opportunity to prove his strength it would be worth the cost.

"You really think a haircut would help?" Ben finally asked.

Fritz reached toward his tool bench. "I don't see what it could hurt."

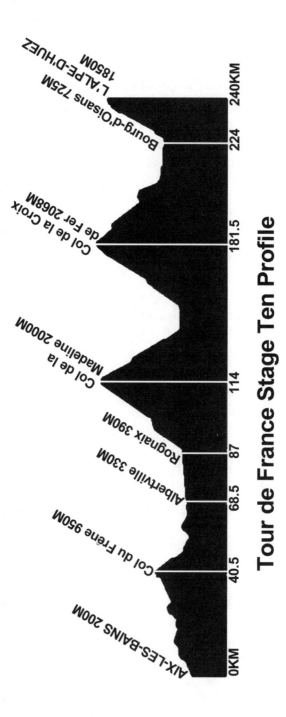

Tour de France Stage Ten Profile

Chapter Eight

Cyclists milled anxiously on the Avenue du Petit Port. Hotels loomed on one side, but the other stretched open all the way to the opposite walled shore of Lac Du Bourget. Heat pervaded. High humidity congested things even further. Perspiration glistened on the brows of spectators.

From here the lower foothills of the day's first climb, the easy one, were visible. The real battle would unfold four peaks and nearly 150 miles away. Often it was difficult to grasp the massive scale of this event. It could only be dealt with one pedal revolution at a time. Stopping to think about the twenty-one stages in twenty-three days totaling over 2400 miles was just too overwhelming.

Ben swallowed the last bite of his millefeuille. He could never get enough of the sweet custard layered croissants or other French patisseries. Why couldn't he find such creations in America? He wiped his hands, then he pulled his stage profile map out of his jersey pocket and studied the terrain he was about to confront—four enormous peaks to ascend today, the final three climbs rated among the most difficult in all of road cycling. Did he have what it would take?

The echoing words of the public address announcer were mostly unintelligible, but the enthusiasm pervading his voice supercharged the pre-race atmosphere.

Ben ran a hand over his uneven, stubbly hair, then replaced his cycling cap. It wasn't the best haircut he'd ever had, Fritz clearly had a better eye for true wheels than even sideburns, but Ben liked it. Today, he felt as different as he looked. For the first time in a long time, he saw himself as an elite athlete. He stood on par with anybody in this race.

Albert and Pierre stared at Ben from twenty meters away. Were their expressions of disdain directed toward his haircut? Probably not.

Ben completed last minute preparations, then moved into place for the start. Soon the grinning race director, standing out the sunroof of his red sedan, swept his white flag downward.

Cleats clicked into pedals and gears clacked up as the peloton came to life. The cyclists started off almost lazily, hoping against hope that no one would be crazy enough to launch a serious attack early on. Ninety-seven percent of the field would be overjoyed if the race didn't begin in earnest until only the final pair of the day's four climbs remained. Such an outcome was unlikely.

The peloton was an unpredictable three hundred legged monster—a beast unlike any other. Built of men, each with a different agenda, it existed for their mutual benefit, yet its existence consumed their independence.

To the peloton, weakness equaled opportunity. If its pace slowed, pieces of the monster would scheme to break free of its gravitational attraction. They would morph into smaller, more agile creatures called breakaways and burst onto the open road, intent on defeating the very being on which they normally relied.

Only one driving dynamic of the peloton's behavior was predictable: On any given day there were a couple of glory-seekers who would bust a lung in order to capture their moment in the sun. That meant everyone else had to spend the day chasing. Such ambition fueled the Tour's relentless engine and assured no easy days.

The riders usually collapsed in shell-shocked amazement at the end of the day: "How the hell did we go so fast?"

With such a treacherous tenth stage looming, it seemed almost possible that the opportunists, whoever they were today, would hold off their attacks for the first few hours.

The course made a loop through Aix-les-Bains, giving the locals a last chance to see the colorful jerseys.

Ben nodded toward a toddler licking a large sucker. "You ever want to have one of those, Thierry?"

"A lollipop? No. I'm a Popsicle man myself, but if you want I can get you one. The sponsor caravan flings them out by the hundreds."

"Very funny. I meant the kid"

Thierry chuckled. "A child is what you're after? You, *mon ami*, have a nose for trouble."

Ben nodded. "True. You know, the lollipop does bring a question to mind."

"Yes?"

"It's a rolling circus around here. Not just lollipops—waves of commercialism."

Thierry laughed. "You don't like traveling a route blazed by a junk train? Is it the squadron of yellow rubber ducky cars that offend you? Please don't tell me you have a problem with the supermodels tossing key chains."

"No. That I like."

"What do you object to, then?"

"I don't object, but why does Pierre worry about American commercialism when Disney should be taking notes?"

Thierry shook his head. "You think too much. He's French. You're a Yankee. That's enough."

The peloton swept around a flower filled roundabout, interrupting the conversation. The vibration of men and machines on the uneven road sounded like children playing on a washboard slippery slide.

The field navigated the dangerous stretch without incident.

The scent of freshly baked bread wafted from a storefront, filling the quaint passage they now traveled. The aroma nearly dragged Ben from his bicycle. He narrowly avoided a huge hole in the road.

He pulled alongside his team leader again. "You'd need a ladder to get out of some of these potholes. In America, lawyers salivate over trouble like that."

Thierry chuckled. "In that case, I'm with Pierre. Keep American influence away. Beneath the wheels of the peloton the roads become something more—a romanticized version of themselves. That hole you're talking about is probably a civic treasure around here. I would bet the mayor is devastated no one fell in this time through."

"A sad day in Aix-les-Baines," Ben answered.

He'd long ago heard the French love the tour because it harbors the remarkable power to transform the everyday into the extraordinary. French farmers were known to recount the simple pleasure of watching the colorful swath tear a seam past their particular verdant field. Those magical moments when Le Tour comes within arm's reach, whether tactically significant or not, were said to mean everything to locals. Now that he'd experienced it firsthand, Ben understood why. The Tour had already surpassed his highest expectation.

"By the way, did your hair get caught in some heavy machinery last night?" Thierry asked.

"Yeah. Fritz's clippers."

Thierry's eyes went wide. "A mechanic? You're not as smart as I thought. Why?"

"Speed."

"Who would give such advice?" The team leader chuckled. "*Non*, let me guess. A jealous bald guy?"

Ben shrugged. "Turns out, I like the way it makes me feel."

Thierry regarded him again. "Makes you look different. More determined."

"I am."

"Different or determined?"

Ben smiled.

A traffic island forced the riders to split into two parallel groups. Ben veered left at the last moment while Thierry went right, again ending their conversation. The sound of the turbulent air changed as the peloton became temporarily thinner, but for the moment, there were no urgent concerns.

Ben turned his attention to the people on the roadside. A plump woman in a purple dress reminded him of an enormous grape. A group of young boys straddling their own bicycles, their eyes glowing with admiration, seemed to be dreaming of a day they would take their place in the peloton.

Ben loved segments like this where the race moved at a

reasonable pace and he could actually focus on the spectator's faces. He liked to imagine their stories, to dream of the things they had experienced. Above all, it honored him to be a part of a spectacle they would sacrifice so much to see.

The routes reconvened. At the same instant the road bent slightly downward and the pace surged. Spectators cheered as the angry rainbow spilled from town and onto the battlefield of the rural roads.

Cyclists bumped shoulder to shoulder as the road constricted. Curses and the clatter of metal on stone echoed from the middle of the peloton. Looking back, Ben saw dispossessed riders clambering onto their bikes or hurrying to navigate the mess. A crash so early in the stage was unusual given the relatively moderate speeds, but it wasn't unheard of since there were so many distractions.

Ten meters ahead of Ben a hyena-like laugh erupted. Kyle was looking over his shoulder at the delayed cyclists. Ben's gut sank as he returned his attention farther up the road.

A lone cyclist streaked away, already opening a gap on the field of a couple hundred meters. As usual, the peloton contained a rider unable to resist the opportunity to gain time. An audible groan escaped as the pack realized the day's race had officially begun.

"It's that mountain goat Luigi," Ben heard a competitor mutter. "Why's he running away so early?"

No one needed to explain the little Italian's motivation to Ben. Luigi was a strong climber, but his team wasn't capable of giving him a real chance at overall victory. He'd therefore put his eye on the prize of the red polka dot mountain climber's jersey. Bonus points were awarded to the first three to fifteen men who conquered each peak, depending on its classification. The more difficult, the more points available. Luigi probably figured if he got out front while the going was easy he could crest the first three peaks in first place. Given that these were severe climbs, that accomplishment would award him more than enough bonus points to take over the King of the Mountains competition lead, even if he reserved only enough strength to limp the day's final climb.

Ben wiped sweat from his brow with the short sleeve of his

jersey.

If Luigi didn't extend his lead far enough to be a real threat as stage victor, Ben figured the breakaway rider's strategy might work out well for Banque Fédérale. The Italian's presence up the road would serve as disincentive for anyone else to launch a strong attack.

In no time Luigi disappeared around a series of bends, evaporating like a mirage. Once out of sight, it wasn't long until he was out of mind. In the oppressive heat, rhythm was hard to establish. Ben slogged along with the pack, more concerned with staying at Thierry's side as promised than anything else. Each time he looked at the team leader he thought about his words from the night before. "There is something holding you back."

The idea resonated somehow, but Ben couldn't put his finger on an explanation.

As the road left Sainte Reine, the climb ratcheted up. The shallow rapids in the roadside stream became foamier. Ahead at the sweep of a distant corner the day's first categorized climb, the ascent of the Col du Frêne, began in earnest. Ben recognized the brilliant yellow time-gap motorcycle waiting for the pack to make up the distance. The motorcycle passenger would write the interval to the breakaway on his board and hold it up for all cyclists to see.

"*Cinq minutes au maximum,*" said Thierry.

Ben nodded and silently prayed for a number starting with four. If the pack remained within five minutes of Luigi all would be well. They could continue their plodding pace without fear for the time being. If not they'd instantly adjust their tempo.

As the motorcycle neared, Ben strained to see the writing on the chalkboard … 10:41. Could that be right? The number became clearer. Yes, ten minutes and forty-one seconds. Ben's gut clenched.

Luigi had put way too much time between himself and the main pack. If he were allowed to expand on such an advantage he'd become a significant threat. Banque Fédérale must react.

"You know what to do," Pierre said over the radio.

Let the suffering begin.

Chapter Nine

In unison the Banque Fédérale riders rose from their saddles and accelerated up the hill. The pace leaped several notches even as the gradient increased.

"It's suicidal to work so hard so early," came a voice from behind.

"Then give up," Thierry suggested.

Effort soon overwhelmed the early stage lethargy that had encrusted Ben's muscles. Today the warm-up had been cut short.

Now committed to the hard work, he craved the fight. He didn't need to look back to sense the weaker climbers spat out the back of the pack, finding themselves casualties far earlier in the day than they ever would have imagined. The feared stage would surely be even harder than anticipated. The peloton stretched like fresh dough: the group surrounding the maillot jaune in a clump at the front, a progressively thin string of riders in the middle, and then another clump forming at the back.

This last group, known as "the bus," normally became cooperative rather than competitive. Before the stage ended the vast majority of riders would find themselves in the bus, simply working together to survive the ride.

Speech became rare in the lead group, but the more primitive human sounds, labored breath, and grunts, increased. Ben concentrated on the task. Unconsciously his breaths, pedal strokes, and body sway became rhythmic. Bit by bit he defeated the road.

Revolution after revolution the cyclists pushed. The remaining elite climbers were men accustomed to outlasting their competition. They rode, not for pleasure, but for pain. They were men driven to prove they could endure more than any other. Time and again one would throw down the gauntlet, pushing into the lead and establishing a gap. Each time the pace increased, a smaller group found the strength to respond.

"*En avant, la moto,*" a nearby competitor said.

Ben looked up to see the yellow time gap motorcycle, the chalkboard just getting near enough to read. Eight minutes and fifty-three seconds. He did a double take. Luigi must be superhuman today. He wouldn't allow himself to be reeled in. Ben powered along with the other elite climbers up the series of switchbacks that topped the long climb.

After cresting the Col du Frêne the route plummeted down a wicked, speedy descent. A parachute would be a more appropriate way off the precipitous wall. Visions of the grape-filled valley below strobed through the rapidly passing foliage. Ben avoided focusing on the serrated sharks teeth lining the lower jaw of the Central Massif just beyond.

In no time, the cyclists streamed off the foothills and joined the highway to Albertville. As the remnants of the peloton swept through long tunnels of overhanging trees, they again settled into workman-like rhythm.

All too soon the route veered from the highway onto the gray ribbon of countrified asphalt leading up the Col de la Madeleine. The mood of the athletes took a less bucolic turn. The first of the out-of-category Alpine climbs had arrived. Despite an uncomfortably brisk pace, the time gaps to Luigi were holding firm. The elite cyclists were becoming agitated.

As the group of the maillot jaune moved into the heart of the stage's second peak, most of the peloton had been dropped. They had a long, lonely ride ahead.

They entered the village of Bonnevau Tse. Here the road was nothing more than a narrow asphalt-covered cart path glued to the doorsteps of the rickety houses and barns. Red and pink begonias planted in guardrail pots lent color and aroma to the town.

Ben grabbed his water bottle and squeezed it. The last of the liquid squirted out in an indignant hiss. He tossed the container aside.

The brutal pace had shelled six of the nine Banque Fédérale

riders from the lead pack. Despite all the work, or rather, thanks to it, the gap still stood at over five minutes. They could live with that number for a while, but at this rate, who would have strength for the final climb?

The grade eased as the road stretched into a deep canyon. Ben stole a furtive glance at his team leader. Thierry's face exhibited calm concentration as usual. He climbed with an easy, rhythmic motion. If Luigi's lead worried Thierry, there was no outward sign.

Ben drew confidence from his teammate's businesslike approach to the situation as he considered his unaccustomed position of being Thierry's last reserve. For much of the day he had ridden right behind the leader's wheel while teammates set pace in front of them. In the last quarter of this climb he had taken up residence in second position, just ahead of Thierry and just behind Albert, the current pace-making teammate.

As the canyon closed, the road steepened, zigzagging up the face of the headwall. Ben kept his upper body relaxed, allowing tension to flow downward and burn off in the punishing gyration of his legs. Like a sled dog in the traces he savored the work. He focused on the powerful sensation of smoothly cruising up the hill, while blocking the actual task from his mind. It was a sort of denial of reality, focusing on the result while ignoring the cause, but the technique often worked well for him.

Unexpectedly, Ben found himself overtaking Albert. His cyclometer showed eighteen kilometers an hour, a bit under the pace Albert needed to maintain. In fact, Albert must be going slower than fifteen. Something wasn't right.

The two men shared a glance as Ben moved by. Albert's hollow expression confirmed Ben's worst fear. Yet another member of Banque Fédérale had cracked. Albert had pushed too hard, and now his body would rebel. Ben knew the helpless sensation well. Like every pro cyclist, he'd experienced it himself many times, sometimes purposely on training rides, other times by mistake in races like this. A man would have as much success running a car without gasoline as leading a race up the mountains after bonking. It simply couldn't be done.

"*Désolé* … Thierry," Albert gasped. "I don't have … legs today."

It must have killed Albert to admit defeat on the day of his demotion. Ben felt sorry for him. He was also impressed that Thierry anticipated Albert's decline before it cost him.

Even without looking back, Ben sensed Thierry's answer had been a calm nod. The team leader would be silently evaluating strategy rather than regretting a circumstance he couldn't change. The two biggest climbs of the day lay ahead, and Ben now sat as Thierry's only ally. Four other teams had more members in the lead group than Banque Fédérale. Two had four riders—twice as many as the defending French squad. What's more, cyclists were likely to join forces in attempts to unseat the reigning champion.

"*Au revoir* friend Albert. Banque Fédérale's nightmare has begun!" The words were delivered in clumsy French. A deep bass voice. Kyle.

Ben turned. He glanced at Kyle's confident scowl, then eyed Thierry. He couldn't waste energy putting his question into words.

Thierry nodded ever so slightly.

Now was far earlier than they had planned on making such a move, but circumstance left little choice. As was usually the case, actual conditions forced strategy-room theory to be chucked out the window.

Ben clicked to a smaller chain ring, simultaneously easing for a moment on the pedals. He didn't want the metallic clatter of a gear change to alert anyone to his plan, so he dampened the noise as much as possible. The instant the chain settled into the more difficult gear, he stood on the pedals and danced up the mountain. He felt Thierry right behind, almost as if the team leader blew on his back at each exhalation.

Ben's focus constricted. The pavement immediately ahead of his front wheel eclipsed the stunning terrain around him. He traveled as parallel as possible to a faint seam in the asphalt, evidence of a steamroller's passing. Hopefully his competitors would meander all over this road.

Ben's heart, legs, and lungs screamed for relief, but it was a plea he couldn't grant. Searing pain confirmed he was well beyond anaerobic redline. Ben promised himself he'd endure the torture for at least another thirty seconds. The task would be easier for Thierry, as following required so much less effort, both mental and physical, than leading.

In fifteen seconds or so Ben needed to ease off to allow recovery or his muscles would shut down. The trick was to scale back without the trailing riders noticing. Deception, convincing rivals you are simply too strong for them, is an integral part of the chess match. Anything to coerce them into mentally raising their white flag. As any athlete can attest, battle at full effort becomes impossible once you "know" you can't win. In this respect at least, there was no more cerebral contest than cycling. God, he loved playing the game again!

They rounded a turn past a quaint chapel, and Ben lifted his gaze. He didn't know this particular climb, the Col de la Madeleine, nearly as well as he wished. Positioned so far from the end of a tough stage, he hadn't expected decisive riding to occur on its face. He prayed for a fortunate break, then saw what he wanted.

His spirits soared. Ahead, the road made a 180-degree turn as it climbed the steep hillside. The switchback would allow him to view the damage he'd inflicted on the trailing group while also showing their competitors how strong he and Thierry still were. He hammered even harder toward his objective, energized now that he had a visible goal.

Somewhere well behind him, a competitor cursed. The misery of another only energized him more. He charged into the hairpin turn. As he navigated the tight bend he steered close to the inside edge, taking the steepest but most direct route.

On the road below, the chase group lay in shambles. Cyclists littered the battlefield like discarded confetti. Bikes wobbled dramatically from side to side as their pilots tried to tease effort out of throbbing legs. Even Gunter von Reinholdt had been dropped. Only Thierry, Kyle, a likeable Spaniard named Pablo Lopez, and a quiet Lithuanian called Frankas Butkus still remained on Ben's wheel. Other than Thierry and Ben, no two were from the same team. The balance of forces, moments ago arranged solidly against Banque Fédérale, had now tilted undeniably for the good.

Ben moved to the other side of the road, out of sight of the majority of the trailing pack, then settled into the saddle and concentrated on a technically sound pedal stroke and gradual recovery. The power of his attack had surprised him. He wondered whether the weight he'd lost in hair, or even the greater ability to shed heat as a result of the bad crew cut, had increased his abilities. It sure felt like it.

"Bold move. *Très bien*," Thierry panted.

Ben gulped air. His screaming muscles craved oxygen, and the thinning atmosphere didn't help.

The temperature must have dropped as they gained altitude, but Ben couldn't feel the difference. Sweat flowed down his face, back, and arms. The patchy snowfields near the summit looked deliciously cool. Maybe a breeze would waft chilled air over their bodies as they passed.

"Can we pause … to pick a bouquet?" Thierry asked.

Ben chuckled as he admired the abundant purple, white, blue, and yellow wildflowers against the soft green background of the treeless slopes.

"Boo," hissed a fan as the duo approached.

Other spectators whistled.

Ben, used to the treatment, paid no attention.

The moment he passed, the fan changed his tune. "*Allez Thierry, Allez.* Drop the murderous Yankee."

"*Troglodyte*," Thierry whispered.

With about a kilometer to go to the top of the hill, and the final brutal switchbacks remaining, a message came over the headset. "Why have you men relaxed? There will be time for that on the descent."

Pierre's words angered Ben, but in a good way. He gritted his teeth and dug deep, accelerating again. Speeding up meant he'd feel the invigorating wind of the descent sooner anyway.

He crossed the anaerobic threshold, this time with the knowledge his muscles could recover on the long, fast downhill to come. By maximizing this surge he should be able to inflict enough damage to prevent the dropped riders from rejoining his group on the descent. Maybe Kyle would join the list of casualties.

"You're more than lucky. You're good." He recalled Thierry's words from the preceding evening and felt renewed strength.

He replayed the statement over and over in his head. Then he allowed himself to imagine Le Directeur's most frustrating phrase, "Benjamin, *plus d' eau*," and he pushed even harder, feeling proud he could transform every indignity to the positive.

The pain pleased him. Only through suffering could he separate himself from the masses. As they crested the hill and approached the aptly named Restaurant Panoramique he stole a glance under his left arm at his teammate. Twenty meters farther back he saw the other three riders struggling to gain the summit.

"Take the bonus, Thierry."

The team leader passed him smoothly. Ben watched the Frenchman from behind, now. Thierry exuded strength. What a leader this guy was. Again Ben considered the honor of working for such a strong and just competitor. Pride welled within him to be such a significant player in Thierry's upcoming historic accomplishment of a fourth tour victory.

Thierry surged across the summit line, collecting the valuable second place climbing time bonus. Luigi, of course, had absconded with the first place bonus several minutes earlier.

As Ben crossed the line picking up third place bonus, he stole another glance at Kyle and the other two cyclists. They looked hammered.

The team car pulled alongside. "*Magnifique!*" said Fritz.

Pierre looked less enthusiastic, but enthusiasm was never Le Directeur's strong suit.

Ben gave both men thumbs up, then accepted the supplies being handed across the gap. He loaded up on food, drink, and lastly, a helmet. As he strapped on the head protector he moved aside for Thierry who gathered the same sort of gear.

Thierry spoke as he fastened his helmet. "I've never been whistled at before. I don't like it."

"In my country it means they find you attractive," Ben said.

"Not that sort of whistling. You know that."

Ben shrugged. "I'm used to it."

Thierry clicked into his large front chain ring and accelerated. Mont Blanc scratched the sky directly in front of them. They rode hard into the shark's teeth of the Central Massif.

A flimsy guardrail of weathered wooden stakes driven in at ten-foot intervals and laced together by twine seemed an odd attempt at keeping vehicles on the road. Apparently the ease of pulling the pegs to clear the wintertime ski slope took priority over driver safety.

It wasn't long before Kyle and the other two riders rejoined their group. The higher the speed, the greater the drafting advantage a large group had over a smaller one. This same formula that spelled doom for Luigi, still all alone out in front, also lessened the disappointment that Kyle hadn't been dropped. The five riders could increase their lead on those behind while also chewing into Luigi's gain. The cyclists snaked down the mountain, passing the sticks faster and faster as they plummeted toward the tree-line.

Fans were more widespread now. A herd of cows with gently clanging bells took their place.

As they passed the yellow time-gap motorcycle parked beside the road the passenger wrote on his chalkboard. Moments later the motorcycle accelerated to match the cyclist's speed. The passenger held out his chalkboard. It read: 2:38.

They'd done even more damage to Luigi than Ben hoped. This group of five was certain to take over the lead on the next peak, and then reach the base of Alpe d' Huez in position to battle out first place.

The descent dropped more steeply and Ben riveted his attention as his bicycle screamed faster and faster. Caution was the immediate casualty as the group plummeted from their laboriously gained altitude at breakneck speed.

On a sweeping right hand turn Ben sensed dust. He tapped his brakes to test traction. The bicycle shimmied. The chilling sensation of high-speed vibration triggered terrible memories. He froze momentarily in fear.

Beyond the rapidly approaching "guard twine" lay nothingness. The void seemed to yawn, sucking him in. This was no time to allow bad memories to seize him. He shoved the recollections away and threw his weight against the turn. The wheels bit the road as the arc tightened. The air-tone screamed an octave higher. Man and machine barreled through the corner, using every centimeter of available road.

In the euphoric moment of success, images of downhill disaster again battled for supremacy in Ben's mind. Negative thoughts now could be catastrophic, but the sensation of a twisty descent was like a Pavlovian trigger to contemplate failure.

The road swerved quickly left, right, left. Ben concentrated. Moving with all the agility he could muster, he navigated the difficult stretch, still holding fear at bay. Then, on a brief straightaway, it all rushed in on him.

Ever since his accident at age fourteen, a road that bent steeply downhill conjured images of the disaster on Boulder Mountain: crashing through the underbrush, tasting blood, smelling the antiseptic hospital room where he'd begun his recuperation. Descents were the one situation that robbed Ben of his power to focus.

He shook his head, dislodging the hallucination and looked for the best line through the approaching turns. Rapid adjustments in position were necessary to maintain the lowest center of gravity as he moved through the challenging section. He made certain his wheels tracked as straight as possible whenever he had to cross potentially slippery wet or dusty pavement. The road vibrated in his handlebars, seat, and pedals.

The wind roaring past his ears made hearing difficult, but from behind, the whine of brakes caught his attention. What did that mean?

A terrible clatter arose- crashing, scraping, and the yelling voices of several men including Thierry overcame the hurricane-like din.

"*Putain!*"

Whose voice was that? Ben couldn't look back. He executed the final turn in the sequence, narrowly dodging rock and debris recently fallen from above. As they passed between the ski resort's skyscrapers, he turned. There were only three men on his tail, none of them dressed in yellow. Where was Thierry?

Ben sat up, allowing the wind to catch him full in the chest. The rushing air made a hollow sound as it slowed him. "Thierry?" he yelled into his radio.

Kyle and the other two cyclists rocketed past. In seconds they were a full turn ahead.

Thierry must have fallen. It was just like Kyle to take advantage of what could easily be a serious injury. He would almost certainly have seen the accident as he was probably behind Thierry in the draft when it occurred.

Ben scrambled for mental clarity. He could either maintain contact with Kyle's group and attempt to disrupt its rhythm, or he could wait and attempt to pull Thierry back toward the lead. Go or no go?

"I demand decisive action." Thierry's words echoed in his ears. Go!

Ben gripped the handlebars and leaned low. Pierre might be furious about his decision, but Thierry would understand. The team leader made it obvious the evening before that he didn't want Ben giving up position unless something could definitely be accomplished in return. This time nothing could.

Albert and others would soon reach Thierry's position and, having recovered on the descent, could lead him back. Once Thierry was again within reach of the lead Ben could drop back and assist him in the final chase.

Ben's poor downhill ability was the biggest knock against him when he entered the European circuit, but in this moment such concerns evaporated. Kyle had made himself such an easy target to hate that …

No. Another of Thierry's admonitions came back to him. "Let go of your anger toward Kyle."

Ben cleared his mind. Kyle and the others must be caught for strategic reasons. He could slow them down if he could rejoin their group. He must overcome his fear of the downhill because he had given his word to Thierry. Time for courage, not carelessness.

He gritted his teeth. "Here I come."

Chapter Ten

Garbled French sputtered in Ben's earpiece. With only a few hundred meters between him and the chase car, the transmission should have been clear, but the wind screaming past his ears and the increasing amount of rock between him and the transmission point made understanding Le Directeur impossible. Mostly he got static.

His line drifted precariously close to the outside edge of the road. Fortunately, the street below the ski area was more modern than what had come before. Nevertheless, he couldn't spare concentration to make out Le Directeur's words.

It would take hard work to re-establish contact with Kyle's group. Once there, the descent would be easier in the company of the three other riders. Maybe he could hear the transmission then.

On straight-aways Ben spun his legs as fast as he could. The wheels moved so rapidly his efforts hardly added any momentum, but every little bit counted. He tore through villages so fast the buildings blurred to streaks of brown and gray. Outside of race conditions, such a descent would be suicidal. Only on a closed road could he take such risks. Gradually, he rejoined the other three riders.

Once in their draft he paused to consider the situation. For the second day in a row, despite vastly differing terrain, the tactical choice that made most sense to him was to "sit on," forcing everyone else in the group to work while he rested and even impeded their progress. This time, victory wasn't an option. The goal would be to interrupt this group sufficiently that Thierry could rejoin, then win the day.

As the road flattened a knot formed in Ben's gut. Had his decision to follow Kyle been right? He'd put his career in peril as the result of a single decision. It was the sort of dilemma he'd faced many times in his youth. Only back then, Dad had been the one slamming his dreams with the same wild abandon Pierre did now.

Thierry's advice jolted him, and again it forced his thinking into a new groove. The team leader would be angered by Ben's defeatist logic. Look forward, not back. Ben certainly preferred that philosophy at a gut level, but hard-learned lessons of obedience weren't easy to break.

After the valley bottom village of La Chambre, the route bent slightly uphill into the narrowing Arc River gorge. Team cars for the other riders in his group handed out supplies. With no support, Ben decided to make a deal. "Trade you my helmet for an energy bar and water bottle," he yelled into the window of a passing vehicle.

The driver chuckled, handing out the food and drink, but didn't wait to take his helmet. Ben smiled as he stowed the supplies. Then he removed the head protector and tossed it near a young spectator. The little boy cheered as he grabbed his souvenir.

Refreshing wind blew through Ben's stubbly scalp. Grabbing the water bottle from its cage, he squirted a quarter of the liquid onto his face and wetted his head. Enough self-doubt. He couldn't possibly perform at the level he needed to with such a mindset.

While, dramatic scenery aside, the next several miles might be routine, long portions of this day would demand all of his mental resources. He needed to keep his faculties as refreshed as possible. For now, he may as well hide from the wind. Time to play follow the leader, waiting until he received word that Thierry needed him to drop back and assist his return to the lead. He must arrive at that moment as relaxed as possible because the effort required would be epic.

He allowed his thoughts to wander, but they entered forbidden ground. His Dad's face loomed in memory, stern expression cut in stone, confident voice drilling doubt into Ben's head about being able to win a bicycle race, any race. Ben redirected the thought before it settled into his physique. He tried to transform Dad's stern face into Bridgette's loving one, but it morphed into something else. Suddenly Dad's defeatist words shot from Pierre's mouth.

Ben shook his head to clear it and then released his mind again. Dad reappeared, but this time Ben let the memory play out. Maybe this is where his thoughts needed to wander.

* * *

"Benjamin! Customer out front. Get your eleven-year-old butt out there," Ben's dad yelled.

Ben laid down his dishrag and stepped to the window beside Dad's recliner. Pulling to a stop out front at their service station was a Winnebago towing a cabin cruiser.

Ben sprinted from the trailer home, anxious to get a closer look. It was the most amazing vehicle he'd ever seen. It wasn't that he'd never seen a big boat or a big camper. Living in this little town of 129 people seventy miles from Bullfrog Marina, he'd seen thousands of boats and hundreds of campers. In fact, Hanksville's economy would collapse if not for the constant stream of vacationers heading to and from the lake. But this boat and camper were different. The paint scheme on both vehicles made up a continuous desert mural—red rock cliff, sand dunes, a coyote, a small Indian village, a great blue heron, lizards, prickly pears in bloom, and more. An awfully lot of activity for a desert scene, but interesting nonetheless.

The door to the vehicle opened, and a fit man in his mid-forties jumped out.

Ben was about to greet the stranger when he heard his dad's voice from behind. "What can I do you for?"

Ben looked back. Apparently Dad couldn't contain his curiosity about this vehicle either. Normally, once he'd sat down to watch the evening news he wouldn't get up for anything.

The stranger scanned the service station. What must this man think of the dirt lot? No asphalt, no grass. The open garage was a jumble of half completed projects. Candy counter and cash register were barely visible through a dirty storefront window. The run-down station made Ben suddenly self-conscious, even though it blended in with the rest of the town.

Heck, even the water source the city was built on, the Dirty Devil River, contained the precious liquid only about half the time. Ben had seen the big city and its lushness and knew his hometown must register as less than impressive to knowledgeable travelers.

Hanksville was God's earth, undressed. Whoever coined the phrase 'God's green earth,' clearly hadn't taken a look at the real thing. Here the earth was red, rugged, and unforgiving.

"Mind if I drink?" asked the stranger, nodding toward the hose.

"Be my guest," Dad answered.

The man turned the spigot. Water flooded across the thirsty dirt. The man lifted the end of the hose slowly, feeling the liquid with his finger as he waited for it to cool. When it did he took a brief sip, then held the stream away from his body. "I blew a fan belt about fifty miles out of town. I've been limping in for the last several hours. Can you get me running again?"

Ben's gaze remained fixed on the ribbon of crystal water spilling onto the dirt lot.

"You want to finish up with your drink and then turn that thing off?" Dad asked. "That stuff is gold 'round these parts."

The man's eyes widened in surprise. He twisted the spigot closed.

"You say you lost a belt. What kind of engine you got in this thing?"

The stranger shrugged. "I'll pop the hood."

Dad walked to the front of the vehicle, Ben at his side, while the man climbed behind the wheel. When the hood sprang open they found themselves staring at a shiny Big Block Chevy modified to fit into the tightest compartment Ben had ever seen.

Dad let out a long, discouraged whistle.

Soon the stranger stepped back around front. He stayed arms length away, regarding the engine the way a bachelor does an infant. "So, what do you think?"

"I think you're going to be spending time in Hanksville. I don't have a belt like that in stock. Getting one will take two days, maybe more."

The stranger tensed. "I don't have two days."

Dad shrugged. "Everyone's got two days."

Ben looked at his father. Didn't Dad know in the city things moved a lot faster? He could be so embarrassing.

"Isn't there anything you can do to get me out of here today?" the stranger asked.

"How far you got to go?"

"Two hundred and fifty miles."

Dad clicked his tongue on the roof of his mouth. When the familiar sound slowed, Ben knew his father had devised a plan— that's the way it always worked. Dad could fix anything if he just thought on it a moment.

Dad unhitched his belt and pulled it from around his waist. "I'm not promising anything, but I'll do my best. Why don't you go grab a bite? There's a burger joint down the road a piece. It's a short walk."

The stranger let out a breath. "All right. I'll do that."

As Ben leaned against a pump, concentrating on slicing his dad's leather belt down to the necessary width, the man emerged from the motor home carrying a shiny green Schwinn Varsity ten-speed bicycle. Ben twisted to watch. He tripped over his own feet and stumbled into an oilcan display pyramid.

Pinned above his nightstand was a magazine picture of this very same bicycle. He'd always dreamed of owning a bike … any bike. But, for him, a Varsity stood at the pinnacle of all bikes. He had spent hours staring at his photo. Now, here was his bike. What a glorious sight. If only he could take it for a spin.

The stranger, apparently oblivious to him, climbed onto the bicycle and pedaled away. Ben dropped to his haunches and started gathering cans, but he didn't take his eyes off the bike until it carried its rider out of sight.

"Can you imagine, Benjamin? That fellow is so rushed he can't even take a leisurely walk when it's forced on him. He's got to race around on that contraption."

"It's not a contraption," Ben said.

Dad shook his head.

Ben picked up the belt and walked to his dad's side. Why couldn't Dad understand that busy city people deserved admiration and respect, not ridicule for the hurry they were always in?

"Sure seems like a nice guy to me. Probably got important things to do."

Dad looked at Ben. "Sure he's nice … but he's a man who hasn't received his jolt yet."

"Huh?"

"Life has a way of administering electroshock therapy, Son." Dad dragged a greasy hand across his moist forehead. "About when you start thinking things like matching murals on campers and boats are important, God reminds you to keep your ambitions in check—to make sure your dreams fit inside your wallet." He stepped to the side for a better view of the murals. "Back before we left Topeka I might've painted my boat like this."

"You?"

"Sure. I used to be a dreamer. But I learned my lesson later, and I intend for you to learn it sooner." He stuck his head back into the engine compartment. "There are better things than being in a hurry to get to tomorrow. You always remember that."

Ben shook his head. It didn't strike him as a lesson he wanted to remember.

Dad's voice echoed out from under the hood. "I left my Allen wrenches on the workbench. Get them for me."

Ben set down the belt and knife and headed for the garage. He went to the workbench but didn't see the tools his dad had asked for. He looked beneath the scattered magazines but still couldn't find the Allen wrenches. He walked back to the Winnebago.

"I can't find them Dad. Are you sure they're there?"

"I said that's where I left them, didn't I? What do you mean you can't find them?"

Ben couldn't think of an answer.

Dad strode in his direction. "Aren't you good for anything? Do I have to do everything myself?"

Ben walked backward. He wanted to run.

"Did you expect them to jump out and bite you?"

Sweat rose on Ben's brow. Why hadn't he looked harder? Dad grabbed Ben's collar as he strode past and dragged his son into the garage. He shoved Ben into the corner and turned toward the workbench.

Dad started shuffling the magazines and papers around. "You've got to move things, Benjamin! You've got to move things."

It relieved Ben that the Allen wrenches didn't appear. Maybe Dad would calm down, realizing they weren't where he thought.

But the man got angrier. With his big right arm Dad swept a tool chest onto the ground. Ben jumped to avoid getting hit. Tools clattered and clanged.

Dad pulled out a drawer and overturned it onto the chest. Pens, a stapler, a ruler, and a bunch of paper clips went all over the place. Dad threw the stapler at a wall and it clattered to the ground in three pieces.

"Am I the only one around here who can do anything?" Dad asked.

Ben took a sideways step.

"Get back here, Son. I'm teaching you a lesson."

Dad spun around and spotted a cardboard box in the corner. He lifted the container and dumped it across the table.

The Allen wrenches fell out among the debris. Ben stepped forward to grab them, but his dad got there first.

"Do you see? I told you they were here." He thrust the wrenches toward Ben's face, and held them only inches from his eyes. "That's what they look like. Remember that. Now, next time I ask you to do something for me, how about just doing it and not coming back with some worn out excuse?"

"Okay. Sorry."

"Sorry. That's all I hear from you. You spend your time dreaming, Ben, while the real world passes you by." He shook the Allen wrenches in Ben's face. "This is reality, Ben. That broken fan belt and the need to fix it is reality."

"I don't know what you want, Dad."

Dad stared at him. He spoke calmly. "I want you to be responsible." He turned and left the garage.

Ben's whole body felt clammy. He went back to the knife and belt to finish what he father had asked of him.

* * *

Alouette, gentille Alouette
Alouette, je te plumerai.
Je te plumerai la tête
Je te plumerai la tête
Et la tête,
Et la tête,
Alouette,
Alouette,
O-o-o . . .

A children's choir stood in orderly ranks on the steps of their small schoolhouse. The singers wore bright smiles and sharp uniforms. Their melody filled the narrow valley.

"Let's stop and listen. We can wait for Thierry," Ben said.

"How I wish you would," Kyle answered.

"Any news of his condition?" Ben asked.

"*Non.*"

No one had heard anything, but news would come soon. It had to.

On the opposite side of the road, wedged between a cloudy glacial river and another soaring peak was a fertile strip of cultivated land. Whispering winds sent shivers through a thriving wheat crop. The plants seemed joyous in the stifling heat. At times like this, it was hard not to fall in love with France. What a job he had.

And he had it because of Bridgette. Her loyalty as his career shattered and his dreams disintegrated told him all he needed to know about her feelings for him. He'd hoped she felt that way. She'd proved she did. In standing by a disgraced athlete she had made a great sacrifice. Without her support he wouldn't have made it through the tough times. He missed her. He owed her.

Kyle spat at Ben's front tire as he drifted back in the echelon, putting Ben into the lead position. "C'mon Barnes. Do some work this time!"

Ben tapped his brakes. "Huh?"

"Damn it!"

Ben smiled.

* * *

By the time the stranger returned, his engine had a leather component. Ben watched his dad wipe grease from his hands with a yellow rag as he explained all the reasons the temporary belt wasn't going to last fifty miles. Ben stayed quiet, even though he knew for certain it would last several thousand. Dad's work always lasted. You could count on that.

The man asked how much he owed and Dad told him he wasn't willing to charge for a job he couldn't guarantee. The men argued. In the end no money changed hands.

After the vehicle left, Ben noticed the green bike leaning against the wall of the station.

"Hey! Look what he forgot."

"He'll have to pick it up next time through town. Roll it around back."

"Do you think he left it behind as payment?" Ben asked.

"Nope. People who own lots of things forget stuff all the time. He'll be back."

Ben walked over to the bike, his heart racing. When he reached the bicycle he dropped to his haunches.

For a long time he marveled at the simplicity of the gear mechanism. He'd seen ordinary bikes before, but never one with gears. For himself, he'd never even owned a tricycle. Why did he feel as if this beautiful machine was his? He couldn't shake the thought, yet he didn't dare share it with Dad for fear the man's answer would break the spell.

The summer passed without a return appearance of the stranger. Finally Ben couldn't resist asking his dad if he could take the bike for a spin.

"I wish you wouldn't," Dad said.

"Please."

Dad stared at him for a long time. "Do you realize you're getting more bull-headed every day?"

Ben didn't answer.

"You do any damage, you'll pay for it out of your own pocket."

"Yes!" Ben jumped and swatted at the doorframe on his way out of the room. He missed as usual. "I won't hurt it," he yelled over his shoulder.

He rolled the bike to the side of the building. He dragged a milk crate beside it, positioning the bike and crate so he could climb to the saddle while holding onto the wall for balance. He edged his way onto the seat, then tottered there, grasping the wall.

He wobbled atop the machine. Like a king ruling a tumultuous realm, it seemed he could see over everything, but it did him no good. His feet couldn't reach the pedals. Sooner or later he'd have to ease himself down to where he could work the crank with his feet, then he'd find out if these things were as hard to balance as they appeared to be.

He hesitated. As much as it might hurt to fall, the greater risk was an accident damaging the bike. Ben weighed the alternatives. Then he lowered himself until his feet touched the pedals. He pushed off the wall and stepped down hard on the higher pedal.

The bicycle surged forward. Ben's groin hit the crossbar before the pedal reached the bottom of its stroke, but the opposite pedal had risen high enough that he could step across to it. That pedal in turn descended like an elevator headed for the basement.

Ben gripped the handlebars, trying to control the direction, but producing only a drunken zigzag pathway. Somehow he remained upright clear to the roadway, but now he could see if he didn't turn quickly he'd head right off the other side of the street.

From out of nowhere a car appeared. Its horn blared as the driver swerved in front of the bike. Ben jerked the handlebars in the proper direction. He gained control.

Wind played in his hair as he watched the tiny town's outlying buildings approach with amazing speed and ease. The magic of the moment would have overwhelmed him if his concentration weren't focused so completely on the road.

As he passed the last dwelling in Hanksville, a troubling thought sprang up. How could he get this thing turned around? Or at least stopped? So far he couldn't even figure out a way to quit pedaling. The self-preserving act of stepping from pedal to pedal whenever his platform descended too far kept him accelerating.

The road seemed too narrow to turn the machine around without falling off one side or the other. Finally, Ben decided he had no choice but to drive into a sand dune, then walk the bike home. He swerved off the road. The wheels bogged down in the red sand. He toppled into the soft dirt.

Ben bounced to his feet. He picked up his vehicle, his wings, his treasure. He looked the machine over, brushing off sand and examining the components for signs of wear. He'd long ago memorized every feature of the Schwinn so he easily confirmed all was well.

Until moments ago all that had remained was to ride. That act turned out to be better, both more thrilling and more liberating, than he'd ever dreamed.

He held the bike at arms length as he crouched, looking into the magical sprockets. He'd completely forgotten about changing gears! What must that feel like?

Ben walked his bicycle back along the road, searching for a place to remount. He realized he wore a wide grin. No wonder. Today the world had changed.

* * *

"Go Kyle! Go Ben!" A group of Americans waved flags and cheered as the cyclists charged past.

Ben savored the sense of motion, of freedom, of being one with the machine. He loved sailing past cheering crowds. This was the reason he was here. Not for politics or for a career, but for the sheer exhilaration of riding. How had he let himself forget?

He needed to rediscover that joy. With it, he just might retrieve his edge.

Chapter Eleven

The next group of fans spewed jeers long before Ben arrived. A small boy even ran into the road, spat on the asphalt, then ran back. Ben ignored the insult. He would work on recapturing the joy of riding, instead. That happiness was a key piece of the puzzle he must reassemble.

Through contemplation he had learned a lot about himself while at the same time keeping his mind refreshed and ready. It was his secret weapon. There was a lot more to learn, and Ben strongly sensed his career might depend on figuring it out quickly

* * *

In his twelfth year, Ben figured he could reach the pedals while seated if he dropped the saddle to its lowest position. He did that, plus brought the seat forward and handlebars down, choosing to ask forgiveness instead of permission if Dad ever noticed.

On the newly adjusted machine it wasn't long before the boundaries of Hanksville and its tiny supply of asphalt were far too small. He ventured farther and farther out of town in each of the three possible directions, eventually reaching the ghost town of Cainville, Utah, and claiming it as his own.

At age thirteen, Ben's dad assigned him the late shift at the gas station. In return for watching the pumps from five until eleven at night Ben got to have his days free. That summer, despite the oppressive heat, the new schedule meant Ben had lots of time to ride. In the following four months he added a half dozen widespread communities to the list of places he'd reached by pedal power. His enjoyment of his newfound freedom was exceeded only by his desire to ride still farther.

Dad wasn't so energized by Ben's sudden mobility. "You know, Benjamin, some people who travel those highways might not be to trustworthy if they come across a young kid and a shiny bike. Besides that, there's drunk drivers."

Ben didn't respond. He'd learned long ago that arguments on such topics were unwinnable.

A month later, when his dad finally announced they were making a trip up to Salt Lake City, Ben begged him to strap the bike to the car roof so he could enter a bicycle race while in the big city. "It's a heck of a lot safer than any of the riding I normally do. They close the roads to everything but bikes. Think if I won!"

Dad rubbed his forehead as if it ached. "I hate seeing you set yourself up for failure, Son. You won't have much of a chance against those city kids. You'd do better to play it safe."

In the end, Dad couldn't talk Ben out of his plan to race. Ben wore an ear-to-ear grin as his father cinched the green bicycle to the top of their simulated wood-paneled Ford station wagon.

At the race, Ben entered himself into the eighteen and under division. Small, ill equipped, and feeling nervous, he rolled his bike to the start line. The waiting competition chuckled while making snide remarks about his size and cut off overalls.

"Hey Opie! You call that a biking outfit?"

Ben didn't mind. The packaging didn't count, just what's inside. You didn't need a Lycra clown suit to win. He would show them.

The starter's gun went off and Ben sprinted into the lead. He opened a big gap quickly as he charged through the industrial park where the race was held. As he passed the spectators at the start/finish line on the first lap he felt he'd explode with pride over his father's surprised expression.

By the time they'd completed five of the twenty laps he could already see the pack ahead of him on the long straightaway. He would have caught them before another trip around the course had spectators not warned the field.

If he'd lapped the other riders, he later realized, he might easily have ridden to victory. He could have remained in their draft and forced them to drag him across the finish line a lap ahead of them.

Instead, between circuits eleven and seventeen, every rider in the field caught and passed him. Each time a group of cyclists approached from behind and then breezed past he experienced renewed humiliation. He despised the feeling of being beaten, though he couldn't summon the strength to stay with the older riders. He'd spent most of his energy on his long solo breakaway.

As he struggled toward the finish line he considered heading off in a different direction so he wouldn't have to face the others. That made it all the more surprising when loud applause and cheers erupted at the finish line.

Afterwards, one by one, the entire group of racers and spectators came by and congratulated him on his "heroic performance." Ben wondered what was so special about coming in last. He certainly didn't like it. City people could be hard to figure

"I hate to say I told you so," Dad said as he stood on the station wagon's rear tire and lifted the bike back onto the roof rack.

Ben pushed dirt clods around in the gutter with his toe.

"It hurts to have your dreams smashed, doesn't it," Dad said.

"Yeah. Hurts real bad."

Dad stepped back onto the ground. "Now I bet you understand why I tried to talk you out of it? There's no sense letting yourself get crushed when there's nothing to be gained."

Ben, his gaze still on the pavement, noticed a pair of running shoes step beside him and stop. He lifted his head. There stood the man from the desert mural Winnebago—the guy who owned Ben's bike.

"Uh … uh … I took real good care of it. Honest. When you didn't come back I just had to see how it rode."

The man scratched his head with his left hand. Between the thumb and forefinger a blue ribbon dangled. Then he looked at Ben's dad. "Well, I'll be. You're that mechanic from Hanksville, aren't you?"

Dad looked confused. "Have we met?"

"Yeah. You installed your leather belt into my motor home a

couple years back. It worked like a charm."

"Really? That's good."

The man nodded. "I can't tell you how happy I am to see the bike's gotten use."

"We'll be pleased to give it back," Dad said.

Ben's stomach knotted.

"Are you kidding? How else was I supposed to pay you? Besides, I just took that old bike off a customer's hands while dropping off their new Bianchi. I was taking it home to strip for parts, but I noticed your son admiring it and figured it would have to do as payment since you were too bullheaded to take a check."

Dad looked at Ben. "That's what he figured you'd done."

"Do you realize how incredible this boy of yours is?" The stranger looked toward Ben, extending his hand. "I'm Bill Mathews."

Ben shook it. "My name's Ben."

The man held out the blue ribbon. "Congratulations, Ben."

"Are you serious?" Ben asked.

"Of course. I just decided to add a division for thirteen-year-olds."

"Can you do that?" Ben's dad asked.

"My race. I can do what I want."

"Gee. Thanks." Ben took hold of the ribbon. The gold print shone on the silky blue background. He read it aloud. "Wasatch Cyclists Criterium Series. First Place."

"Listen. I'm putting together a cycling team. My bike shop is the sponsor and I'll be the coach. You've got a ton of raw talent, a little guy like you lugging that tank around. Why, until now you didn't even have a set of pedals with toe cages and cleated shoes."

"Until now?" Ben asked.

"That's what I said. I've got an old pair in the back of the truck I'm going to give you."

Ben looked toward his dad—no apparent objection. He turned back to Bill. "Thanks! Will they make a difference?"

"Oh, I guarantee it. The shoe clips right onto the pedal, and a leather strap fastens it so you get 360-degree power. Everyone in today's race used them except you. You have no idea how much you have to learn about cycling, Ben. Are you interested in joining us?"

"Can we come back again, Dad?"

Dad shook his head. "This is our first trip to Salt Lake in three years. We're leaving this afternoon and I doubt we'll be back for another three."

Bill scratched his head. "We can come up with something. How about I coach you by mail?"

Dad squeezed his chin between thumb and forefinger. "Why do you want to coach my son so bad?"

"You have to ask? The kid's drowning in potential. He's got a future … with some work. I've been in cycling my whole life—even rode professionally—and I've never seen a boy with such promise."

No one had ever given him such a compliment. Ben's bloodstream felt carbonated. He glanced at his dad.

Dad stared at him. "Hmmm. I don't know. If you start taking bike riding as seriously as this guy wants, are you still going to have energy to do your chores?"

"I will. I promise."

"You know how I feel about time wasted bicycling."

Ben dropped his head.

Bill cleared his throat. "With all due respect, it's not time wasted. These kids learn important life lessons on the bicycle. I'm not asking him to play. It will be work."

"Please, Dad!"

Dad thought silently for a moment. "You'd be making this gentleman here a promise, too. Don't waste his time if you're not going to follow through. A man's got to stand behind his word."

Ben looked at them seriously. "I won't let either of you down."

They shook hands on their deal. In addition to the new pedal system Ben returned to Hanksville, the proud owner of a Lycra clown suit. He felt speedy just wearing it and couldn't resist sleeping in it that night.

* * *

A mongrel dog charged from the crowd, teeth bared. It leaped at Ben's leg, fangs narrowly missing flesh. Ben twisted his cleat from the pedal and kicked. The dog lurched again, this time snagging the cycling shoe with a tooth. Ben kicked a second time and the dog lost its grip.

The mutt fell backward, barking maniacally.

Ben spun the pedal into position with his toe, then pushed the cleat in place. It engaged with a metallic twang. Simultaneously he looked up the road. His three competitors had seized the opportunity to attack. They were a half dozen bike lengths ahead.

Chapter Twelve

Ben hadn't been working nearly as hard as the other three cyclists. He wasn't surprised they were desperate to drop him. The challenge didn't panic him either. He shifted to a higher gear, rose from his saddle, and accelerated smoothly. In less than half a minute he slipped back into Kyle's draft.

The Megatronics team leader turned to look behind him. His eyes nearly exploded out of his head when he found Ben filling his field of vision.

"I'm starting to get real sick of you, Barnes," Kyle said.

Ben chuckled. "Thanks for the compliment."

* * *

After their chance reunion in Salt Lake, Coach Bill Mathews and Ben Barnes began a frequent correspondence. Coach Bill wrote at least once a week; Ben wrote back even more often than that. The mailbox became an obsession. He couldn't resist checking it every time he passed by, even when there couldn't possibly be anything inside.

Whenever a letter came from Salt Lake he tore it open and devoured the contents. The packages contained bicycle articles, training schedules, race fliers, diet suggestions, and more. Ben sent back completed training logs and a healthy dose of questions. Sometimes he'd scribble a note as simple as:

Thanks for everything Coach Bill.
Ben

Then he'd seal it, stamp it, and send it off before heading out to do his work.

His dad was right, as usual, regarding chores. It was very hard to do his regular jobs plus find time to get in all the mileage Coach Bill expected. Ben wished Dad could be proven wrong just once. Not this time though.

There were days Ben returned from a ride and collapsed on the couch only to have Dad rouse him and send him off to his assigned work. Ben would sleepwalk through the tasks, not about to give Dad the satisfaction of seeing him fail in his promise.

One day shortly after his fourteenth birthday Ben decided to add Boulder, Utah to his list of places visited by bike. He'd saved up money for a hotel room and food because the round trip was too far for a single day. Now, to convince Dad.

"I got all my chores done. In fact, you know those weeds that were in the planter around the Chevron sign?"

"I hadn't noticed them," Dad said.

"Well, there were plenty and I hoed them out, plus I hoed all the way around the trailer and I packaged you up a couple of meals that can be heated in the microwave. I stacked them in the freezer."

"At this rate you won't have any work to do for a couple of days."

A huge smile escaped onto Ben's lips.

A cloud of curiosity crumpled Dad's brow. "Just what are you trying to sweet talk me out of, anyway?"

Ben forced his features into a more serious expression. "Well, I was hoping you'd let me go on a long bicycle trip."

"Long? Just how far you got in mind?" Dad crossed his arms and paid closer attention.

"Maybe to Boulder? I've never been—"

"Boulder?" Dad shouted. "That's more than a 200 mile round trip with a big mountain in the middle."

"I've got money for a hotel room."

His father shook his head. "You're planning on staying overnight? Who would do your chores?"

"You just said—"

"Never mind what I just said. What would drive you to pedal half-way into the next county?"

"I just—"

"You're going to be the death of me, Son." Dad fell into a nearby chair.

"So, can I go?"

"I should have gotten myself a dog. At least you can tie them up."

Ben didn't say a word. This sort of sarcasm had preceded permission before. He stared at his dad.

Finally Dad spoke again. "Can you promise to be back before your five o'clock shift tomorrow?"

Ben nearly jumped out of his skin. "You bet! It's a promise!"

Boulder was west on Highway 24 for fifty miles, then south at the junction with Highway 12. From there the big, green mountain loomed ahead. Ben attacked the slope. He pushed the pedals in revolution after revolution up the incline. The road twisted and turned, climbing steadily higher. He kept expecting to spot the summit around the next corner, but each time he instead saw more mountain.

The lush pine forest seemed to whisper. "Climb off your bike, Ben. Relax in one of my shady meadows. Put your feet up. What's your hurry?"

Ben couldn't shove the temptation to stop from his mind. Cool streams tumbled down the rocks and begged him to relent, but still he pushed on. A whispering voice in the back of his head kept suggesting he take a long rest then turn back toward home. This journey was too much. Who but he would know he'd failed to reach his objective? Who but he would care that gravity had won the day?

Ben gritted his teeth. The very thought that the challenge might be more than he was up to angered him. Despite the hollow feeling in his stomach, the sensation that his blood stream didn't carry its usual flow of energy, he dug for a deeper resource.

He focused on the twelve inches ahead of his front tire, concentrated on conquering a foot at a time. His speed hardly kept the bike balanced.

The slope increased and he slowed even more. He discovered that by zig-zagging across the road he could attack it at a lesser angle and at least hold enough momentum to balance. He looked up only occasionally. Finally, through dense stands of aspen and fir, he caught a glimpse of the summit. Surely the road didn't go over the very top. The peak was still so far away.

He rounded a bend and left the forest behind. He'd climbed above the tree line. Now he could see where the road led through the pass. Already the gradient decreased. Success was within reach. He tapped into his last energy stores. He'd been saving a little strength for emergencies such as a blown tire, a gear problem, or bad weather.

And then he crested the hill. Highway 12 snaked down the lee side of Boulder Mountain and onto the spiny terrain of the southwestern Utah red rock desert. In the distance the asphalt strip balanced on Hell's Backbone, then wound its way through undulating red, pink, and white sandstone formations until it finally disappeared over the horizon. Ben had heard people came from exotic places like Germany and Australia just to see this place. No wonder.

He glided the final twelve miles into Boulder, stopped at a small café, and hobbled inside. Walking felt foreign after more than seven hours of pedaling. Ben eased up to the counter and slid onto a stool. He looked at the elderly woman, her hair in a tight gray bun, as she stepped forward to take his order. "Do you sell spaghetti?"

"You that kid from Hanksville everyone talks about?"

Ben crinkled his brow. The woman loomed over him, but in a friendly way. She seemed twice as wide and ten times as soft as his dad. Despite her size, her gentle blue eyes welcomed him.

"That boy who's always ridin' his bike everywhere," the lady continued.

"Yeah," Ben answered. "I guess that's me."

"And you just pedaled over Boulder Mountain?"

"Yep."

She inspected him closely. He'd seen women study quilts that way before attempting to make an even better one for themselves.

"Why do you do it, Honey?" Her voice sounded musical.

He shrugged.

"Why do you put so much energy into something with no

reward?" she pressed.

"'Cause I like to. I wanted to see Boulder and the road to it."

"And next you get to ride back?"

"Yep. In the morning."

"Well, you already know the road between here and there, so what do you expect to learn on that trip?"

Ben thought a moment. "Guess I'll learn what things look like from the other side."

The lady nodded, seeming to understand. "What's your name, young man?"

"Benjamin Washington Barnes."

"Barnes. I don't know of any Barnes in these parts."

"We don't have any relatives around here. My mom died six years ago, and my dad said he wanted to live in a safer place. We left Topeka looking for a new home. When we reached Hanksville he up and bought the Chevron."

"Your mom died?"

Ben looked at the ground.

"She died because the community wasn't safe?"

"She and I were home alone one night when a robber broke in. She tried to grab his gun."

The big soft lady stared at him seriously, thinking things through. "How old are you, Ben?"

"Fourteen."

"Fourteen." She mulled the number as if it carried great significance, like it was the key to a complex puzzle or something. Then she said, "I'll tell you what, Benjamin Washington Barnes. Any time you get a serious enough itch to pedal more than one hundred miles each way over mountain and desert just because you want to know how things are getting along in Boulder, you stop by my café and I'll treat you to all the spaghetti you can eat. Plus I've got a bed for you if you don't mind sleeping on a fold-out-couch. How does that sound?"

"I can pay. I brought money."

"You put them bills back in your pocket Ben. Can I call you Ben?"

Ben nodded.

"How about you call me Thelma? I'm going to talk your ear off" 'cause I'm as curious about Hanksville and the things between here and there as you were about Boulder. Answering my questions will be your payment."

"That's a pretty good deal."

Thelma chuckled. It sounded like hands running up and down a piano keyboard. "Do you realize you're the most interesting visitor this little café has ever had?"

Ben shook his head. "Uh, uh. I thought you got foreigners here."

Thelma's laughter shook the room. It felt good to be near her. "Yeah, I do get foreigners. Not one of them ever rode their bike here, though. Now, how hungry are you?"

"Pretty darn hungry."

The wonderful laugh erupted again. "That's what I guessed. I'll be right back with a heaping plate of spaghetti."

Thelma hadn't been kidding about talking his ear off, but Ben liked it. Before he'd finished his plate he'd decided Boulder was his favorite place in the world. After that, Ben rode to Thelma's every few weeks. Each time he pedaled over Boulder Mountain it seemed smaller than before.

* * *

A stiff breeze hit Ben in the face as Kyle peeled off the front of the pace line and put him into clear air. Ben quit pedaling and tapped his brakes, just as he had each time his turn to pull had come. The deceleration caused a ripple reaction to the two trailing riders.

"*Mierda!*" Pablo Lopez veered past him. "Sitting on is one thing, but you're being a real pain. Can't you have the decency not to destroy our momentum every time you pull through?"

"Nope. I ride for Thierry," Ben answered.

The route left the highway again, this time veering into the tourist town of St. John de Maurienne. Narrow alleyways sliced between five-story hotels. The crowd enveloped the riders. Their cheers reverberated off the sharp angled walls. Even the patrons of a chic looking café stood and cheered.

Ben devoured an energy bar and washed it down with several squirts of warm water. He'd need fresh supplies soon. Would Pierre give them to him?

* * *

One day Ben heard a neighboring farmer in Hanksville had sold his John Deere tractor to a resident of Boulder and would be driving it there. Ben challenged the man to a race. The idea got people so excited that soon nearly everyone in Hanksville, Boulder, and the tiny towns between had money riding on the outcome. The wagering ran heavily in favor of the tractor until Thelma from Boulder covered all bets against Ben.

"You'll win one for me, won't you Ben?" Thelma's optimism was irresistible.

"You bet I will!"

At the startling line, Ben stared into the stiff west wind. This wasn't the sort of weather he'd wanted. He straddled his shiny green Schwinn, waiting for the competition to show. An enormous crowd milled about him. Nearly the whole county had shown up.

A distant rumble slowly built to a roar as the green and yellow tractor climbed onto the road from a nearby field. Black smoke spewed from the growling exhaust stacks. The huge machine came abreast and stopped. Atop it, a perturbed looking farmer wearing a straw hat and missing three teeth loomed over Ben.

"Howdy Mr. Glick," Ben yelled over the racket of the clattering engine.

"You ready, boy?" Mr. Glick answered.

"I guess so."

"On your mark, get set, go!" screamed the mayor.

Off they went. An entourage of pickup trucks and a school bus, each filled to the brim with spectators, played leapfrog with the competitors as the race moved along the highway. Ben's adrenaline surged with the cheers. He had to calm his nerves so he wouldn't burn out too quickly.

For the first seventy miles the route followed the gradual grade of the Fremont River. Neither man nor machine could eek out a lead. Ben worked hard to break away on several occasions, but each time he built a gap the headwind tired him and the tractor reeled him back in.

After the third unsuccessful attempt Ben resigned himself to following in the tractor's draft for a while. Just like in the Salt Lake City race, the going would be much easier out of the breeze.

He had to stay close to the tractor to avoid breathing the polluted air streaming behind it. Every so often the farmer looked down and chuckled. Ben ignored the attempted humiliation. His new game plan was to hang back and preserve energy until the race hit the mountain. Then they'd see who'd be chuckling.

The route turned onto Highway 12 and soon began to ascend Boulder Mountain. Ben stood on the pedals, concentrating as he passed the tractor.

The farmer laughed, downshifted, and retook the lead with ease that surprised Ben. As the tractor breezed past, Ben didn't even have the strength to stay in the machine's draft. Soon he found himself enveloped in its blackened air stream and had to drop back even farther so he could breathe.

The rumbling tractor was faster than he'd guessed. In another few minutes the green and yellow machine got so far ahead that, even on the longest straight-aways, he couldn't see it.

Tension clogged Ben's veins. Then he discovered he could draw on that stress like a new source of energy. As the terrain became steeper he accelerated again. Within a short distance he re-established visual contact. The sight of his rival fueled him even more. He pedaled furiously. The crowds, now picnicking in a grassy meadow, roared their approval as Ben flew by.

He couldn't wipe the smile off his lips as the spectators scrambled toward their vehicles. The gap narrowed rapidly and on the steepest section of the hill he pulled even. He couldn't extract enough torque from his legs to put away the victory, though. He worried about the outcome as the tree line neared. Then he heard a clatter beside him. Mr. Glick banged on the gearshift lever. He struggled to downshift. Ben dug deep, gritted his teeth, and pushed for the summit. As he crested the hill he looked back at the tractor and saw it encased in a cloud of gray smoke.

Ben bent into an aerodynamic tuck. The farm machine couldn't possibly overtake him now. Another cheering crowd awaited him in the parking lot of Thelma's café. Ben rode the last hundred yards with his hands in the air, not even putting them back on the handlebars as the crowd caught and slowed him.

Thelma took his bike as several men lifted him onto their shoulders. The undulating crowd danced around the lot and down the street for nearly an hour before the defeated tractor finally clattered into town.

No one seemed to mind losing their money, and just in case there were any hard feelings Thelma treated everyone to a huge barbecue. On that day Ben became a local hero. It was the same day he became an incurable racing addict.

* * *

Addiction to racing—Ben missed that. He must get it back.

Exiting the village, steep switchbacks climbed to an old square turret that must have been used in medieval times to control passage through the narrow valley. The change in terrain was just enough to slow the speeds and encourage a greater concentration of spectators. On these climbing turns, the fans would have a better chance to see the faces of their favorite riders. This time, because they were so near such a tourist packed town, the group of onlookers was large enough that the riders could hear the tinny report of race radio on the collective transistors in the crowd as they rode by: "… are all still in shock over Thierry Depardieu's withdrawal from the race. He tried valiantly to continue on a broken ankle but simply could not …"

Chapter Thirteen

"Your beloved boss is out. Now help!" Kyle yelled.

Ben looked at his ex-teammate but couldn't think. As the route snaked through a tunnel of trees, he fell to the rear of the paceline to ponder. Thierry had abandoned the race? Was that possible?

Of course it was. Some years only half the riders made it to Paris. Every cyclist knew that on any given day he might confront circumstances he couldn't overcome. This was an unforgiving business.

Now what? He wouldn't even be in this race if not for Thierry. What was he supposed to do? Should he let Le Directeur decide? Would Pierre's orders be the best for the team, for himself? Clearly, Thierry thought not. Everything converged upon this moment.

Numbers ran through his head. At the beginning of this stage he'd sat only five minutes and forty-three seconds off the pace. With Thierry out of the race he was only about five and a quarter minutes behind the man who theoretically held the overall lead, a German cyclist named Gunter von Reinholdt. Gunter had been dropped when Ben led the big surge on the Col de la Madeleine. Ben had no idea how far back the German rode now.

Within his own team, Ben had been in third place when this stage started, well behind Thierry and slightly behind Albert, but today Albert had fallen off the pace even before Gunter. So, the stage would likely end with Ben as his team's highest placed rider in the GC. If Banque Fédérale's goal was the yellow jersey, and that's what they had said over and over, American or not, he represented their only hope. His resurgence in the team time trial now had amazing significance. If not for that, he wouldn't be in the game.

That left Kyle to contend with. When the day started, Ben was four minutes and twenty seconds behind his former teammate. Kyle now appeared most likely to assume the lead at the end of this stage. Ben couldn't let that happen. No way could he allow Kyle to put on Thierry's jersey.

Ben imagined a ghost-rider for Kyle, like the ghost-runners kids use in sandlot baseball when they run out of live bodies. From Ben's perspective this one rode four minutes and twenty seconds up-road from Kyle, for if the two Americans finished side by side in each of the remaining eleven stages, Kyle would still be victorious by a wide margin. Ben had to erase that gap. He must make up the deficit over the remaining two summits and eighty-six kilometers. The most important fifty-three miles he had ever ridden were coming up.

As the route eased left it dug into the limestone wall and bent skyward. Ben eyed the steep road and smiled. This was the perfect spot to launch an attack. At the rear of the paceline he tensed, waiting for his moment to charge the awesome Col de la Croix de Fer, The Pass of the Iron Cross.

He hit the hill and rose from his saddle, increasing the speed from the flats as he assaulted the mountain. He focused his determination onto the pedals.

He rocketed past the three other breakaway riders. He saw everyone as his enemy. He'd make Kyle pay for forcing him to ride away without word from his friend. He'd force Pierre into eating his doubts about his preparation or skill. And he'd take out his rage on this mountain for what the last mountain did to Thierry.

For this to work he had to open a significant lead over his rivals before Le Directeur resorted to drastic measures to slow him down. After all, he was out of water and in urgent need of more food. Without coolant and fuel he had no prayer of maintaining his pace.

It didn't take long to establish a gap as the other three cyclists were apparently in no mood to ride so hard this far from the line. Ben guessed at their thoughts, something like: "The American is throwing a tantrum over the loss of his teammate. He'll go a little way up the hill, blow up, and that will be the end of him."

Such a conclusion would serve Ben perfectly. He settled back into the saddle and rode at a more comfortable pace as he recovered. Ahead, despite the dense greenery, an enormous rock grotto reminded him of his childhood home in the Utah desert. Back then he'd often charged up hills using imaginary rivals as motivation. Now he had real rivals. This ought to be easy.

Just as he got his breath back Pierre's voice came through, loud and clear. "Benjamin, I couldn't be happier about what you've done today."

Unexpected relief eased Ben's mind. "Really?"

"Yes. Your insubordination will make it a simple matter to throw you out of European racing forever. You've proven beyond all doubt that you lack both judgment and maturity. I have much more to say, but first I have a call to patch through to you."

Ben bent a shoulder to hide his lips from the camera ahead. "Wha ... what?"

Another voice, scratchy with the residue of tobacco, came over the radio. "Pardon, Monsieur Barnes. Would you be willing to tell me what in the hell you think you're doing?"

Ben's gut clenched. "Who's this?"

"The man who signs your checks, that's who. I repeat, what do you mean to accomplish?"

Laurent Robidoux, team owner and mystery man. Rumor had him weighing as much as any three cyclists on his team and omniscient besides. Fritz had once said, "Monsieur Robidoux knows everything about me." Then he added, "He knows everything about you, too."

Not likely.

Ben's mind spun. He'd heard rumors that Monsieur Robidoux liked nothing more than floating around the Mediterranean on his yacht making decisions that affected millions. That's probably where he was right now. Ben imagined the enormous man surrounded by beautiful girls as he reclined in his Jacuzzi, ready to decide Ben's fate before moving on to more important matters.

Though Ben didn't want to waste energy talking he had no

choice.

Instinct took over. He straightened his posture, hands off the handlebars. "I'm doing a commercial for your bank." With a wide, cheesy grin he ran a finger under the Banque Fédérale name emblazoned across his jersey, then flashed two open palms like miniature fireworks bursting.

There was a pause, presumably as the television signal bounced through editing rooms and back and forth between satellites, then a confusing sound filled the line. Static? Coughing? Choking? No ... laughter?

"What is this I'm seeing? Do you have any idea how many people must wonder why the bad haircut guy is goofing off at a time like this? They tuned in to enjoy your suffering and you treat them to a ... a ... what do the call that perky American exercise guru?"

In the background Ben heard someone make a comment.

"*Oui*, a Richard Simmons impression, except with *un certain savoir-faire*," Monsieur Robidoux continued. "That shot is sure to run everywhere."

"A good thing for your bank, right?"

"Hmmm. *Peut être.* There is potential. Of course, if you fail it won't play so well."

A smile crept across Ben's lips. "Which means?"

In the brief silence that followed Ben could imagine Pierre lighting up and sucking down multiple Gitane's in rapid succession.

"Which means ..." Monsieur Robidoux said, "you must succeed."

Ben's spirits soared. "And I will. That is, if Le Directeur does not prevent me."

"An interesting gambit, Monsieur Barnes. It piques my interest. If you win this stage, your strategy will be spoken of as genius. Pierre will get the credit. Of course he'll help," Monsieur Robidoux said.

Le Director's voice came through. "But he won't win. He's gone out far too early. The move is not genius. If I allow it, I'll be mocked.
"

"If I lose I'll tell the press that I attacked against your orders.

Your reputation is safe," Ben said.

"Hmmph," Pierre grunted.

"Are we in agreement?" Monsieur Robidoux asked.

"*Oui*," Ben said.

"Grudgingly," Pierre said. "This madness cannot succeed but what choice do I have?"

"Agreement nonetheless," Monsieur Robidoux summarized. "I don't think you can make it either, Ben. How can you keep such a pace from so far out? Still, you intrigue me. And to make this even more interesting, I'll sweeten the pot. A stage win on my team's most disastrous day would be worth millions in publicity. If you pull it off you'll be very happy about the number of zeros on your next paycheck. That goes for you as well, Pierre."

The idea motivated Ben. Hopefully it did the same for Le Directeur. Maybe Fritz had been right, but Monsieur Robidoux's insight was much simpler than Ben expected.

"One more thing, Ben. If you fail, kiss your career goodbye. I won't have my bank embarrassed by that little publicity stunt if you follow it up by limping home as an also ran."

Ben swallowed. It felt like a dirt clod was lodged in his throat. Thierry had probably been right. Pierre couldn't mothball his career, but Monsieur Robidoux could.

Ben spoke into the radio, "Food please."

Monsieur Robidoux chuckled, "Do you hear that Pierre? Get this man something to eat. Anything he wants. Put it on my tab!"

The laughter only increased when the purple and green car pulled up alongside Ben, the motorcycle cameraman still focused on the scene. Ben hadn't even known the support vehicle was in the neighborhood. He wanted to chuckle at Pierre's scowl, but he'd already used enough unnecessary energy and he suddenly felt a bit frightened.

Out of the car window three hands extended, each holding a different item.

"How's that for service, my boy?" Monsieur Robidoux asked.

Ben squirted an energy gel into his mouth. He followed it with a quick drink for fear the thick goop would clog his windpipe and affect his breathing.

"Don't answer me," the team owner said. "Conserve your strength. We'll talk later. *Au revoir.*"

Ben heard a phone clatter onto its hook, then a dial tone. He took a bite of the energy bar and slowly chewed, already anticipating the rejuvenating effects of the food.

Le Directeur looked into Ben's eyes and said, "I agree with him about the bad haircut. It's terrible. Whose idea was it?"

"Yours. Thanks for thinking of it."

Pierre scowled. "I don't know what you're talking about, but let's return to a subject on which there should be no misunderstanding. I advise you to believe Monsieur Robidoux when he says he can end your career."

Ben brushed a hand across his cheek, dislodging his earpiece and letting it dangle. He didn't need any more input from a man who didn't have his best interests at heart.

"Put that back in," Le Directeur boomed.

Ben turned and focused on the road.

Chapter Fourteen

Ben eyed the precipitous road ahead and imagined the even steeper hills he couldn't yet see. But were they his biggest obstacles? The tremendous challenge he'd psyched himself to face this morning paled in view of the chips now on the table. Everything he'd worked for was at stake.

Did he have the necessary strength? He felt good now, but there was a lot of road ahead. A yellow motorcycle pulled past and slowed. The passenger held his finger on the first of two times to indicate it represented Ben. He angled the board so Ben could see it.

Twenty-six seconds. Could he be that close to Luigi?

A car rounded the bend ahead. Why hadn't he noticed before? That had to be Luigi's support vehicle. The Italian climber was close.

The number at the bottom of the chalkboard was one minute, twenty-nine seconds. Subtracting his deficit behind Luigi meant he held a one-minute gap over his pursuers. Was that correct? If he was that far ahead, even after slowing for the conversation with Monsieur Robidoux, it could only mean the chase group considered his pace suicidal. They must believe they'd scrape him up like road kill before the top of this hill.

Ben realized his form had deteriorated. His shoulders wobbled slightly and his pedal strokes weren't smooth. He was pushing on the down stroke, but not pulling throughout the rest of the cycle. He concentrated on the errors and corrected them, then watched with satisfaction as his cyclometer showed his speed clicking up a notch without an increase in effort. He climbed easily into the village of Combe Bérard. At the far end of the town he caught his first glimpse of the Italian.

Luigi was his carrot. Ben approached steadily, all the while evaluating the other man's form and concentrating on his own.

In only a minute of riding he moved within fifty meters of the Italian. In a way, Ben was disappointed by how quickly the gap disappeared. It meant Luigi was moving sluggishly. Ben would have preferred the motivation of chasing a rider for a longer time.

The Italian's form was fine. The problem was obvious. He pushed a tiny gear slowly, as if he didn't care how long it took him to get over this mountain. Ben recalled Luigi's likely goal. He had only the slightest prayer of winning the tour, or even this stage. Instead, by making a suicidal attack over the first three peaks, he meant to collect the lion's share of the King of the Mountain points.

Maybe when he learned his gap had disintegrated so rapidly, he'd assumed the group of four or five riders who had been pursuing him all day were about to pass. That would severely reduce his opportunity for points on the last two ascents. As a result he must have decided there was no reason to exert himself further.

Ben entered a long, cool tunnel not far behind the other climber. He decided to try to lift his friend's spirits. "Hey Luigi!" The words echoed.

The Italian turned his head.

"It's only me, Ben from America."

Luigi smiled, "*Ciao*, Ben! This I didn't expect. You are alone?"

"It's complicated. We can ride together now."

Luigi turned despondently toward the road ahead. "No, I am through."

"Nonsense. Let's get you more points. We'll crest together and you can have first place."

The Italian looked back again, this time with a crinkled brow. "You would do this for me? You are good man, Ben from America. It is a deal."

Ben watched with satisfaction as the bike ahead accelerated. He had to increase his cadence to close the gap. He settled in behind Luigi and let the other rider take over the mental challenge of keeping the pace high.

As they exited the tunnel together, someone booed.

"You have friends here too," Luigi said.

"Yes, they love chanting my name in low tones."

"So, that is what they are saying. I mistook it. Let me take the first pull, Beeeeeeeennnnnn." Luigi looked back, obviously entertained by his own joke. His eyes went wide. "You are not Ben."

"I'm not?"

"Well, maybe. What sort of accident have you had with your hair?"

Ben smiled.

The road swept into another short tunnel, then exited to an explosive vista stretching vertically from fertile floor to craggy summit. Despite the beautiful surroundings, the enthusiastic crowds, and all the tactical considerations, Ben directed his thoughts inward. He had been handed another opportunity to retrieve his edge, and he meant to take full advantage.

* * *

One day, five months after Ben's high-speed wipeout on Boulder Mountain, Bill Mathews arrived at the Hanksville gas station.

"How's the knee?"

Ben lifted his pant leg. A jagged four-inch scar was the only visible sign of the trauma. "Better."

Coach Bill looked around conspiratorially. "Do you think your dad will let me give you a present?"

Ben shrugged.

"It's for your fifteenth birthday. Stay right here."

Coach Bill walked to the back of his truck and returned with a gleaming mountain bike. "I don't ride this baby anymore. I figured a young up-and-comer like you might find some use for it."

"Cool! But Dad, he says no more cycling. I can't change his mind."

Coach Bill nodded, a smile practically fracturing his face. "Then this may be just what you need. These things go a lot slower than road bikes. You can hardly tuck, and it's impossible to reach the sorts of speeds you crashed at."

Ben smiled. "Yeah? I'll talk to him. Let me take it for a quick spin."

Ben lifted a leg over the bike. Just then Dad's Ford station wagon pulled in. The vehicle skidded to a stop in a cloud of dust. Dad stormed out with fury in his eyes.

"What did we agree about bicycles, Benjamin?"

Ben laid the bike on its side.

Dad swiveled toward Coach Bill. "Dumbest move I ever made was not accepting your money to repair that fan belt. Your blasted bicycle nearly killed my son. Now you're replacing it? I want you to leave him alone. Do you understand?"

Coach Bill stepped forward. "I can see how..."

"You can't see anything!" Dad shouted. "Has Benjamin showed you what he did to your last bicycle?"

"Not yet."

Dad snarled. He stormed to the back of the garage and disappeared from sight.

"I brought you a Bianchi too," Coach Bill whispered. "I guess I'd better drop it by Thelma's for the time being."

Ben's heart skipped a beat. "You're kidding! An Italian road bike?"

"With hi-tech Look brand pedals and click in shoes. No more toe cages. At least you'll come off the bicycle the next time you crash."

Dad reappeared, dragging mangled metal behind him. He flung it at Coach Bill's feet.

The green bicycle was totaled. The front forks bent to the right at nearly ninety degrees. Both wheels were so far out of true, there was no hope of straightening them.

"Yard art," Coach Bill said.

Dad shook his head. "Death trap. Now, off my property!"

* * *

High overhead the church bell at St. Sorlin d' Arves rang a welcome as Ben and Luigi fought their way up the battered road. Ben took over lead duty as they entered town.

Within the topsy-turvy village the road seemed confused, searching for a way through. The asphalt path squeezed between oddly scattered buildings and cut across yards. In many places eaves overhung the road. In one spot two even touched, forming an arch overhead.

Ben redirected his mind to the past, even though he knew he was getting closer to exploring the moments he most feared contemplating. He'd avoided these thoughts for years, but he now believed his future demanded him to confront the past.

* * *

It took a month to convince Dad that it made no sense to walk around town when he had a perfectly good bicycle. Once he won that argument, heading off on trail rides was only a small step.

Thanks to Coach Bill, not only did Ben's horizons expand to include mountain biking, but the potential directions for travel quadrupled. Dirt was many times more plentiful than pavement in this part of the country. Within two months he had entered the only three mountain bike races he could find in southern Utah. He won his class in each.

As the season waned, he discovered a fourth event in Moab. This time, rather than hitching a ride with a neighbor, he talked his dad into driving.

Over a hundred riders turned out, but Ben took second overall and easily won his age division.

"How did you do that, Son? Do you realize you were the youngest guy out there?"

Ben beamed. "Want to know my secret?"

"Of course." Dad smiled.

"It's Thelma."

Dad's brow furrowed.

"She expects so much. She's always saying, 'Win this one for me,' 'Win that one for me.' I haven't won yet, but I keep getting closer. She wants me to win so badly, I feel like I owe it to her or something."

"But you have won, Son. You win your age group every time."

"Yeah, but she means overall."

Dad put a hand on Ben's shoulder. "To me this one counts. We should celebrate."

"Celebrate?"

"I brought camping gear just in case we ran into delays and couldn't make it back home."

Moab seemed like an exciting town. Ben wished they could celebrate there, but Dad was all smiles as he loaded the car and drove away. For Ben, anything was better than an immediate return to Hanksville.

The dirt road Dad chose clung acrobatically to a cliff as it struggled to the mesa top. What madman had built this thing?

Once atop the Colorado Plateau, the signs led to Dead Horse Point. They set up their tent overlooking a stunning gooseneck of the Colorado River. Canyonlands National Park, angular and forbidding, sprawled in the distance. The jagged sandstone formations appeared impassable. The broad vista staggered Ben, but his dad surprised him even more. Ben had never seen his father act so carefree.

Dad grabbed a wine bottle from the cooler. Ben had never seen his dad drink before, either.

"Where'd that come from?"

Dad waved him off. "Sparkling grape juice. Figured it might make for a fun occasion."

Ben eyed his father. Had he planned this night out in advance?

Dad produced two plastic cups and poured drinks. Ben took a taste. The juice tingled going down. He liked it.

Dad set up a Coleman cook stove and heated stew from cans. He brought Ben a bowl full.

They sat in front of a small campfire, eating and watching the sunlight play on the giant red boulders.

Fantastic shapes and shadows moved about like in a dream. Ben savored the hearty meal.

"You know I've never been fond of your bike riding, Son," his dad said. "But maybe there's some good in it. It's made you tough.

Colleges lust after long distance runners. I think you'd be pretty good at that."

It surprised Ben to hear his father share such hopes, seemingly focused on making Ben's life a better one than he had lived.

Ben blew a cooling breath over a spoonful of stew. "I don't want to run. I want to race bicycles."

"Not practical. How do you expect to make a living riding a bike?"

"Some people do."

Dad waved a dismissive hand. "Very, very, very few … if any."

"Maybe you should take a look at my magazines. Some of the riders are millionaires. All they do is race bicycles."

"That's not reality, and you know it."

"Coach Bill makes his living off bicycles."

"Don't talk to me about Coach Bill, okay. Besides, Coach Bill is lucky he hasn't killed himself in the process. You already came way too close for comfort." Dad shook his head. "No, I want more for you than that."

Ben thought a moment. He'd prefer yanking his teeth out with pliers to discussing bicycle crashes with Dad. A new argument occurred to him. "I can't make a living running, either."

"No, you can't," Dad agreed. "But you can earn an education. That's much more valuable."

Ben stood. He picked up a flat piece of sandstone and flung it into the abyss. The rock sailed away. Long after it disappeared from sight he waited for it to make a sound. He heard nothing.

"Why are you such a pessimist, Dad?"

His father regarded him for a moment. "I'm not pessimistic. I'm realistic. A man who doesn't rein in his dreams so they don't get squashed simply has no sense."

Ben hurled another rock. "How would you know? You've never dreamed."

Dad held up a steaming spoonful of stew and regarded it thoughtfully. "You know, Son, there was a time I didn't. Not even in my sleep. For a long time after your mom's death I sort of shut things down, convinced my misplaced dreams had betrayed her. If I hadn't wanted such a big house, that thief wouldn't have wanted to get inside. I guess it wasn't until I watched you ride that race up in Salt Lake City that I realized dreaming was good for something, after all."

"But I came in last place, and you said you wished I hadn't tried."

"And look how you've responded. Yesterday you nearly won against competition twice your age." Dad looked like he thought his insults had been responsible for pushing Ben to greater accomplishments.

Ben shrugged. "So then, why are you asking me to give up bicycle racing?"

"Because it makes sense, and since we're on the subject, because I had a dream."

"What dream?"

"I dreamed …" Dad pointed to his mouth, chewed, then swallowed. "I dreamed you won the NCAA Championship running the 10,000 meters for the University of Kansas."

Ben's jaw dropped.

His dad nodded.

"But it's not going to happen. I'm going to keep riding bikes, not running."

"Damn it, Benjamin. There's no reason to make this difficult." Dad's adamancy came as a surprise. "I have a lot more experience than you. I've seen a lot more in life. Would you grant me that?"

"Well, yeah."

"Good." Dad picked a blade of June grass. He regarded the end of the green sprig, then slid it between his two front teeth. "Now take my word for it when I say there's a better path open to you. For years now I've allowed you to have fun, but maturity requires practicality. It's high time you grew up."

Ben stared at his dad for a long time. "I am growing up, Dad. I've learned a lot about my strengths and my weaknesses. On the bicycle I've discovered who I am and what I can become."

"Good. Then you're certain to reach the same conclusions I already have."

If Ben had dared, he'd have reached out and grabbed the bobbing sprig of grass from between Dad's lips. He'd have kicked over the sparkling grape juice, and maybe torn down the tent too. Instead he bit his lip and counted to ten. "I want to race bicycles, not run."

"Listen to sense, Benjamin."

"I'm going to bed."

Ben wanted to growl as he brushed his teeth. He climbed into his sleeping bag, seething mad.

*   *   *

"Nice pull," Luigi said as he retook the lead.

Ben dropped in behind. The climb was passing easily thanks to his reminiscences. The final ascent would be far too intense to handle in this dreamlike way, but for now he'd continue his introspection.

They passed a clanging herd of cattle and more groups of fans. Most cheered. Some booed. The road confronted the mountain more steeply and Ben let his mind return to the Utah desert.

*   *   *

At the Dead Horse Point campground Ben woke to his dad's snoring. Ben inched out of his sleeping bag then climbed from the tent. Outside the dawn crackled with possibility; a perfect canvas on which to paint a great adventure. Pink, yellow, and blue streaks colored the bright but still sunless sky.

He went to the Coleman stove and started breakfast. In moments the smell of fried bacon wafted through camp. What was it about the outdoors that made food preparation so intoxicating? The teapot sang out. Ben carried instant coffee into the tent and lowered it near his father's nose.

The man's eyelids cracked open. "You read my mind."

Ben set the cup on the ground and returned to his preparations. By the time food was ready his dad had crawled from the tent.

Dad stretched his arms wide and rolled his neck side to side. "You ready for the scenic route home?"

"What scenic route?"

"The one we're going to blaze. You up for it or not?"

Ben smiled. "Of course I'm up. What's gotten into you, Dad?"

"Maybe more dreams. For years I ran away from life, away from everything that reminded me of your mother. You remind me a lot of your mother. I ran away from you more than anything else. I'm sorry, and I want to fix things."

Ben nodded. "You want to fix things, huh? Which way to the scenic route?"

"I'll check the map."

In this region it wasn't just the sparse population that explained the lack of alternate routes, but the severity of the terrain. Sheer walled canyons were everywhere.

Ben looked forward to the discoveries the day's adventure would reveal. He was also happy last night's argument seemed forgotten.

With breakfast finished they loaded the car and headed down the highway. After a few miles they turned off on a bumpy dirt road. Far below them the Green River wound through the Labyrinth Canyon Gorge. Dad consulted a map and pointed out geologic curiosities along the way. It surprised Ben to learn his father had the same sorts of interest in the outside world that he'd always been filled with. In his old age Dad had simply decided he had no use for such excesses.

At the Spring Canyon junction Dad decided to head deeper into the unknown. He turned off on an even rougher road. The old station wagon struggled with some of the steeper hills, and several times Ben felt the terrain below the car pushing up on the floor, as if the road saw the vehicle's intrusion as an indignity it meant to thwart.

The route led into a steep walled red rock canyon. Soon only a craggy strip of azure sky remained high above. They were winding through a bizarre region of enormous quill-like sandstone formations, when the left rear tire blew.

Dad climbed out of the car. "Get the jack and lift her up."

Ben scrambled into action.

As the vehicle rose Dad crouched to look beneath. "We're losing transmission fluid."

Purplish liquid dripped into the sand.

Dad clicked his tongue on the roof of his mouth. When it slowed he said, "Tell you what, Son. You know those little V8 juice cans in the cooler? Bring me one?"

It seemed an odd request, but Ben did as he was told. When he returned Dad had scooted under the car. He was cleaning the area around a crack he discovered in the transmission case.

"Do you want to drink this later?"

"Nope. Pass it under here. Hand me that gum you're chewing, too."

"Used gum? Suit yourself." Ben extended the objects beneath the car.

Dad pinched off a piece of gum and jammed it into the hole in the transmission case. He carefully removed the sticky piece of aluminum foil that covered the opening in the V8 can. "Let's both take a swig of this for good luck." Dad raised his head and poured some of the red liquid into his mouth, then handed the beverage out.

Ben drank.

Dad handled the aluminum tab like a precious photograph he didn't want to mar with a fingerprint.

"You've heard of V-8 engines, haven't you?" Dad chuckled, a completely uncharacteristic sound.

Ben laughed, too.

Dad's face turned serious again. He placed the sticky tab gingerly over the gum-filled hole in the transmission; then he set the heel of his hand against the patch and pressed hard. "I doubt it's going to hold, but here goes nothing."

Dad removed his hand from the case. Both of them stared at the spot for a long time. The leak had stopped.

"Whether it holds or not with the engine running will be a

different matter," Dad said.

"It looks secure."

"That it does. Let's get that tire on and skedaddle."

Ben backed up to give his father room to slide out.

A gunshot echoed.

Ben sprang to his feet to look for a hunter. He noticed the station wagon teetering, then realized the explosion had been the left front tire bursting. Maybe the rough road had weakened it, and now the heat had taken its toll. The vehicle swayed like a drunkard looking for a seat, then rocked rearward, toppling the jack. The massive load came down with a sickening crack.

Dad groaned.

The man lay pinned beneath the car. Ben scrambled to grab the jack. He worked as quickly as he could to return it to the compressed position. As he did, he searched for the best spot to wedge it under the car.

"Hel- Help me!"

"I'm working as fast as I can!"

It seemed to take forever, though. When he finally had the jack low enough, he slid it into place.

He pumped the handle furiously, raising the automobile. After an eternity he could finally see space between Dad's chest and the bottom of the car.

The groaning had subsided.

"Dad! Are you all right?"

"I … think so. Good work, Son."

"Oh, good. I was so scared." He scrambled to a position where he could see his dad's face.

When he did he noticed the blood. Not only had it reddened Dad's shirt, but another stream trickled from his mouth. "What should I do?"

"Just give me … a second … to collect my senses."

"I'd better not move you. You'll have shade there. I'm going to ride my bike for help."

Dad stared at him vacantly, then said, "Yeah, good idea."

Ben stood, unlashed his mountain bike from the top of the

station wagon, then crouched back down. "Here's a canteen and some food. You just rest. I'll be back with help in no time."

"Ben, you know I love you, right?"

Tears welled in Ben's eyes. Of course he knew this, or at least he thought he did. Sort of. Why this gushiness? Dad never talked like this, and Ben never cried. Then he noticed tears streaming from his fathers eyes as well.

"Yeah. I love you too, Dad. I'll hurry."

"Hey, Son. One more thing."

Ben peered under the car again.

"You do like I asked last night, all right?"

Ben's throat felt sandy. "You mean …"

"I mean give up the bike. Take up running so you can earn yourself an education."

"Um. Well." He searched for the right words to avoid making a promise he didn't intend to keep.

Dad coughed weakly and squeezed his eyes shut.

"Okay, but …"

The hint of a smile played across Dad's lips. "That's my boy. Whatever happens, I'm very proud of you."

"But …" Ben couldn't continue. He didn't have the heart to retract the one word that seemed to have eased Dad's pain. That could be dealt with later, once Dad was safe.

Ben rose to his feet. Time to go, take action, not waste words. He jumped aboard the mountain bike and headed for Moab, thirty-five miles away. He raced like the wind, flying through rocky terrain as if it were flat pavement. Up and down the undulating road he went. Despite the obstacles Ben drove the bicycle forward at increasing speed. His legs pounded like pistons, relentlessly forcing road behind him.

After yesterday's hard ride, he kept expecting to tire. Each time he imagined doing so, the image of his father, suffering beneath the car, fueled him to greater effort.

He thought pain might eventually force him to relent, but his brain dumped one chemical concoction after another into his bloodstream, deadening the suffering and spurring the muscles.

Even then, a sixth sense told him he must go faster. He'd have to scorch the dirt to fulfill the dreams he'd only just learned his dad had dreamed.

Ben came upon a campsite five miles out of Moab in the dark of night. He steered off the road and skidded to a stop.

"Is there a problem?" A deep voice startled him.

Three men sat around a campfire. By sheer luck, one was a doctor. They loaded up and sped back to the accident site. The return trip seemed endless, but finally they arrived.

After a brief examination the doctor looked up and shook his head.

"No!" Ben screamed. A man laid a hand on his shoulder but Ben spun away. "No." Then he collapsed beside his father, overcome by exhaustion. "Why, Dad? Why didn't you hang on? I needed more time. I went as fast as I could."

Ben would never know at what point he had lost the race. If only he could have pushed himself that little bit harder it might have made all the difference. Instead, he'd failed in the only race that would ever matter.

Chapter Fifteen

Ever since Dad's death Ben had lugged his guilt around, an ever larger supply of remorse shackled to his dreams. Why had his father forced him into that pledge? Ben didn't want to become a runner. Dad had no right to ask such a thing. As a result, Ben's greatest strides toward success in professional cycling had always been tainted by the sense that Dad wouldn't approve.

Almost defensively, other uncomfortable thoughts had taken root. Had Dad let go of life, even slightly earlier than he might have, because he didn't believe his son had the strength to save him? Might he even have allowed himself to die to prevent Ben from straightening out the accidental promise? Having just recalled the circumstances more clearly than ever before, Ben knew the answers for the first time.

No.

All these years he had allowed his mind to play games with reality, to alter events in order to justify actions and feelings. He repeated his father's last words:

"Whatever happens, I'm very proud of you."

He'd forgotten that final comment, tucked in behind the broken promise that had controlled his thoughts for so long. Whatever happens. Powerful words. Very proud. Powerful emotion. That changed things, didn't it?

Ben stared at the razor-like pinnacles on either side of the low point known as the Col de la Croix de Fer. Glaciers and snowfields hid in the deepest recesses. Ahead of him Luigi ground on.

"Do you need me to take a pull?" Ben asked.

"No, I'm still good."

Ben nodded. Inside he felt changed, but in a way he couldn't yet fully comprehend. He'd begun to understand what Thierry had sensed the night before, the reason behind his inability to get everything out of himself, to tap his deepest reserves.

* * *

Ben would never forget seeing the legal document that declared him orphaned. For the next several months the court system busied itself deciding his fate. At first it looked as if he'd become the ward of relatives from Kansas who showed up on short notice to attend the funeral and settle the will. The thought of living in flat country depressed him, though maybe it would be a good area for running. After all, that's what he had promised Dad he'd do. Still, riding hills was his greatest love, and mountainous country called to him.

When Coach Bill offered to take him in, Ben lobbied hard for that outcome. A judge told Ben that as a minor his wishes didn't matter and awarded him to the Kansas relatives. But they lost interest in him when they discovered the estate had little value.

Eventually Ben was transferred to Salt Lake City where they were supposed to be better equipped to care for children than in the rural counties. Ben discovered that wasn't true. At least Coach Bill visited often.

Ben had been living at Juvenile Services awaiting an end to red tape delays for nearly a month when Coach Bill showed up one day.

"C'mon. We're getting out of here," the coach said.

"Can we do that?"

Coach Bill nodded. "Your relatives and I came up with a temporary arrangement. I'll work on extending it."

Ben gathered his things, wondering how long until he'd be shipped away. Bill took him home and pointed him toward a bedroom. Ben opened the door. There was the Bianchi. He dropped his things and went to the bike.

"You ready for a ride?" Coach Bill asked.

After that, despite the cooling weather, they took long rides nearly every day. Often they joined larger groups. Ben loved having so many training options.

He often dreamed of staying with Coach Bill permanently. There were all sorts of complications that were never explained to him, though, and he constantly worried he'd be sent elsewhere on a moment's notice. The situation kept him on edge. He wished he could do something to settle the custody situation.

As spring turned to summer, Ben's cycling flourished. He started winning races, lots of them. Splashed across the front cover of *Bicycle Magazine's* September issue was a photo of him leading the Snowbird Hill Climb. Across the top of the page large print proclaimed, "Prodigy!"

When Ben first saw it he called to heaven. "See Dad. I am a cyclist. That's what I was meant to be. You can't hold me to that old promise. You should've hung on. You should've believed in me."

* * *

Ben's front wheel touched Luigi's rear one, jolting Ben into the present. The Italian's pace had lagged for only an instant, but clearly it was the American's turn to go to the front and pull. He steeled his mind against the pain as it rose in his lungs and legs.

"We've got it made, *il mio amico*," Ben said. "We're nearly up and feeling fine."

Luigi gasped for breath.

Ben increased his pace slightly, passing Luigi. He heard the Italian's labored breathing as he fought to convince his body to accelerate, then felt Luigi settle in behind. The nearly silent exchange told Ben the Italian barely had the energy to hang on.

"You're doing well. Stay on my wheel. I'll pull you the rest of the way to the top."

"Who are you? Superman? You climb better than Luigi."

Hearing such talk from a man regarded as the premier climber in this particular race boosted Ben's confidence. Besides that, he knew he had more in the tank. He had to calm himself to avoid accelerating.

Ben reached into his back jersey pocket for food. He bit off another large hunk of the energy bar and held it in his mouth, not willing to expend any effort chewing. He would simply allow it to soften, then suck it apart.

The whine of a motorbike engine sounded from behind. There was already a cameraman in front of them, so this must be the bike with the time gap info. Ben silently prayed that the effort expended thus far had preserved their one minute lead, but he was prepared to see that they were about to be closed down.

When the chalkboard came into view Ben glanced at it, then stared. It said one minute and fifty-one seconds! He couldn't believe it.

Learning of such a gap must have spurred the chasing cyclists to increase their effort. Ben had made up nearly half the gap to Kyle's ghost-rider. Surely the news of such a deficit had motivated Kyle to lift his pace. Ben couldn't allow his enemy to take back any of the space he'd put between them. Time to dig deeper.

He glanced back at Luigi, ready to urge the other man to attack the hill with him again. They'd have to fight hard if they were to retain this margin.

Luigi's cadence slowed as he lifted a hand from his bars, kissed the fingertips, and opened them toward Ben.

Disappointed, Ben pivoted toward the road ahead. The Italian's actions revealed his feelings clearly enough. He'd already acknowledged Ben as the stronger rider and saw no point in wasting energy trying to stay with him. With an advantage of nearly two minutes, he could spin to the top and still beat the chase group. Therefore, his result would be pretty much the same whether he went all out or took it easy.

Luigi would collect second place points on this mountain, the Col de la Croix de Fer, to go with first place points he had earned on each of the climbs before. Cumulatively, that would guarantee him the polka dot jersey at the end of the stage. His goal accomplished, he was through.

Ben envied Luigi. There was a lot more pavement between Ben and his objective than between Luigi and his.

He evicted the thought with a shake of the head. The epic stretch of gravity he now battled had produced some of the most memorable moments in cycling history. Would today bring another?

Winning this stage would be paid for in currency, just like anything else. Either he had it or he didn't. In this case the payment was pain. How much was he willing to experience in compared to his rivals? How much had he already invested in training compared to the other athletes? Now was the time to prove his bank account was the biggest.

Chapter Sixteen

Ben upshifted, then stood on the pedals again.

He clawed his way alone, toward the summit of the Col de la Croix de Fer. The road ascended a steep valley as it closed in on the rocky headwall. Massive numbers of wildflowers sprouted between the numerous boulders, but the odor of skunkweed overwhelmed their scent.

A unique sensation washed over Ben. So, this is what it felt like to lead a Tour de France stage all alone. He'd experienced a similar feeling long ago on the Snowbird Hill Climb, and before that when he took the lead against that John Deere tractor near the top of Boulder Mountain. It was the sensation of breaking trail.

The majority of the time, no matter what's going on behind, a bicycle racer reacts to what's happening in front of him, either within his field of vision or sometimes far beyond it. There's a quantum shift in experience in that moment when everything is behind him, when he's alone to set the tone of the race.

The stakes multiplied the sensation. Might a fox pursued by hounds experience this phenomenon? Maybe … in a sense, at least for that portion of the chase where adrenaline flows freely into its veins.

The leader is the scriptwriter, tacitly deciding how fast the others must complete every section of the course to put themselves back into the game. At the same time, the leader has the constant disadvantage of laying his cards on the table first. In this case, Ben also felt an unimaginable number of eyes on him, staring through the media's various lenses as they tracked his every move.

There were cameras on motorcycles, in helicopters, and even recording the faces of analysts as they dissected his performance. There were televisions in living rooms, on team owner's yachts, in rival support vehicles, and nearly everywhere else. At this moment a staggering percentage of the world's population, millions upon millions of people, had focused on the tiny piece of real estate Ben Barnes happened to occupy.

Often he had tried to imagine the moment such attention might focus on him, but now he realized he had never truly comprehended how it would feel. Like nearly everyone, he'd become much more accustomed to being the viewer than the player. He tried to imagine what it might feel like to recline on the sofa, drink in hand, analyzing whether this particular athlete had what it took to reach the line first, but he could not.

Other than a possible short respite in the final valley, the remainder of this race would require him to focus on the present more intently than he ever had before. He needed to be in tune with his body, in tune with his environment, and in tune with his rivals. While he'd ridden with Luigi he'd known if anything important happened the Italian would be informed by radio and would tell him. Now he had to rely on Pierre. Was there enough trust to make this relationship work? He glanced back at Le Directeur in the trailing car as he reinserted the earpiece.

"I knew you'd want me soon. I'm not accustomed to being treated so disposably."

Ben couldn't expend energy on soothing egos. Le Directeur had a lot to gain and little to lose if Ben could pull off a victory. That ought to be enough for him to set pettiness aside. He was anxious for one piece of information: "How is Thierry?"

"Gossip is what you want?"

"Please tell me."

"I have no real news. I'll let you know when we hear something."

"But you must ..."

"I said I would let you know. Now concentrate. That's the biggest favor you can do Thierry."

As irritated as the delivery made him, Ben recognized good advice. He continued his assault of the steep mountain road at a speed that surprised even himself. His heart thumped along, well within acceptable range. His confidence rose as he recognized he was probably gaining time while remaining below anaerobic threshold. His biorhythms were apparently in sync today.

Ben recalled the sensations of his youth when he fell in love with cycling. He remembered the experience of reaching a new town for the first time, of sticking a new pin in his internal map. Long ago he'd learned that no matter how many times he visited the same place, he added to his understanding each time he traveled there.

He thought about Alpe d' Huez, and smiled at the way that location's meaning would change forever for him on this day, provided he won. He couldn't let up because he didn't want to face the consequences of a loss.

The hot air had been relatively still all day. Now in the formerly empty sky, small cumulus clouds gathered. Ben took a drink of water, washing down the last of the energy bar. He made some quick calculations in his head. The food he'd taken on when the support vehicle last visited totaled 800 calories. At near 400 watts of energy for the last thirty minutes, he would have burned approximately 850 calories. That meant he was headed into deficit, forcing his body to break down fat, what little he had, into glycogen. More likely his system would turn to converting muscle into the precious fuel.

As difficult as it was to chew, he had to eat. "Food," he said into his radio.

He squirted the remainder of his water bottle onto his head and tossed the container aside. He couldn't help smiling as spectators, the same ones who might have booed him, ran to claim the souvenir.

The support vehicle pulled alongside. Le Directeur wore a scowl. "*Plus lent.* You're riding too fast. The last climb will take a great deal of energy. You must prepare for it now. Your history in these situations is not good."

Ben frowned.

"You don't have to take my word for it. Here, listen to this. The commentators are talking about you now." Pierre reached toward the television and pressed the button to increase volume.

Ben looked at the video of a cyclist riding alongside a Banque Fédérale team vehicle. It took a moment to register that he was the rider.

A familiar voice came over the speaker. "… is Ben Barnes' history of going out too early and hard. This unpredictable American has blown up before. I believe he will again today. He's simply riding too fast. In fact, the chase group has relaxed noticeably now that it's obvious they are about to bring Luigi into the fold. They're content to let Barnes go up the road and self-destruct."

Ben fought to control his anger over the analysis. There was so much it failed to take into account. "That's bull."

"*Non*, this is good. At least if you're as strong as you claim to be," Le Directeur interrupted. "If they underestimate you, so much the better. Maybe your history of failures has laid the foundation for an upset."

History of failure? Hot blood rushed into Ben's face, but he shut his mouth and thought this through. Unexpectedly, he saw the sense in Le Directeur's words. He couldn't afford to waste energy arguing, anyway. He took three gels from Le Directeur's extended hand and tucked them into his jersey pocket. Only liquid calories from here on in. He accepted another water bottle and stuck it into his cage.

Ben glanced at Fritz in the back seat. The mechanic flashed a wide grin and a clumsy thumbs up. "For all you do, this Bud's for you." Then he pretended to drink his extended thumb.

Pierre slapped his forehead with an open palm. "Oy. Am I to be the vehicle that destroys this beloved event through American over-commercialization?"

"If I don't win this stage, Kyle Smith will. He's also American, and a lot more popular over there than I."

Pierre nodded. "Yes. It seems there's no denying the Yankees today. Don't worry. I said I'm on your side, and I am."

"How's my gap?" Ben asked.

"Increasing slightly. A moment ago a helicopter shot panned

134   DAVE SHIELDS

from you to the chasers. I estimate two minutes."

"I want three at the summit."

Le Directeur thought a moment. "It's reasonable to try for more, though I don't see gaining so much. Wait until I signal, then we shall see how you do. Just remember, there's no point in pushing if it comes at the expense of the final climb."

"I understand."

"I admit you look strong. That doesn't mean you won't cramp. You have a history."

Ben gritted his teeth, but took no offense. There was no denying his reputation. Not only had he lost the United States Pro Cycling Championship to Kyle partially as a result of the weakness, but in the past his calf muscles had seized into excruciating and useless knots on several other major climbs as well.

But now he had the awesome massages and the magic tablets. That would make all the difference. No doubt Kyle counted on cramps stopping Ben. Ben could hardly wait to disappoint his foe.

Pierre jolted him from his thoughts. "Ben, are you listening?"

Ben nodded.

"It would be best not to try extending your lead until the climb's final two kilometers. That way the others will believe you're tiring. They may truly relax. Despite what television said, I doubt they're as complacent as the commentator suggests. Remember, he's praying for a French winner."

What irony, to be warned of nationalism by Pierre. "I'll remember."

"*Très bien*. Gather your energy. I'll watch the other riders and let you know when to go. When I do, don't make it obvious you're changing your pace."

Anxious to repair his relationship with Pierre, Ben answered, "Good advice." He thought differently. He wanted to go now. He had the strength.

Obeying orders was strategic, though. The Frenchman's tacit admission that his nationalistic feelings conflicted with his role to aid Ben signaled a good first step. Le Directeur's full support could be a major stepping-stone to success.

Ben veered wide of the vehicle and continued toward the summit, settling into a comfortably sustainable pace. Ahead, the chalky colored road slithered up the side of the massif like a huge, lazy snake. The terrain beyond boggled the mind, a jumble of gray pinnacles, rock upon rock. White snowfields and patches of low-lying greenery broke up the predominant impression of crushing limestone. Otherwise, the only relief was the gatherings of spectators dotting the trail, splotches of lively and incongruous color in a brutal landscape. What a place to ride a bike.

A scowling spectator leaped into his path. Ben approached at a steady pace, certain the man would move out of the way.

"Murderer!" the man screamed.

Ben steered wide. The man moved to cut him off.

"Have you not brought enough misery to the Depardieu family? First, you killed Nicolas. Now you topple Thierry and seek his glory! It is too much!"

There was no road left. Ben squeezed his brakes and skidded to a stop.

Chapter Seventeen

The irate spectator grabbed Ben's handlebars. "You will pay for the pain you have caused France."

Ben twisted his foot from the pedal and put it on the ground. "You have it wrong. Let me go."

He overheard a nearby radio. "... an unprecedented scene. Ben Barnes is blocked by a partisan. The most unsportsmanlike act I've ever witnessed. Precious seconds tick away. Something must be done."

Shouting men rushed from all sides.

"Drunken fool!"

"Lunatic!"

"What do you mean to accomplish?"

"Get out of the American's path, you embarrassment!"

Two men tackled the obstructionist. Another gave Ben a running push up the road. It felt like being expelled from a bad dream.

Ben tried to re-establish concentration and rhythm as he pedaled past a crowd of spectators, now unnaturally silent. His legs quivered while adrenaline, needlessly expelled, subsided. Fans stared curiously, and he stared back.

Ben heard the radio as he rode. " ... can deny the American handled himself with dignity. I haven't been a fan of his, but ill will has gone too far. No athlete can be expected ..."

Ben couldn't regain his form. Maybe if he stood and sprinted he could put things back on track. He felt desperate to recover the seconds he had lost in the confrontation.

"Let me go now."

"*Non.* Wait."

It took more effort to stay than go, but instinct told him to repair things with Pierre by following his instructions.

With his patience thinned by physical stress and his emotions running high it wasn't easy to keep his pace in check. A fan ran alongside pouring water on his back. It was a compliment Ben hadn't experienced since before the catastrophe involving Nicolas. He smiled and nodded at the fan.

The cold water turned down the physical heat. Now he must will his mind to reduce the mental intensity. He concentrated on his upper body, focusing on one muscle at a time, relaxing. He'd wait, he'd simmer, until the moment came to attack. Then he'd unleash more fury on this mountain than it had ever before seen.

The nearer he came to the peak, the larger and more frequent the outcroppings of spectators became. Would someone else try to assault him?

The fans gave him surprising space, inconsistent with typical tour mountain stages. The radio announcer's words must be having some effect. He heard only scattered cheering, but at the same time boos and derogatory whistles were entirely absent. Despite the lack of noise, he felt an electric intensity.

As if in response to the supercharged air, a breeze freshened behind him. The abundant flags stretched out. A few were American, but most banners were European. Their shadows flapped across painted white letters on the road. Fans waiting to see their favorite stars had written the cyclists names on the road. Ben didn't look for his. He was no favorite.

Finally the road reached the headwall. He turned right on the first of the switchbacks leading over the last, but most fearsome barrier to the pass.

Ahead, he saw more stars and stripes. Four cheering American girls wore tee shirts that said: "Kiss me Kyle."

The next time he saw his country's flag up the road his emotions rose higher. He wanted to hurry to their position and prove he wasn't Kyle. Of course, they must already know that.

Why wasn't Le Directeur signaling him to go? He was inside three kilometers. In the remaining distance it would be a gargantuan task to gain the time he coveted. The longer he waited the more difficult the job would be. He squirted the remainder of his water bottle into his mouth and tossed the container aside.

He keyed the microphone. "Go?"

"*Non.* I'll tell you when."

He shook his head, trying to clear it of cobwebs. He had decided to give Le Directeur a chance. He still would for now, but only because the information the team car could feed him would be invaluable on the ascent up Alpe d' Huez.

Like Dad before, maybe Pierre would become supportive once he understood Ben's grit. But Dad's well-intentioned help had ultimately proven off the mark. Would Pierre's be the same? Maybe. When it really mattered, Ben would count on himself.

At an altitude of 1900 meters, nearly 7500 feet, the air had become rarified. He took deep breaths and held them in his lungs, giving his blood time to extract oxygen and rush it to his aching cells. He thought about the organized mayhem going on inside his body. His chest shuddered with the powerful contractions of his heart as the big muscle pushed blood throughout the entire network. He estimated it beat at 170 contractions per minute. His Anaerobic Threshold was 180 and he could push his heart to over 200 beats per minute for short periods under the right conditions, but that would have to wait.

The narrowing road barely clung to the mountainside. It crossed the steepest sections balanced on ancient stone retaining walls. In other places, the route picked it's way through splotchy, lichen-encrusted boulders.

He passed the marker telling him the summit was two kilometers distant.

"Now?"

"Wait."

Ben struggled to rein himself in, battled the urge to accelerate. He felt so capable of powering over the summit from this range, why wouldn't Le Directeur let him go? He'd be lucky to extend his lead to two minutes and thirty seconds at this point. Soon even that would be out of …

"*Il est temps!* Now, Benjamin! Now!"

The words were like liberation to an imprisoned man. Ben eyed the cameraman on the back of the motorcycle and saw him taking crowd shots. Ben ratcheted the gears up one at a time, keeping his cadence steady but pushing successively larger gear ratios. The readout on his cyclometer climbed. Eighteen, nineteen, twenty, twenty-one kilometers per hour. He started passing the motorcycle on the left side, the cameraman still filming the other way.

"*Merde!*" yelled the driver. The motorcycle leaped forward.

The cameraman clambered for balance, then locked eyes with Ben, only an arms length away. "*Zut!*"

Ben couldn't contain his smile. Twenty-two, twenty-three, twenty-four—despite the brutal gradient. Ben had wings. His legs drove hard while his upper body remained steady as a marble bust on a podium. The crowd rocked back on its collective heels, giving him an even wider berth as he screamed up the slope. He passed the one-kilometer marker.

Whatever had allowed him to ignore the pain in his legs to this point seemed to be wearing off. As the searing sensations increased, Ben fought to control his focus. He would not succumb to pain.

Twenty-five kilometers per hour. No way would anyone else cover this section of road at such a speed. He rounded the final switchback, no more turns between here and the summit. Each pedal revolution brought Ben closer to his objective, but it overwhelmed him to focus on a goal so far away. He looked up the road a shorter distance. He spotted an American flag, then another, and another.

Each time he reached one he focused on the next and pressed on, telling his muscles he might be willing to relent if they got him to the intermediate objectives quickly, but knowing deep down that nothing would stop him until he crested the col.

He became aware of the roar of the crowd, far more intensified since his acceleration. Somehow it seemed the deafening sound emanated from his muscles, his legs, and his heart. If they subsided in effort, so would the screams. If they increased, the cheering would as well.

He clicked onto his large front chain ring, a cog normally reserved for down hills and flats. He kept his cadence steady. Twenty-six, twenty-seven, twenty-eight, twenty-nine. The crowd exploded. Thirty. The summit arrived.

He flew across the brief flat section. The Banque Fédérale car pulled alongside.

"*Magnifique!*" Fritz yelled.

Warm satisfaction flooded Ben's body, the result of both the compliment and the hard-won respite for his legs.

He grabbed a fresh water bottle, a second bottle containing a sugary electrolyte drink, and two gels. The extra weight wouldn't hurt him going downhill. He tucked each item into its appropriate place and reached back again.

This side of the mountain was entirely different than the other. It began long and relatively straight, with an almost constant grade. He gained speed rapidly, even without pedaling, but the poor road surface made control difficult. The pathway curved ahead just as Fritz handed his helmet across. Ben fumbled, caught it, then lost it again. The plastic head protector clattered down the road behind them.

"Another one, Fritzy!"

"I'll have to retrieve one," said the mechanic. "That was the only one I had ready."

"Then forget it."

"But ..."

Ben stomped on the pedals. This time it was easy to accelerate. With gravity's assistance the road flew beneath his wheels. He recalled the way he had caught Kyle and the others from behind on the previous descent. He hadn't even considered his old fears as he screamed toward his objective. If only he could duplicate the effort on this slope.

He needed similar motivation. He imagined Kyle's ghost-rider somewhere on the road ahead, but where? The objective was too vague. He must find a concrete target.

The cameraman's motorcycle sped along in front of him. That was it. He told himself he must catch them, that everything depended on it. He told himself he was the last person capable of stopping them, that everyone else had given up the chase.

His story felt immediately urgent. Maybe it was due to fatigue, maybe desperation, but catching the motorcycle became his one and only concern.

His legs responded, driving like combustion driven pistons, pushing the pedals at a faster and faster rate. These men must be stopped at any cost. His personal safety was of secondary consequence.

Soon the wheels spun so fast that even in his highest gear, pedaling as rapidly as he could he no longer felt resistance. No amount of pedaling could increase his speed. Still the motorcycle maintained its gap. It looked like they were going to get away!

Ben moved his hands from the handlebar drops to a position side-by-side against the stem. He hadn't done this since that terrible accident on Boulder Mountain. How ironic he'd attempt it on the same descent Franco Chioccioli had been pictured navigating on page thirty-four of his old Italian cycling magazine. Ben still had that publication somewhere. He ought to dig it out next time he got home.

He glanced at the cyclometer. Ninety-five kilometers per hour and still the motorcycle maintained its gap.

Ben moved his head forward until his cheeks touched the backs of his hands. The wind sound mutated like the musical note from a child's slide whistle.

His cyclometer hit the century mark. Still he accelerated. Ben's Boulder Mountain crash had come at much lower speeds, but he couldn't dwell on that now. A hazard sign warned of a difficult sequence of curves ahead.

Ben eased his hands back onto the handlebar drops, praying the shape of the road roughly matched the arrow on the sign. He set up on the extreme outside edge of the pavement. The shoulders were dangerous because of possible debris or even spectators, but they were vital when rounding corners at high velocity. By using all the available pavement the cyclists could ride a straighter line than the road actually took.

Ben reached the first turn in the sequence, and according to the road sign the sharpest. A jumble of light and shadow made it difficult to be certain exactly what path the road followed, but Ben aimed for what appeared to be the inside of the curve. He rocketed through the corner. He had never taken a turn at this speed.

He shifted his weight to the right, lifting his right foot to the top of the pedal stroke, pointing his right knee toward the pivot point of the turn, and leaning his shoulders and torso as far as he could in the same direction. He carved the smoothest and widest arc the asphalt would allow, then sensed the dark patch on the road ahead was water, not shadow. He righted the machine, knowing at speeds like this he'd lose traction instantly on wet pavement.

The spinning tires sprayed a thin mist of water over him. He immediately resumed the turn, tighter than before to make up for the moment he had straightened the wheel. Still he avoided the brakes.

His arc wasn't tight enough. He must either slow or complete the turn on the hard packed dirt shoulder. He tensed as he chose the latter. A sharp rock or thorn would be the end of his tire. Even a momentary loss of traction could shatter his career. And his body.

The wheels threw up a talc-like explosion as they hit the dirt. In another instant they returned to solid pavement. Sweat burst from every pore—a million glands releasing liquid in response to his close call. He shivered as the water immediately evaporated from his skin.

The gamble had paid off, but there was no time to reflect on success.

Ben adjusted his weight and body position for the second turn, noticing as he did that the gap between him and the motorcycle had narrowed considerably. They hadn't expected him to maintain such high velocity through this section. Good.

The last two turns in the sequence were, as the road sign had indicated, milder than the first. The bike tracked perfectly. The road straightened, and on a fresh stretch of pavement he reached even higher speeds. Ben couldn't believe how in tune with his machine he felt as he zipped past an enormous waterfall, then down toward a cloudy, glacial filled reservoir. She was good, this bike. Fritz had been right.

Along the reservoir shore the route climbed. With all the speed Ben carried he was able to cruise up the hill. Once the road cleared the dam, the route plunged downward again.

A yellow warning sign indicated switchbacks. He returned his hands to a more traditional position, poised over the brakes. The increased air resistance slowed him and the wind noise scaled to a lower note.

Ahead, the road dropped sharply as it turned back on itself. He saw the fear in the cameraman's eyes as the motorcycle flew down the mountain. He didn't want to lose ground now. Ben positioned himself at the extreme edge of the road. His head felt mere inches away from the cliff screaming past on his right side. Rocks, branches, tree roots, and other plants whizzed by dangerously close to his face, but he riveted his attention on the upcoming turn. He positioned his left pedal at the top of its arc and shifted his weight to that side of the machine.

Instinct told him he could never make such a tight corner at this speed, but maybe the terrain zipping by at eye level made things seem faster than they really were.

Unfortunately he couldn't glance at the cyclometer for even an instant to check his speed. He tapped the brakes. If the bike slowed it was imperceptible, but the gesture calmed his inner voice.

The moment to turn came. He leaned hard and tilted the handlebars in a smooth motion. He sensed the tires biting the asphalt almost as if he had nerve endings in the rubber. Centrifugal force fought to throw him and his machine over the void beyond the turn. As he approached the inside of the corner he realized his arc wasn't tight enough.

He must touch the brakes again … or lean harder. He leaned, even as he sensed the failing grip of his tires. He teetered as never before on the razor's edge separating brilliance from insanity.

The bike scribed an inconceivable line across the asphalt, but still it wasn't enough. The far edge of the road approached too rapidly. He considered squeezing the brakes, embracing safety, but resisted.

The wheels lost traction and instinct begged Ben to put his right foot out. He spun the pedal a half turn to feel the road with his foot.

BANG!

A shock wave blasted up his right leg. The rear wheel leaped into the air, then screeched as it bounced sideways several times before regripping the road. Ben threw his weight forward, almost as if riding a unicycle. What had gone wrong with the rear end of his bike? He struggled to control the one reliable wheel. With all of his upper body strength he wrenched it onto a straight track. Somehow, he'd made the turn.

He zipped down the straightaway toward the next switchback. Ben eased weight to the rear of the bicycle. Everything felt all right again. He glanced at his rear wheel. It looked fine.

In an instant Ben realized what had happened. He'd dug a pedal, big time. His right pedal hadn't just touched asphalt, it had gripped it. The contact threw the rear wheel off the ground. Miraculously, the tire hit the pavement and regained traction, only in a better position for completing the turn. He'd clipped the ground with a pedal many times before, but never so solidly or at such high speed.

He had just survived a one in a million shot. He would never attempt it again. The next 999 thousand plus attempts couldn't possibly end so well.

In the midst of the thought, he zinged past the motorbike.

He'd done it! Now what?

He looked at his cyclometer: eighty-one kilometers per hour. No time to shudder, but these speeds through this terrain was unthinkable. He yelled triumphantly. Adrenaline pumped full bore, and so did his legs.

As he approached a media car he made eye contact with the driver in the rear-view mirror. The vehicle jolted forward, wavered, and then steered too far to the right hand side of the road. It skidded down an embankment and crashed into a tree. Through a haze of dust and pollen Ben saw the driver and passengers scramble from the destroyed vehicle as he screamed past.

Ahead, another switchback, this time to the right. The approaching turn didn't appear quite as sharp, giving him more roadway to work with. He set up as before. This time at the nadir of the turn he was again short in his arc. He leaned harder. He teetered, a fraction at most, from dropping into a dry slide and ending his race, then ejected cleanly from the turn.

Ben had entered a zone he'd never been in before. Every nerve ending was dialed in. In all the thousands of descents he'd ever executed, he had never put together one that came close to this. His newfound ability to take a faster line gave him an unbelievable sense of power.

He returned to his most aerodynamic position atop the bike. He reached yet another windy sequence but remained in the unstable posture. The action came to him at lightning speed but his reactions were up to the task. The bicycle cruised through the turns as if on rails.

He shot onto the ensuing straightaway and found himself dangerously close to the rear end of the official's sedan that led the race. The car leaped forward, trying to re-establish the usual spacing.

The bicycle, caught in the vortex of the slipstream, accelerated as well. Technically Ben was illegally drafting the vehicle, but the fault wasn't his. If anyone would be penalized for his proximity to the car it had to be the official driving. At the head of the race the biker had the right-of-way.

The computer now read ninety-three. The brief draft from the vehicle had sling-shotted his speed up yet another increment. Judging by the distance covered and altitude lost Ben knew the worst of the road was now behind him. He concentrated on slicing through the wind as fast as possible.

"… some good … for …"

Ben cupped a hand over his earpiece to block out the wind noise.

"… is reporting your gap over the summit timing station at two minutes and fifty-three seconds …"

Ben wanted to throw his fist in the air in celebration. Almost half a minute more than his highest expectation. How much more time might he have added on the descent? It would be a while before he learned … the longer the better.

Another rapid turn sequence loomed ahead. Ben concentrated on the road. Right, left, right, harder right, wobble, correction, more wobble, brake tap, still wobbling.

Chapter Eighteen

The bike screamed out of the sequence, spitting used road from beneath its tires like a pitching machine ejecting fastballs. Ben's pulse pounded.

The rear wheel had tracked poorly through the last turn. No surprise there. The ultralight sew-up tires had endured more than their fair share of stress. Sometimes the glue adhering them to the rims gave way. Tires could peel right off under such conditions.

Fortunately, good 'ole Fritzy Boy had done his usual excellent work in gluing tire to rim. Ben resolved to kiss the silly looking Frenchman. That would show how deep his gratitude ran, especially because the mechanic knew full well how hard it would be for Ben to kiss a man, even the traditional French *bise*.

An abrupt four-switchback climb to the hanging village of Le River de Allemont increased his blood flow again; then came the descent. Thankfully all but the final two high-speed switchbacks were now safely behind him. The tire was unlikely to fail at the slower speeds once the descent was complete. Ben knew the remainder of this course well. Fifteen kilometers down to and through the scenic Romanche River Valley, then just under fourteen kilometers up the storied lower face of Pic Blanc to the famous finish line in the ski station of Alpe d' Huez. In less than an hour, he'd be done.

He careened around the last few bends in the mountain road. The rear end of the bike shimmied slightly, but made it out of the corner intact. Ben wiped his brow, only then recalling he had no helmet. If he had crashed—no, he shouldn't even contemplate that at the moment. He breathed a sigh of relief. The gambles had paid off.

As Ben's legs caught up to the spinning wheels, a wave of

satisfaction broke over him. He had just reinvented the descent. That had to be one of the greatest downhill sequences of all time.

No time to reflect now, though. He must prepare for the final climb. If he handled it like he had the descent, the two other knocks against his ability—his tendency to cramp and his rumored inability to finish the job—would be history.

The night before, Thierry claimed his reputation as a star was the result of a single performance. He said the outcome that day exceeded even his own expectations; that the results caused others to reassess who he was. Had the Frenchman been aware of these shifts in attitude as they occurred? Ben certainly was.

Even if no one else saw him differently, his self-image had undergone a dramatic rehabilitation. It wasn't simply a return to the leadership role he once knew himself capable of. He'd found a dose of maturity he never imagined possessing, an ability to calmly assess situations under extreme pressure. For the first time he truly understood the advantage of sound decisions over quick conclusions, of cool nerves above abrupt action, of total concentration versus merely paying attention.

Deep inside, Ben now knew he was the most capable player in this race. It seemed as if he'd always known that, even though he could recall doubting his own ability earlier in this day.

In this young and abrupt mountain range, foothills were nonexistent. The mountains formed a near ninety-degree angle with the valley floor. The awe-inspiring walls of the Central Massif towered on all sides as he followed the course into the center of the narrow Romanche River Valley. This would be the last portion of the race where he could allow his mind to wander even slightly. In fact, he must force distractions on himself. If he expected his senses to be sharp when he needed them most, he had to give them a break while they weren't in such demand.

He thought of Bridgette. She deserved credit for this ride every bit as much as he. She'd stuck by his side when many others jumped ship. This weekend when the race left the Alps and spent a day on the Riviera, she'd visit. Ben couldn't wait.

He recalled bringing her to Utah to meet his friends after

being kicked out of professional cycling. He'd been giddy about their relationship for months, only to be humiliated by Kyle's claim that she'd spent an evening with him.

* * *

When Ben and Bridgette's flight touched down in Utah's capital city shortly after his expulsion from European racing, both Bill and Thelma were at the airport to pick them up. Excitement illuminated Bridgette's eyes as she greeted the friends he had told her so much about.

"*Bonjour*," she said.

"Likewise." Coach Bill extended a rough hand.

Thelma had no such formality in her veins. She drew both her guests into a tight hug and squeezed them against her fleshy body.

"I warned her about this," Ben said, gasping for breath.

Thelma released them.

Bridgette smiled. "It's even better than you said it would be."

"Oooh, I like this girl already," Thelma said. "These two were made for one another. Do you sense that, Bill?"

Blood heated Ben's cheeks. He glanced at Bridgette. Her eyes were on him. They exuded confidence.

Coach Bill scratched his head. "I don't think men are much good at seeing that sort of thing. At least I'm not. I'm just glad to have Ben back. How are you, my friend?"

"I wish the circumstances were better," Ben answered.

"Pshaw. What's done is done. You stood your ground with the top cyclists in the world. You'll be back among their ranks sooner than you can whistle Dixie."

On the flight Ben had contemplated leaving professional cycling behind forever. "I can't whistle."

Before anyone took his hint of retirement, Bridgette expertly trilled the tune of, "Oh I wish I were in the land of cotton …"

Thelma broke into a wide grin. "Hang on to this one, Ben! She's a keeper!"

Ben looked out the concourse window at the Wasatch Front.

"It's sure good to be home."

Thelma squeezed his shoulder. "Are ya all going to make it down to Boulder for a dish of Megatronics Pasta?"

"I think you should consider changing the name of that dish," Coach Bill said.

Thelma covered her mouth with a hand. "You're right. Which team will you join next, Ben?"

"You say that as if it's my choice. No one clambered to offer me a contract before I left."

"Well, we've got to come up with a new name. How about you go out and win a race for me. Remember how you used to do that in the old days? I'll re-name the pasta after your next victory."

Ben shook his head. "It's not as easy as you make it sound. I can't just go around promising victories. It doesn't work like that."

Thelma frowned and sagged her shoulders. She looked as if she'd just learned Santa Claus didn't exist.

"Aw, Thelma, you've got to be realistic. How about letting me enjoy being home for a moment before we plan the future."

Thelma tousled his hair. "Whatever happened to that unstoppable little guy I once knew?"

Ben's gaze fell to the ground. "He got stopped."

Bridgette waved Ben off. "What he meant to say is, of course we'll be by for some of your cooking. In France he brags about it nonstop."

Thelma perked up. "He does?"

Ben kept his eyes down. "Yeah. I think about home constantly. In fact, who says I'll return to Europe? I'm considering retirement."

The suggestion met with ear-shattering silence.

Finally, Ben looked up. His three companion's formerly wide smiles had overturned.

"You can't quit," Thelma said. "I've been saving pennies so that one day I can go over there and watch you race."

"Jeez, Thelma. Please don't complicate it like this. I'm just thinking aloud."

Thelma frowned.

"How serious are you?" Coach Bill asked.

Ben swallowed. He looked at his friends. "This is home for me. You don't realize how difficult it is over there. It's not just biking. Sometimes the stuff that goes on while you're out of the saddle is the really tough part."

"I do realize. I did it myself. Remember?" Coach Bill said.

Ben shook his head. "Not like this. Things have changed."

"It's just politics. You'll get the hang of that stuff," Coach Bill's voice held an urgent edge Ben hadn't expected.

His own tone involuntarily raised an octave. "If the politics on an American team were too much for me, how would I ever survive a European squad? A foreign team is the only choice, you know, and I don't even speak more than a smattering of any other languages. I can't tell you the number of times I'd have gotten into trouble if not for Bridgette translating."

"And I'll rescue you a thousand more times if I must … starting now." Bridgette kissed Ben's cheek. "This is supposed to be a time to relax and enjoy. I can't wait to see why you love the Utah desert so much. Let's concentrate on that."

* * *

"*J'ai l'information.* The chase group just reached the bottom of the descent. Your margin is three minutes and thirty-seven seconds," came a message over the radio.

Ben smiled. Kyle's ghost-rider was only a little more than half a minute up the road.

"You have performed adequately so far. The question is, will you be able to climb the final mountain?"

The smile evaporated. Was it beyond Pierre to congratulate him on anything? "*Oui.*"

"I know you can ride ordinary hills. But do you have what it takes to lead the Tour de France onto hallowed ground?"

"I said I could climb!"

"I don't think you can imagine the humiliation you would bring to us if you failed. You have forced me to risk a lot today, Benjamin. A stage win is now within our grasp. If you do exactly as

I instruct I believe I can lead you to victory."

Pierre had risked nothing. Did he really believe he had? If so, maybe he'd help. But Ben still wasn't convinced of that.

He turned left onto the highway paralleling the Romanche River. The ninety-degree adjustment put him face on into a stiff breeze. The wind immediately slowed him. The time-gap motorcycle sat beside the road, and the passenger started his watch. It gave Ben an idea.

How would his rivals react if he performed exactly as they expected? They believed he'd cramp, didn't they? He quit pedaling.

"What's the problem, Benjamin?" Concern stressed Pierre's voice.

Ben resumed pedaling, but slower than before. "After the timing station I just passed, is the next time-split taken at the base of Alpe d' Huez?"

"That would be my guess," Le Directeur answered.

"At that point, how much time do you think I need to win?"

"As much as you can get. What is your point?"

"How much time do I need?" Ben squirted an energy gel into his mouth and chased it with water.

"You told me you had the strength for this final climb. Now you're slowing and the climb is still distant."

"I'll bet three minutes would be enough. Tell me what the commentator says to this." Ben unclipped his left foot from the pedal and massaged his calf.

Urgency flooded Le Directeur's voice. "What do you think they'll say? Hold on. They're already talking."

There was a pause.

"Exactly as I guessed. They're explaining that you deserve your reputation for cramping. Moments ago you promised you were strong. Which is it?"

Ben pushed the bike forward using only the right pedal, continuing to knead the lower left leg. "I am strong."

The cameraman ahead aimed his lens directly at Ben. Ben imagined he had zoomed in tight. He grimaced, recalling the excruciating pain of cramps.

"Damn it, Benjamin. You keep saying you feel well, but I can see that isn't the case. You're giving your rivals confidence. Please be discreet!"

The motorcycle dropped alongside the bicycle. The television photographer held his camera low and took a shot of Ben's right leg struggling to keep the bike moving forward while the left leg dangled uselessly.

Ben turned his head. "I'm bluffing. Don't you play poker?"

"It doesn't look like a bluff to me."

"If it looked like a bluff, what would be the point?"

"Don't lie. I can see you're cramping. This, after you joined our destinies so that your poor performance can cost me my job. I tell you now: Get it together! One more cramp and I pull the plug on this experiment."

Ben wanted to laugh. Le Directeur's lack of confidence frustrated him, but it was tempered by his newfound, or at least rediscovered, faith in his own gut instinct. "I should bust my butt into a headwind?"

"No. Your energy will be better used battling gravity once the climb begins, but it's not the time to allow pain to defeat you either."

Ben nodded. "Since the chasers can draft they're going to gain on me through here, anyway. Why not let them think I'm about to fail? Maybe they'll begin racing against each other instead of cooperating."

The radio stayed silent for a long moment. "*Oy*. You make many assumptions. Your mind is not as agile as you think. The stress of riding takes much out of it."

"What assumption is wrong?"

"I don't know which one. Do it your way and we'll find out."

This felt reminiscent of arguing with Dad. Ben clipped his left foot back into the pedal. "So how much time do I need at the base of the final climb?"

"*Trois minutes* sounds good. If you're still three minutes ahead at the base of the climb maybe you can hold on to win the stage."

"My goal is not to win this stage," Ben said.

"*C'est quoi?* Are you kidding? You're too much for me! What is your goal?"

"To wear the maillot jaune."

"*Vous?* Ridiculous."

"Tonight."

"Don't be obscene," Pierre raged.

Le Directeur's doubt fueled Ben's internal fire. "I can. Giving up time here means building energy for later. If I take a rest while eating and digesting I'll reach the mountain ready to climb."

"I'm not playing this ridiculous game with you."

Ben stared at the massif looming in front of him. "Very well. If I win without your help I'll let everyone know."

"Aaarghhh. What choice am I left? I have nothing more to lose. Let me calculate." A pause followed. "Maintain thirty-five KPH across these flats. That might leave you three minutes gap to start of the climb. There's no way to be sure, though."

Ben slowed to the target speed. "Good, now I can relax for a while. Wake me if anything good happens, Honey." He closed his eyes and rolled his head against his shoulder.

Hopefully the rest of the world, or at least his main rivals, would interpret the visual punch line to his joke on Pierre as extreme pain and exhaustion.

Le Directeur didn't laugh. "Benjamin, you are going to lose this race."

Chapter Nineteen

Riding into the wind on the flat highway from Allemont to Bourg d' Oisans would be Ben's final opportunity to relax his mind. He felt mental clarity far beyond what he'd known when the day began. He could now recall the joy of riding, the pain of loss, his father's dreams, and his friends' support. If not for each of them he would not be here.

An image of Bridgette's face, her vibrant smile, and silky hair, drifted through his mind. With the image came her aura, that infectious enthusiasm she wore like perfume. He thought back to their Utah trip.

* * *

The second day home Ben drove Bridgette south from Salt Lake for five hours to Thelma's place in Boulder. Bill and other Northern Utah friends headed south too.

Much to Ben's embarrassment, he found the town strewn with banners and posters praising his accomplishments. The entire populations of Boulder and Hanksville, as well as large segments of several nearby communities stood cheering along the roadside. No single establishment could contain the party. Well-wishers flooded businesses and homes on both sides of the highway.

Why so many people? What made him responsible for such unrealistic expectations? Didn't they know he'd left Europe suspended and disgraced?

As the rising full moon perched like a gigantic ping-pong ball on the sandstone formations to the east, Coach Bill drew Ben aside. The old cycling guru put a hand on Ben's shoulder and walked him toward Thelma's garden. "I can't get it out of my mind. Are you still thinking retirement?"

"I've all but decided on it."

Coach Bill shook his head. "You've experienced success, Ben. Now you must learn to overcome it."

"What's that supposed to mean?"

"It takes a lot more inner strength to endure good fortune than bad. Few people realize that."

Ben regarded his friend carefully. He'd always admired Coach Bill's grasp of philosophy, but he doubted this was true. "I've experienced my share of both. Success is awesome and failure reeks. You know that."

"When I rode professionally, if I'd understood what I'm telling you now, I'll guarantee you my accomplishments would have been greater. It's one of the secrets of life. It's a concept great men master."

"What concept?"

"Think of it this way." Coach Bill rubbed a weathered cheek. "Each of us has an internal thermostat. If we don't live up to our self-image, the burners kick on and heat things up until we get comfortable."

"Sounds simple enough. What's the point?"

"What do you think the thermostat does when it gets too hot?"

Ben watched moon shadows shift on the rolling rock landscape. "I don't know. I assume the cooler clicks on."

Coach Bill chuckled. "Right. But air conditioning is not a good thing when we're after success."

Ben looked at his mentor with a crinkled brow.

"Don't you see? Your self-image believes it's doing you a favor by keeping your success in check. That's why you want to give up on pro cycling."

Ben patted Coach Bill on the shoulder. "I appreciate your concern. I really do."

Coach Bill nodded. "Think about it. You'll understand."

Ben walked away shaking his head, his resolve to quit European racing solidified by the fear he was bound to disappoint his wonderful friends.

The decision left him feeling empty. Now that he'd given up on his longstanding dream, what would he do? Why hadn't he followed through with the promise he made his father? He should have become a runner. He could have competed as an individual and avoided all the team politics. Maybe he should do that now?

Hopefully, he could untangle his thoughts in the backcountry. He'd promised Bridgette an adventure in the untamed desert, and now he looked forward to it more than ever.

Out in the silent wilderness he'd get in tune with his deepest feelings, as well as the feelings of the one he truly loved. Yes, loved. It was an emotion he'd only admitted to in the remote recesses of his mind, but he now realized Bridgette was more important to him than anyone or anything else.

She'd taken the desert southwest by storm. Her enthusiasm for life drew people toward her like children to a fuzzy yellow chick. The resulting aura created an increasingly magnetic attraction for Ben. He couldn't imagine their friendship—or love—ever ending.

* * *

Tents dotted the fields. Camping trailers plastered with pictures of favorite cyclists were everywhere. Still several kilometers out of town, cars were parked in any available spot, most of their owners nowhere to be seen. That meant the town had to be packed with vehicles as well. What must lie ahead? Apparently an enormous crowd on Alpe d' Huez. Ben had heard of crowds exceeding half a million on that eight-mile stretch. How many would be there today?

* * *

After the party in Boulder and a night on Thelma's hide-a-bed, Ben and Bridgette headed for the Hole-in-the-Rock-Trail to begin their camping trip. They clattered down the bumpy dirt road in a borrowed pickup truck. This route had originally been established in an ill-concieved attempt by Mormon pioneers to construct a more direct route to their settlements on the other side of the Colorado River. The problem was, in this vicinity the river ran at the bottom of 2000-foot deep Glen Canyon. To cross, the travelers had to blast a route through the cliffs. The pioneers had anticipated their journey would take six weeks. Six months later the surviving members of the trek hobbled into a location short of their planned destination.

Ben and Bridgette stopped twelve miles before the point where those earlier travelers had begun their descent into the gorge. Ben savored the scent of sage as he stepped out of the car. The smell of home.

He stared across the vacant expanse of desert. "This is the Coyote Gulch Trail Head. I've never taken this hike, but I've always wanted to."

Bridgette climbed from the vehicle, scanning the area skeptically. "Are you sure this is where we want to go? The street sign back there said, 'Middle of Nowhere.'"

"Very funny. Trust me."

They put on their packs and headed into the forbidding desert.

From their very first steps the noontime sun baked down on them, dry and relentless. No wonder there were no animals in sight and the tallest plants didn't even reach knee high. The undulating terrain immediately around hid all clues of an environment that might contain diversity or interest.

They followed scattered boot prints in the sand. The route eventually ended at the brink of a sheer walled ravine. Bridgette looked even more doubtful as she peered over the edge.

Ben scouted along the ridge. "Here's the route."

At his feet a narrow defile cut between two enormous rocks. The opening was only two feet wide in most places, even narrower in some. Its floor angled gradually down, through the cliff face. "You'll need to take off your pack and hold it above your head to squeeze through. I'll lead the way."

The sandstone made a static sound as clothing and packs slid against it.

Half way through Ben glanced back at Bridgette. "You look

like the tasty part of a rock sandwich."

"I'm not certain how to interpret that, but I can't believe you got me here by bragging of wide open spaces."

Ben laughed. "Just a little bit farther. I can see the other end."

Once they wiggled through the remainder of the slot they stood below the cliff that had previously prevented them from entering the canyon.

Ben put a finger to his lips, then pointed into the distance. A herd of five mule deer raised their heads high, sniffing the wind, then bounded over the hill.

"Now what do you think of the middle of nowhere?"

"Not bad."

Far below, huge cottonwood trees hinted at an oasis. Bird song drifted toward them—the trilling of some exotic breed.

They resumed their descent. On the canyon floor they discovered a sun dappled Eden. A lively stream, its banks lush with ferns, saw grass, and Mormon tea cut a serpentine path through the soft red sand. Bridgette removed her shoes and walked in the water. Clouds of pollywogs swam for cover as she approached, obviously sensing the tremors of nearby footfalls.

Bridgette kicked droplets into the air. "Who could ever have dreamed a place like this existed?"

"The desert is full of surprises. Just wait."

They walked upstream silently. The seclusion relaxed Ben, just as he'd hoped. He had looked forward to returning to canyon country for a long time. Eventually they reached the spot Ben had been looking for. Coyote Natural Bridge spanned the stream, the rock opening easily large enough to drive a semi-truck through. Cut out of a sheer wall, it looked like the decorative entrance to a giant's garden.

Not far beyond the passage, the stream veered right. Ben continued straight ahead into an enormous grotto. The cave yawned 200 feet wide and 75 feet high at the opening. It continued back for at least 150 feet.

Ben dropped his pack into a firm sand shelf. "We'll set up camp here."

By the time the sun set over the canyon wall they each held pots of hot stew. Beside them sat a bottle of French wine. They watched the light of a descending sun explore the cracks, undulations, and desert varnish on the red wall at the other side of the canyon.

A small fire crackled at their feet. Ben tossed a pinecone into the flames. "Do you know why I like being with you so much, Bridgette?"

"I have my suspicions, but no, I guess I'm not positive."

"I was raised by a pessimist." Ben smiled and looked back at her. "I don't know if I'll ever be able to soak in enough optimism to make up for it. Your sunny outlook does more for me than you'll ever know."

"*Merci beaucoup.* But each one of us sees the world in the way we see it. There's not necessarily anything right with me, or wrong with your father. Still, I'm glad you like me the way I am."

Bridgette steered the conversation to his bike-racing career. "I understand your frustration with cycling, Ben, but I can't allow you to give up."

"What do you mean?"

"You have a gift, and it's my job to see that you use it."

"Your job?"

She smiled her dazzling smile. "Self appointed, but you're not getting rid of me."

A shiver ran down his spine. "Should I be worried?"

"No. You're a man and you don't know any better than to do what your woman tells you."

Ben laughed. "And you're my woman?"

"Damn right. What do you think I'm doing following you here, of all places? We're a team."

"And I suppose you have a plan."

She lifted a spoonful of stew and put it into his mouth. "Very perceptive."

Ben shielded his mouth with a hand so he could talk. "Are you willing to tell me what the plan is, or am I just your victim?"

She pushed another spoonful in. "Just answer this. If I could deliver you a contract from one of the top three European teams, would you promise to sign?"

Ben choked. "Top three?"

"That's what I said. If you got a contract from one of the big boys, would that convince you to stick with cycling for another season?"

Ben thought about which teams would qualify as the top three. There was no one in the top ten he'd reject, but neither did he expect them to make him an offer. "Yeah. But I can think of reasons they might not want me on their teams."

"I'm willing to ignore the last part of your answer this one time. We'll work on your attitude later. The important part is that you agreed to the plan."

"And that's all you're willing to tell me about it?"

She smiled. "No. Now I'll tell you the rest because I know you're a man of your word."

Ben crossed his heart with two quick swipes of his right index finger.

"I've never told you about my Uncle Pierre. He's a crafty fellow who on many occasions has tried to convince me to use what he calls 'my sexual charms' to lure a superstar cyclist from a rival team over to his camp. I've always refused, but lately I'm thinking maybe he has a good idea."

"His camp? Are you talking about Pierre LeBlanc of Banque Fédérale?"

Bridgette nodded.

"He's your uncle?"

She smiled. "Small world, no?"

"Yes, but your plan won't work."

"Why?"

"Not only is his anti-Americanism well known, but Nicolas Depardieu was on Banque Fédérale when—"

Bridgette put a finger to his lips. "Leave this up to me, okay? I'll tell him I can convince one of the top rated young cyclists to join his team as a domestique if he'll extend a minimum contract. You're not going to get picky about wages, are you?"

"Well … no."

"Good. Then it's all but done."

A warm sensation flowed through Ben's veins. "But … I don't know French."

She purred with the satisfaction of triumph. "Lessons begin tonight."

* * *

Pierre's voice crackled over the radio. "*Accélérez!* Now you aren't even going as fast as we agreed. What is going on Benjamin?"

Ben looked down at his digital display. It registered thirty-one kilometers per hour. "Sorry, daydreaming."

"Hmmph. Let's see if you can pay attention when we head for the summit. Otherwise the result will be sure to embarrass us both."

Chapter Twenty

Mountains erupted from either side of the valley floor like barricades set out by God. The peak that interested Ben was on his left, La Grand Sure.

The portion he could see from his current position was a sheer limestone wall. Further east, there was a spit of precipitous slope reaching all the way to the valley floor. The angle of incline may have been milder than the cliff he could now see, but only by a tiny increment. Nevertheless, the decreased slope allowed a finger of vegetation to stretch down from the towering heights. Apparently that had been enticement enough for road builders to blaze a path to the summit. Little could they have known the twenty-one switchbacks they blasted from the rock were destined to become cycling's greatest Mecca.

Ben inhaled deeply as he allowed his gaze to travel toward the peak. The craggy summit had snagged a wispy cloud. Could he overcome an obstacle capable of grabbing hold of the sky?

He thought about the finish line and his anxiety to cross it. He'd practically memorized the route to the final destination, but for that matter, everyone associated with the race knew the remaining climb intimately. After all, this was Alpe d' Huez. Legend after legend had been born on that fabled patch of pavement. Would Ben Barnes be next?

How many could ever attain such a goal? The Tour de France climbed this mountain only once every two or three years. If a cyclist had a long and fortunate career he might find himself in such a race five times in his life, on each occasion pitted against nearly 200 other men harboring the same dream.

Ben stopped dwelling on the treacherous asphalt pathway connecting his present location with the goal. He'd have to take it one pedal revolution at a time. Instead, he drew inspiration from Bridgette.

She had forced him to extend his reach, pushed him beyond his capabilities. Together they imagined a life where their dreams had already come true. Bridgette had been right. They were a team, a good team. She was the most valuable piece of his life, yet he couldn't bring himself to make the relationship permanent. Why? What did he fear?

The road entered Bourg d' Oisans, the village at the base of the final climb. After reaching the fountains of the town square, the route turned left ninety degrees. Ben noted with satisfaction that he now faced a cross wind instead of a head wind. The chase group's major advantage had expired, and he still held the lead. More important, he felt fresh.

Only a hundred meters ahead a banner stretched over the road with the inscription "*Départ.*" Next, he'd head for the heavens. He'd ridden the climb from this point many times, but never alone. This would be unlike anything he had ever experienced. When he crossed the line beneath the banner he'd be awarded the bonus time for winning the intermediate sprint, but he had no interest in the green sprinter's jersey that accomplishment counted toward. He couldn't care less about what ended there. Rather, his concern was what began.

At the same point the clock would start to time the ascent of Alpe d' Huez. Equally important in Ben's mind was the gap back to the chase group. How much time had they made up?

He stood on his left leg and unclipped his right foot. He reached back and grabbed his toe, stretching it until the bottom of his foot lay against his buttocks. This act was his last shot at convincing the chasers he wasn't fit to climb.

"Please don't do that," Pierre moaned.

Ben returned the foot to the pedal. He steeled himself for the challenge.

The road confronted the looming cliff head-on. It hit the obstacle and deflected ninety-degrees to the left, but bit into the hillside and climbed. The initial twelve per cent grade soaked up most of Ben's momentum.

As his speed decreased, the mass of spectators crowded from all sides, leaning in behind the race officials' cars and camera motorcycles he followed. The vehicles used their horns to warn the crowd to step back. The trilling tunes and screaming fans made the entourage seem like some sort of happy traffic jam.

A spectator sprinted at his side. "Is this is as fast as you can go? The French chasers will devour you!"

Ben didn't even look at the man, but he couldn't control his response. He accelerated, leaving the runner behind and producing a roar of appreciation from some of the spectators. The response was more enthusiastic than he'd expected. That made him feel good. He established a comfortable cadence, enjoying the sensation of his muscles under stress.

The radio crackled. "*Mon Dieu!* You were bluffing, after all."

Ben realized if Pierre had changed his mind, everyone else might have done the same. He slowed a bit, slumped his shoulders, and tried to make his labor more obvious. Hopefully the pursuing teams would forgive him a brief energy spurt on such a historic stretch of road. The camera would be on him a lot through this first segment as everyone tried to judge just how capable he was. He needed to look as pathetic as possible, at least until the chase group passed under the banner and learned how rapidly they were gaining on their quarry.

"Just as I feared. Merely a brief burst of adrenaline," Pierre groaned.

"Have faith. Give me the time gap when you have it."

Ben resumed his previous speed, but this time disguised the acceleration with a pained expression and swaying technique. It was difficult to send external signals so contrary to how he felt. So powerfully did body language affect him, trying to look like he was suffering made him feel poorly. He began doubting his strategy. He reminded himself that the moment the chase group reached the mountain he could abandon his ruse and put the hammer down in earnest. That's when his outlook would improve. He could hardly wait.

Ben kept one eye on the digital readout of his cyclometer. So far he'd been able to keep his speed high despite his acting job. He looked forward to the moments the camera wasn't in position to catch his expressions. It felt good to relax his facial muscles and concentrate on racing.

He reached the sign indicating switchback number twenty-one. The final countdown had begun. Twenty more famous hairpin turns remaining, then the finish line. He rounded the corner, both looking forward to and dreading to hear when the chasers began their ascent. More spectators ran at his side for whatever distance they could keep up, but these seemed inspired by the joy of the moment instead of any sort of intimidation.

"The chase group just crossed the timing line. Your lead is down to two minutes and forty-nine seconds."

So, there it was. Ben felt thankful for the portion of mountain he'd already put behind him. Hopefully his pursuers believed they had him pegged.

"Are you happy now? You have burnt your opportunity and what have you gained for it?"

Ben ignored the negativity. "Who's coming?"

"Still the same: Kyle Smith and two others. They're strong and confident. No sign of panic. The next group is less than two minutes behind them and driving fast. Now do you see what I was saying? You're blowing your chance through pure foolishness. The pursuing riders far exceed your caliber on terrain like this. Our only hope is to strategically use your remaining margin to …"

"I'm blowing nothing. My margin will grow from here on out."

"Benjamin! You aren't thinking clearly. Strategy is my job, but I can only help you if you will obey my orders. Do you agree?"

"No."

"*Imbécile!*" Ben could almost hear Pierre's spittle stinging the microphone. "Are you still fantasizing about taking the maillot jaune today? That can't happen. Your cumulative time is too far behind the riders chasing you. To prevent Kyle Smith from wearing yellow, you must add a minute and a half to your lead over some of the toughest terrain on earth. Even that might not put you at the top of the General Classification. Gunter von Reinholdt had five minutes and fourteen seconds on you when the day started, and he's in the group behind Smith. Just concentrate on not blowing up. Ride within your abilities. Make certain you cross the finish line first. If you can hold on to win this stage, it will be glory enough."

Ben's blood boiled. These were things his dad would have said. Was his frustration with Pierre the result of his deep-seated hatred of pessimistic thought? He paused, counted to ten, but couldn't cool down. Despite Pierre's "told-you-so" attitude, the reality was that events were playing out just as Ben had hoped. What good was the negativity doing him?

None.

Ben passed a Winnebago. Big speakers blared the radio broadcast for all to hear. The amplified voice was Thierry's.

"Il est comme un frère pour moi ."

Who was like a brother to Thierry? Him? Ben heard no more before he rolled out of earshot. Why hadn't Pierre yet told him a single thing about the team leader? He keyed his microphone. "What is Thierry talking about on radio?"

"Do not bother me with irrelevant concerns."

Ben's blood heated. "At least tell me how he's doing. You promised news of his condition."

"We have more pressing concerns."

"Try this for an concern. I'm through with you, Pierre."

"You're what? You arrogant fool. If you don't think you need my help to complete this race then you know nothing. Your career is finished! You are ..."

Ben pulled the listening device from his ear for the second time today. He couldn't stand the negative energy. It reminded him too much of the side of his dad he didn't like.

The directeurs of the other teams would be shouting encouragement, admonition, challenges, and motivation into their riders' ears all the way up the hill. They'd be driving their athletes harder than the cyclists were capable of pushing themselves. Some riders swore they could turn off their minds and allow the messages pouring through their earpieces to override the protestations of pain their brains struggled to transmit.

It would have been a huge advantage to receive the assistance of a physically unstressed mind. That's why Ben had tried so hard to forge an alliance between himself and Pierre, even lopping off all his hair at a suggestion apparently so whimsical Pierre didn't remember he'd made it one day later. That their partnership had collapsed because Ben asked about Thierry was clear evidence it had been too tenuous to ever survive.

Contrary to Pierre's reaction, there had been nothing irrelevant about Ben's question. Thierry considered Ben a brother! That's what the team leader must have been telling the world. The thought electrified him. In a small way, it made the tragedy with Nicholas more bearable. What's more, Ben felt the same way toward Thierry.

He could do this without Pierre. The trick would be to relax and accept the pain. All that mattered now was how hard he could drive himself over the next half hour or so. Ben must drive Ben.

The cameraman motorcycle had been shadowing him a couple meters to the right. Ben turned toward the journalist and projected his voice into the microphone pickup. "I dedicate this climb to my mentor, Thierry Depardieu, and to his brother Nicolas!"

The eyes of both the cameraman and the motorcycle driver bugged out. Ben understood why. Such things weren't done. Now the pressure was really on.

Ben shut his eyes most of the way and drew a deep, relaxing, breath. It was an exercise he'd perfected long before, transporting himself mentally to his secret spot, a place to inhale a dose of confidence and serenity. He blew out the spent oxygen, expelling with it contemplation of Pierre and what might have been.

He pictured his campsite beneath the grotto looking out toward Coyote Natural Bridge, the place where Bridgette had begun changing his outlook on life. He glanced toward the gurgling stream at the foot of the sandy bank where he stood. He listened to chirping birds and heard the wind rustle in the cottonwood trees. He noticed mosses, lichens, and ferns where spring water seeped from a nearby sandstone wall … and he felt Bridgette at his side. She whispered to him. "Now prove to the world what I've always known about you."

A sense of power washed over him. It refreshed and invigorated him. Time to close the deal.

Chapter Twenty-One

Hundreds of thousands of fans covered the mountain. Bicycles littered the roadside. Cars and campers parked in every available spot. More fans had walked from their vehicles parked far below. These people deserved a show, and Ben planned to deliver.

He remained seated as he escalated the pace, increasing his cadence another ten revolutions per minute but not adjusting gears. It felt liberating to abandon his bluff and test what he really had. The bike accelerated effortlessly, almost as if there were a strong hand at his back.

He focused on his heart rate. The powerful muscle throbbed within his chest at about 180 beats per minute, right at his anaerobic threshold. If he pushed any harder, his muscles would plunge into oxygen debt and lactic acid would build up too rapidly.

He must keep the pain high, but remain at a sustainable level of effort. What remained was essentially an uphill time trial, the sort of test cyclists feared, even despised, more than any other. Those who followed would probably be riding in groups, a circumstance that made maintaining high effort a far easier task. That was simply how things had played out, nothing worth dwelling on. Now was the time for intense concentration, for tunnel vision.

He pushed several increments harder than he normally would at this point on this hill. For the remainder of this ride physical misery was good and recovery was bad. Convincing himself to push the pace no matter how uncomfortable things got would require every bit of resolve and concentration he could muster.

He knew he had the ability to suffer the pain of pushing massive gears alongside anybody, but he'd have to prove it today without another rider to pace him and with the eyes of the world on his every move.

The sting of lactic buildup seared his thighs and calves. The toxin came as a byproduct of burning massive amounts of energy. Ben would not allow discomfort to stop him.

Beyond the drop-off to his right, Bourg d' Oisans already resembled a model train village. He searched for pursuing cyclists on the road below but couldn't see any before he had to cross the pavement and pivot around switchback twenty.

As he continued riding the crowds increased. He couldn't believe the numbers. Many of them cheered, others stood silent. None booed.

Switchback nineteen came quickly. The road clawed higher. It felt like the route to the moon.

Ben gulped air, lungs bursting. How could he take in so much oxygen, yet feel increasingly thirsty for air?

At switchback eighteen he fought the temptation to take the corner wide, giving himself room to enjoy the rare flat section of road.

Once he rounded the bend, a long imposing stretch to the next turn loomed over him. Climbing this slope would hurt. He put his head down, preferring not to see so much difficult road all at once.

The gradient increased to fourteen percent. Ben concentrated on keeping his speed constant. He fought the pedals through the throbbing misery of quadriceps begging for relief.

Someone booed. Ben glued his gaze to the ground just ahead of his wheel. He wouldn't give a lone detractor the satisfaction of acknowledgment, however slight.

Weeds encroached into the asphalt near the shoulders. Cracks and irregularities revealed frost damage. White words hastily stenciled on the black asphalt scrolled through his field of vision: "*Allez!*" "King Thierry," "Luigi the Great," "von Reinholdt," "Kyle Smith." He didn't see his own name, though the words "Banque Fédérale" gave him satisfaction.

Some fans crowded in so close Ben could see their arms and legs even though his head was down. They seemed incredibly enthusiastic. He looked up.

A man with an enormous red, white, and blue afro and holding a French flag on a pole ran beside him. "*Allez* Ben! Go, Go, Go!"

Ben couldn't help smiling at the man as the runner began to fade. "*Merci*," he breathed.

It seemed the number of his supporters had increased dramatically while the ill wishers had all but disappeared. The change in the crowd's mood refreshed him. He knew it could change in a heartbeat if he made a mistake.

He kept his head up, watching the multitude of waving flags. Regardless of the country they represented, he drew encouragement from the banners. He dug deeper.

The fans without flags pumped fists or raised glasses in salute. A man in a Superman costume squirted water on Ben's head. A heavyset man in a red devil costume shook his trident and screamed encouragement.

"*Allez! Allez!* Up! Up!"

"Go, Barnes, go!"

Ben thrived on the good sportsmanship.

The grade decreased slightly, and he shifted to a higher gear. A man in a bright orange shirt ran at his shoulder. The colorful clothing indicated he was from the Basque region, an area of Spain near the French border. Residents there were known for their fanatical support of cycling, particularly over mountainous terrain. The man spoke in Spanish but Ben understood enough. "*Su forma es excelente.* Keep it up. You can win!"

Basques had produced many great climbers. Obviously, this man and others like him had been hoping for one of their own to lead the charge up this legendary Alpe, but they were outgoing people who were ready to throw their enthusiasm behind any rider who caught their imagination.

Ben accelerated involuntarily. The faster he went the more enthusiastically the crowds cheered. His only way of expressing appreciation was to accelerate even more. As he did so, he felt the crowd's enthusiasm increase.

The road relented another increment. Ben became conscious

of his pulse. His heart was racing too fast, probably near 190 beats per minute. It was so difficult to maintain concentration under these circumstances. He had worried about the sorts of lapses where he might begin taking it too easy without realizing it, but now he recognized he was in equal danger of pushing too hard if his attention wandered. The only way to conquer this hill was to spend energy in reasonable doses. He shifted to an easier gear despite the decrease in gradient.

"No, no!" yelled a roadside supporter.

"You must attack," said another.

"Do not relax," screamed a third.

Ben looked forward to reaching spectators who hadn't seen him back off his pace. After all, he was still climbing the mountain at a far higher speed than he'd anticipated when the day began. To this point he'd gained over 200 meters vertical in a kilometer and a half lateral, or 700 feet in a little over a mile. Few paved roads anywhere in the world began so harshly.

He navigated switchback seventeen and drove toward sixteen. Here the grade relented again as it passed the church and village of La Garde. The road seemed almost flat, even though it still climbed at over eight percent. His heart rate was back in control. He flew past people at increasing speed on the relatively long and straight stretch.

After switchback fifteen an eleven percent grade confronted him. The bicycle bogged down. He felt the first ripple of exhaustion. With it, the unique sensation of leading he'd experienced when he left Luigi behind returned, stronger than ever before. Voracious wolves snarled at his back, watching his every move. He knew how badly they wanted to leap forward and devour him.

He tried to convince himself that his rivals were tiring at the same rate he was, but the image wouldn't stick. His fatigue energized the wolf pack. That's how it worked.

"*Allez, allez, allez!* Your lead is three minutes and forty-five seconds," yelled a spectator.

Could this be true? Unofficial sources couldn't be trusted. How he wished he had a directeur to keep him informed.

He drove the bicycle around switchback fourteen. The next seven straightaways, he knew, were shorter—almost like swimming laps—and just as hard to keep count of. Back, forth, back, forth.

Because of the tight proximity of the turns he soon felt encased within the crowd, inhaling their screams, exhaling so they would have the oxygen to scream again. The roar deafened.

Partisans loomed above, screamed below, and squeezed in from both sides of the road until the pathway appeared nonexistent. Grown men jumped into his route with the enthusiasm of young boys. Some cheered maniacally; others put him in the crosshairs of camera lenses. Few moved before he'd pushed within arms length. At the last moment they would leap to safety.

Instinct told him he should slow to allow the humanity to move out of his path, avoid a potential collision, but desire overrode everything. He must press the pace, forcing the spectators to abandon their positions as quickly as possible.

It worked. Like blowing leaves on a highway, the fans scattered from his path as he pressed onward. A man wearing a Banque Fédérale jersey and a French beret but with an American flag tied around his neck like a cape sprinted up the slope beside him. "Go Ben! Go! Go! Go! Go!" They made eye contact. The man slapped him twice on the back. "Win! You can win! Do it!"

He had a real fan!

Twenty meters behind Ben the Banque Fédérale support vehicle followed. As tough as it was to get a bike through, the car presented an even bigger challenge. Pierre used his horn as a weapon to clear the path. Like an M-1 tank commander he sprayed wave after wave of sound into the crowd before him. Ben could only assume the strategy continued to succeed because, no matter at what rate he dealt with the hill, the same horn always trilled from the same distance behind. If only he could find a way to surf the sound waves.

On second thought, that wouldn't be necessary. The vortex of cheering sucked him forward. He'd never experienced anything like this. The starving hoards devoured him. His effort to satisfy them only increased their desire.

Many of these men, women, and children had staked claims to their favorite piece of roadside days in advance. Now they were insatiable in their hunger for cycling heroics. Ben pedaled into the mouth of the beast. He had nowhere else to go. He drove his thighs like pistons, pounding downward then pulling upward with every ounce of strength he possessed.

Despite the yelled exhortations, the painted names on the road, the cool water periodically poured on his head and back, the flags waved in his face, and all the other massive sensory input, he found himself inexplicably able to concentrate intently on the climb. He flirted with disaster as he pushed his muscles to their utmost capability, sucking in oxygen so hard his lower teeth ached from the wind he created over them.

He had lost count of the turns, but it didn't matter. The appearance of the St. Ferre'ol church steeple would reorient him soon. That monument marked switchback seven, approximately five kilometers from the finish.

He gathered in terrain as quickly as possible, anxious to spot the church spire. His performance drove the crowd to the brink of pandemonium. Shouts of "*Allez!*" and "*Pédalez!*" rained down on him. The energy from the partisans fueled him to even greater levels. The roar ahead brought to mind the screaming tractor he'd raced up Boulder Mountain. He strove to catch up … but couldn't.

He rounded yet another hairpin turn then glanced over the heads of the crowd. The St. Ferre'ol steeple loomed above them. Once again he could put his finger on the map, mentally charting his progress up the hill.

This was the orange corner, domain of the Dutch. If any group of fans knew how to have a good time, these were the ones. Orange paint covered the road, orange clothing covered the people, and throbbing rock music pervaded all. "Hup, hup, hup!" the crowd yelled.

Ben lifted his gaze. The ski station was finally in view, directly ahead but high above. Had he allocated enough energy so far, or too much? Just as he convinced himself he'd done the right thing he perceived the faintest sputter in strength, the earliest precursor to bonking.

Then he remembered he still had an energy gel. He grabbed it from his jersey pocket and ripped the packet open. How had he forgotten to use the gel earlier? What else might he be forgetting? Did he need Pierre's expertise despite the pessimism?

He squeezed the gooey concoction into his mouth and chased it with his remaining water, then tossed the empty bottle. Would the sugar enter the bloodstream quickly enough to save him? Everything depended on it.

Chapter Twenty-Two

The feelings of an emptying tank grew. Low blood sugar threatened to topple him. Maybe if he lay off the pace slightly. There were limits to the punishment a man could put himself through.

He shook his head violently. His mind was playing tricks, trying to woo him into accepting defeat. He reminded himself he'd dedicated this ride to the Depardieu brothers. He must make it a worthy gift. Beyond that, his own goals demanded he withstand the pain.

Ben steered through switchback six. This segment was short but very steep. There was no way of knowing what sort of gap he had on the chasers. Even an instant of inattention might make the difference between a yellow jersey or not. Such a lapse could even transform victory into defeat.

The crowds surged in on him. Someone said, "*Il vacille?* He's faltering."

Were they referring to what they saw in his form? He assessed his technique. He had allowed it to deteriorate. Ben corrected his posture, concentrated on smooth, even pedal strokes, and minimized the bike wobble. He must push. He must maintain efficiency. The sooner he crossed the finish line the sooner the pain would end. He wanted to burn this thought into his consciousness, but his mind had difficulty clinging to even the simplest concept.

Ben rose from the saddle, leaned forward of his handlebars, and pushed onward. The slight change in muscle groups felt good, like tapping a new energy source. But how deep was it? He noted with satisfaction as his cyclometer ticked up to a higher speed.

A voice on race radio blasting from speakers atop a car said, "… Barnes is pedaling *avec de la classe.*"

Classe, a compliment reserved for the rare merger of raw

talent and efficient style. Ben had never received such high praise in European cycling circles. A lot had changed today.

Ben heard the announcer again from another speaker. "His performance defies description. From out of nowhere, the American is the current GC leader on the road!"

Could that be true? Leader in the General Classification, fastest cumulative time of any rider in the tour? That meant if he could maintain this gap the maillot jaune was his. He stifled a cheer as he passed beneath the four kilometers to go sign, but couldn't keep a grin from his lips. A last dose of adrenaline flooded his veins, and along with it, nourishment from the gel.

He sped up even though the slope didn't relent. Revolution after revolution, terrain rolled behind him, cheering fans dropped into the background, and the next switchback came closer. But then the euphoria wore off, and in its place pain returned greater than ever.

Ben's thighs screamed, his calves quivered, and his lungs ached from near asphyxiation in the thin alpine air. His heart hammered at 185. He knew his body well enough to know that, but how fast did he want it to be? He couldn't muster the mental acuity to come up with simple answers. Was he pushing too hard? As much as he hated to admit it, he needed a directeur. But the negativity—he definitely didn't need that.

Cheers rained down from a gondola car directly overhead. So thick was the throng surging from all sides that if not for the vehicles leading the way in front, he might not have guessed the road turned at this point. He steered around the hairpin curve called 'virage numéro cinq,' turn number five. The gondola moved up the hill with him.

An imposing wall of humanity confronted him at ground level. Men shook fists, children danced, banners waved. People seemed stacked upon one another. Could the road really be as steep as it appeared? Now above tree line, the remainder of the climb to the village was exposed, swarming with people. Thousands upon thousands of screaming voices rained down on him.

From this point the underlying slope eased, but the road

builders had bitten off larger and larger hunks of hillside to compensate, so the gradient didn't relent. He rose to attack, bearing down on the pedals with full weight, pulling on the upstroke with everything he had. He practically turned himself inside out searching for every last ounce of power. He leaned into his pedals. Then he failed.

He fell back in his saddle, flabbergasted at his lack of power. His legs felt leaden. It took a gargantuan effort to maintain enough momentum to keep the bike upright. Ben battled the hill, stunned at how thoroughly he'd bonked.

Images twisted in his mind. He felt dizzy and confused. The air throbbed. He needed someone. Even pessimism would be preferable to this bizarre sense of isolation while drowning in adoration. He couldn't pedal, plan, and perform. He must not fail.

Slowly he slipped the earpiece back in, bracing, yet yearning, for the assault of Pierre's advice.

"Please Ben, please. Push. Push." The hushed tones couldn't possibly belong to Le Directeur. The heartfelt encouragement was being whispered by a true supporter. He listened a while longer. Bridgette! How had she gotten hold of a transmitter? Where was she?

Finally Ben spoke. "*Salut Minet.*"

"Ben? Is that you?"

He wiped a hand across his brow. "What's left of me."

"Oh, thank you God! Thank you for answering." Bridgette's voice crackled with gratitude. "Dig deep, Honey! I can see you on television now. You're close. You'll wear yellow tonight. You've made your dreams come true."

"How did …"

"No. Don't waste energy asking questions. Concentrate on your form. Pedal on my command. Push. Push. Push. Push. Good. Keep going."

Ben navigated around the tight left hairpin of turn four. The crowd, seemingly hovering on all sides, screamed encouragement.

"Remember what Bill told you about your internal thermostat? You never knew he shared that conversation with me, did you? Don't answer. Listen. We had to coax you back into cycling, Bill, Thelma, and I. You resisted some pretty good arguments, even Bill's air conditioning theory. That one was genius."

Ben recalled his old coach's words about overriding the internal thermostat. Did they make sense now because there really was something to them, or because he couldn't think clearly?

"Bill knew there would come a time when you'd be ready for that wisdom. That time is now. We don't need air conditioning."

Ben turned the thought in his mind, and as he did he sensed the tiniest new reserve, an ounce of energy. Was there more? He reached within.

Something was there. A new reserve, unlike any he had ever drawn on before. Strength—supplied not by adrenaline but by desire—the desire to live up to the expectations of so many friends. He sensed their faith in him as a real thing, his own, private tailwind.

A television helicopter hovered at eye level above the spectacular Saranne Gorge. The sight highlighted the precipitous nature of the wall he continued to scale. He riveted his concentration back onto the road.

"Push. Push. Good, your cadence is much improved. Keep it up."

Ben felt it, too. He'd regained rhythm.

"You'll never believe it, Ben. Laurent Robidoux called and asked me to hurry to his downtown office. He told me his star racer would soon be in need of a carrot. I guess that's me. Are you motivated?"

"Yes."

The camera must be capturing his goofy smile. Viewers wouldn't believe where the happiness came from.

Ben glanced uphill to his right. The ski station's hodge-podge buildings were no longer far away.

He smelled fresh paint. On the road ahead, someone had hastily stenciled "BARNESTORMER." Ben smiled. When he rolled through the "S" his tire picked up white paint. It left a thin, dashed line behind for the next several revolutions.

"Push. Push. Push. Great work Ben. Keep it up. I'll be waiting for you at the top. Push!"

"You're here?"

"I'm here, yes. The team helicopter brought me. I'm waiting for you at the finish line."

Ben stood on his pedals and accelerated. Fritz had described Monsieur Robidoux as the master motivator. He'd been right. What experience could exceed celebrating victory atop this hill with the one he loved?

The ghost-riders for both Kyle and Gunter were very close, but behind him now. To remain ahead he must use every last ounce of energy.

The helicopter rose, then sailed over Ben's head toward the finish line. The machine made it look so effortless to cover the remaining terrain. Ben listened to Bridgette's continuing encouragement as the aircraft moved about for different angles. Meanwhile, other cameras on motorcycles tracked his progress from a more intimate range.

Ben turned hard right at switchback three and headed back across the hill. Bridgette's voice still urged him on over the headset. "You're the most powerful man in this race. Prove it. Give everything."

He needed to see her. Slowly, the hollow feeling of bonking returned. His muscles screamed. Still, energy from his new reservoir kept his wheels going round. He pushed on, not knowing how he kept up the effort. Was he burning muscle? How much would he pay for this tomorrow?

Ben's lungs seared as if liquid fire flooded his windpipe. His heart banged within his ribcage like a convict rattling cell bars in a prison riot. His thoughts dangled incomplete, and incompletable, threatening to spin out of control at any moment. Much as he tried to concentrate on Bridgette's voice and the inspiration it delivered, his consciousness was a cacophony of conflicting argument.

He battled to grab onto a single idea and let it pull him to the finish line. "This is for Thierry, for Nicolas." He repeated the mantra again and again.

The road zigged around switchback number two. Only one zag left! He passed beneath the three kilometers to go sign, the finish line now theoretically within reach. Shortly after the next switchback the road would level considerably. He put his head down and pushed.

A cartoonish pink painted ghost passed beneath his tires. A similar red ghost followed. Next came PacMan heading for the little white pills the video superstar craved. As the dots passed under Ben's tires, the crowd chanted, "Wocka, wocka, wocka, wocka!"

Ben fought his way up the incline, knowing his form was now miles from perfect, but resigned that he could do nothing about it. If he could access strength from minor muscle groups by using odd angles of attack, that's what he must do. He wrenched his bike and body into whatever positions seemed to create useful leverage.

He steered to the extreme inside edge of switchback one. Fans crowded in on him, obscuring the route. The noise deafened. Ahead, a man in a plaid shirt faced the wrong direction, staring up the road. What was he watching?

"Push Ben, push! Dig deeper!"

The oblivious man in plaid stepped backward. They collided. The spectator spun, seemingly in slow motion, an incredulous expression on his face. Ben toppled sideways and slammed into the ground.

Chapter Twenty-Three

The man in plaid fell on Ben and his bicycle, pinning Ben face down against the pavement. Something about the texture of sound had changed. He couldn't put his finger on the difference.

He tried to rise, wrestling with the bike and the clumsy man. Finally the fan rolled out of the way, but the composite tubes, gears, and sprockets still seemed to fight back. Ben struggled to free himself. He unclipped his cleats from his pedals. He pushed the machine away and stood.

His head spun as he fought for equilibrium. He found himself facing another rabid fan, this man's face red and screaming. What had he done to make this person so angry? Everyone seemed mad. The entire crowd screamed. In this confusing moment he couldn't translate their words.

Then he realized they were begging him to continue, pleading with him to complete the race. They seemed to sense they'd become part of one of the epic moments in cycling history, if only they could exhort this American athlete to wrap up what he'd nearly finished.

The resort hotels of Alpe d' Huez stood only a short distance up the road. Then he realized why the sound had changed. His earpiece had fallen out. He replaced it.

"… are you doing? Please *Minet*, hurry! You only have only two kilometers to go. Get on the bike!"

A fan held his machine upright and pulled him toward it. Ben lifted his leg over. His left calf seized.

"Get on, Ben! The others are catching you."

Catching him?

He obeyed the words flowing in through his earpiece instead of the message blasting out of his brain. The thought of being overtaken after such work reignited his hatred of losing. He had despised the feeling of failure since that day in his very first race in Salt Lake City when the entire pack caught and dropped him. He clipped his shoes into the pedals as fans gave him a running start.

"Now pedal!"

Normally he'd work out a cramp by slowly extending the range of motion, but he had no time. Searing pain flooded his left leg. His right leg had to both push the bike up the hill, and battle his left leg in its determination to contract. For half a pedal stroke only, the left leg did useful work as it contracted ferociously, but each time the left foot reached the top of the stroke the muscle became more than useless. It became an impediment to progress. Ben had to contract the right leg with all his might. Each time it felt like the left calf muscle would shred before it returned to the extended position.

"Pedal! Pedal! Pedal!"

He could barely hear the words over the screaming protestations of his brain.

The incline gradually relented. Ben picked up speed as he raced through the town. The cramp gradually subsided. He switched onto his big chain ring as he entered the village square and swooped beneath the "*flamme rouge*," the one-kilometer to go pennant. The small red plastic triangle hung from a huge inflatable archway positioned over the road.

Both legs were working correctly again, driving, surging. His speed continued to increase as the finish line approached. The last left turn was near, a tight ninety-degree corner. He squeezed the brakes, skidding momentarily, and nearly overshot the bend. Fatigue had disintegrated his handling skills.

Finally his eyes locked on the finishing banner. It read, "*Arrivée*," a word he'd been so desperate to see for so long. Bridgette was somewhere in the crowd beyond. He drove for the line.

"Just a bit farther!"

He saw her. Auburn hair shimmering, walkie-talkie in hand, she stood frantically gesturing in the press area, just beyond the finish line.

"Come to me! I'll make the pain worth it. Pedal! Pedal! Pedal!"

Ben pushed the bike forward, oblivious to everything except the distance between him and his girlfriend. The gap collapsed on itself.

His front tire broke through the beam of light. The clock stopped. Ben raised his arms and punched at the sun. He screamed at the spectators, and the spectators screamed back. He had done it! Ben Barnes had etched his name into the history of *Alpe d' Huez*!

He rolled into the crowd at the back of the finish chute. Hands grabbed and escorted him, still seated on his bicycle, toward the press area.

Sweet relaxation flooded his consciousness. Contentment and exuberance swirled together in a rainbow-like emotion, while the desperate feeling of being the race leader, of being hunted, evaporated like recent rain on a sunburned highway.

His body tingled, and momentarily one thought overrode all others. He had become a character in his own dream, only it was better than his wildest imaginings: the flags, the music, the enthusiasm, the weather, the painted road, the view, and so much more. How could this be real?

He'd visualized a moment like this so many times over so many years. Now, here he stood, lifted to this Herculean accomplishment as the result of a billion tiny actions—his actions—stretching over a decade and all oriented in the same direction. There had been moments over the years when he'd lost sight of the goal, but something in his subconscious always pushed him back on track. Never before had he so vividly experienced the absolute connection between thought and reality than in this wonderful moment. Never before had he felt such control over his future. If he could create reality from a dream, was there anything outside the realm of possibility?

The thought proved too powerful to keep hold of, at least in this moment. His mental focus shifted to the obstacles he'd overcome rather than the destination he'd reached. In a strange way, the goal now seemed hardly significant compared to the journey. The sights he'd passed to get here were everything—the largest obstacles far greater treasures than the easy times.

The journey had been the reward. He hadn't expected this either. Who could have known such sensations existed? Feelings washed over him, lifted him, and cleansed him. If he could bottle them, the potion would change the world.

Since his first day on a bicycle, cycling had taken him to extremes. The experience had both lifted him to the highest of highs and plunged him toward the lowest of lows. Middle ground seemed nonexistent. He loved sport for that. Everyday life simply couldn't compare to the extremes he attained through athletic competition.

Reporters swarmed, but he ignored them, searching for Bridgette. She bowled into him from behind. Hugging. Squeezing. Kissing. He shrugged off his escorts, twisted a foot from its pedal and propped himself against an outstretched leg.

"Oh, Ben! You did it! I knew you could!"

He laughed uncontrollably as she kissed his arms, face, and chest.

"You're my hero! You did it, you did it, you did it, you did it."

Ben vaguely sensed the pandemonium about him, people streaming in from all sides, cameras clicking, recorders humming.

"Bridgette. Bridgette, stop a moment, will you?"

She made eye contact, quizzical lines crinkling her face. She spoke before he could. "Ben, I need to ask a question I couldn't distract you with during the race."

"Yes?"

"Who does your hair these days?"

He smiled. "Very funny. Marry me, okay?"

The message raced out to the entire world, probably registering in the consciousness of astute viewers on other continents before it made sense to Bridgette or even Ben. Still, it seemed the most intimate moment in earth's history.

She stared at him numbly. "Of course."

They kissed.

"We need to clear this area," said an official.

Ben opened his eyes but Bridgette's lips remained locked. He tried to use his expression to tell the race steward he was sorry for being in the way, but he didn't know if the message got through. When Bridgette finally let him go he again attempted to move, but his muscles had seized.

He wanted to ask for help, but race leaders can't afford to show weakness. He forced his leg up and over the seat, then walked as normally as he could. A mechanic hurried off with his bicycle. Bridgette grabbed his hand and walked beside him.

The photographers and reporters moved with them like metal filings chasing a magnet under glass.

"How did it feel to have Thierry refer to you as a brother?"

Ben smiled. He had guessed right. "It makes me feel great. The feeling is mutual."

"How do you feel about your performance?"

"No regrets."

Other reporters elbowed in. "*Excusez-moi.* Are you saying you feel fortunate Thierry was injured and created an opportunity for you?"

Ben glared. "No. We're teammates. My role was to assist him. Circumstances forced adjustment."

Another journalist crammed his question in. "*Êtes vous heureux d'avoir fini?*"

"Of course I'm happy to be finished." Must they ask the obvious?

"Was it harder than you expected?"

Bridgette stepped between Ben and the main body of reporters. "Give him space, *s'il vous plaît.* Ben will answer everyone's questions in a moment."

Pierre approached, his mouth creased defiantly. Fritz hurried to his side.

Le Directeur growled. "Never have I been so..."

"Here come the men who guided me to victory today." Ben projected his voice in an attempt to drown Pierre's foaming approach and conceal their conflict from the press.

At his words Ben watched a nearby journalist's expression go from bloodthirsty to perplexed. Ben wondered if his strategy had worked. Tomorrow's headlines would tell him.

"Have you calculated the gaps necessary to take the lead in the General Classification?" Ben asked.

Fritz waved a piece of paper. "Kyle should finish second. After accounting for today's time bonuses you need four minutes and ten seconds over him."

"And von Reinholdt?"

"He's charging fast. If he gains the eight second bonus for third you must defeat him by four minutes and fifty-six seconds."

Ben looked toward the two digital clocks mounted at the top of the finish gate. The upper one had frozen at 6:39.58. That was his time. It had taken him over six and a half hours to complete the course today, a gargantuan chunk of time even by tour standards. Yet he'd still finished well ahead of the fastest projected time for this particular leg of the race. What a stage. No wonder his muscles ached.

Below the digital display of Ben's time, a second clock counted up, second by second. It would record the deficit between each rider compared to the time set by Ben. Already it had reached 0:01.38.

"I'd like to watch them finish." Ben nodded toward the line. He looked at the reporters. "Can your questions wait?"

Many of the journalists turned gratefully toward the racecourse, obviously also anxious to see how things played out as well. Pierre and Fritz moved with Ben and Bridgette toward a group of chairs apparently abandoned by the press. Ben sat, then looked down the street. The last twenty or so seconds of the course were visible.

Fritz nodded toward the giant television screen on their left. "There is your nemesis."

Kyle Smith cruised through the town square, the difficult portion of the course now behind him. It wouldn't be long until he came into view. The timer indicated two minutes and thirty-five seconds had passed since Ben's finish.

Ben turned to Fritz. "What's the news on Thierry?"

"Shattered ankle, good spirits. Just what you'd would expect from The King."

Ben smiled. "Yeah, just what I'd expect."

The television shot changed to Gunter. A caption confirmed he now held third position. He looked to be only a couple hundred meters behind Kyle.

"The German looks very strong," Fritz said.

The clock had reached three minutes and twenty seconds. Kyle had about fifty seconds to cross the line to beat Ben's cumulative time. Gunter still had a little over a minute and a half.

Ben turned from the monitor and watched the road. Seconds ticked by like hours. Fifteen seconds: no sign of anyone. Twenty seconds: still nothing. Twenty-five seconds: Ben looked at his fiancé.

"There!" Bridgette's outstretched finger pointed down the road.

Kyle charged toward the line as the clock plodded forward. Three minutes and fifty-six seconds, seven, eight, nine. Ben's heart sank. Kyle was going to cross the line in time to beat him.

Kyle dug deep. As he broke the finishing plane Ben looked at the clock. It read four minutes and twelve seconds.

Somehow he had bested Kyle in the General Classification by a mere two seconds. Ben collapsed back in the chair, looking skyward with his arms spread wide.

Bridgette squeezed him, then clung to him as she looked down the road. Her touch felt heavenly.

"Here comes Gunter," Pierre said.

Ben lifted his head and stared at the road again. Gunter von Reinholdt rounded the final corner and drove toward the finish. The crowd roared. The seconds rolled by even more slowly than before. Then he crossed the line.

Fritz jumped to his feet. "Four minutes and fifty-nine seconds! You're ahead of Gunter by three seconds, Ben! You lead the Tour de France!"

Bridgette sprang from her seat. "My heart can't take this!"

Ben wondered whether his could either, but he lacked the strength to say so.

Each of the top three men had accomplished great things on this mountain, and while their efforts had knotted the race, Ben had come from nowhere to best the other two. Tomorrow's stage could hardly have been set up better. That is, if he could still do battle.

"Looks like we saved each other's careers, Pierre. Now it's time for you and I to switch to a new chain ring. We must work together." Ben looked left. Le Directeur had gone. He was nowhere to be seen.

Fritz shook his head. "The boss is pretty conflicted. He'll get over it."

Ben nodded. "I hope so." He stood to move toward the interview area.

"Need a hand?" Fritz extended his arm.

Ben shook his head. "I wouldn't give Kyle the satisfaction."

Fritz slapped his back. "*C'est l'esprit.*"

Reporters converged again. "Did you leave anything for tomorrow, Ben?"

The vacancy in his legs screamed out, begging him to answer "no." Had he burned irreplaceable muscle in those last few kilometers? Would there be anything there the next time he went to the well? He needed something for tomorrow, didn't he? And something for the day after that. And the day after that. And all the days to follow.

The stage just completed had brought them near the halfway point in this year's tour. Ten stages and nearly twelve hundred miles had passed under the peloton's wheels. Eleven stages and just over twelve hundred more miles remained. As a domestique it had been possible to spend a stage recovering, cruising to the finish concerned only with beating the cut-off time. Contenders never had such a luxury.

"I'll find out how strong I am when everybody else does. I believe I can hold my ground."

"It's well known you and Kyle don't get along. Was it satisfying to beat him?"

Ben hesitated. What purpose would it serve to give this journalist the answer he wanted? The last thing Ben needed was to escalate their confrontation in public, no matter how many newspapers such a response might sell.

"I'm grateful to win."

"Can you do it again?" the reporter pressed.

"Tomorrow is another day."

"How does it feel to defeat the man who forced you off your former team?"

Ben tensed. The questions triggered the sort of animosity toward Kyle he had avoided the entire day. These guys were fishing for the sound clip they wanted.

"Do you want to know true satisfaction?" Ben asked.

A newspaper reporter poised his pen over his pad. "*Naturellement.*"

"It's getting off the bike after so many hours of grueling work. You know the feeling, don't you? Making deadline, then slamming the pressroom door behind you."

Several journalists laughed.

Ben fielded question after question, some insightful, many ridiculous. Through it all he watched riders trickle across the line as the clock counted higher.

Finally a race official escorted him behind the assemblage of flat bed semi-trailers that made up the stage. Ben grabbed Bridgette's hand and pulled her into the waiting area with him. At nearly every step a fellow racer, an opposing coach, a reporter, or a fan congratulated him on his rare performance.

Cyclists still rolled in as the awards ceremonies started. At some point the disparity would result in disqualification. Time cut-off rules forced every athlete to push every day.

Soon Ben was called on stage. He accepted a dozen roses and some kisses on his cheeks from the podium girls for winning the stage. The crowd voiced their approval at his tenacity as he flung the flowers into their midst. Then, gathering great effort to hide the discomfort, he hobbled down the stairs. How would he ever get his legs in condition to ride tomorrow?

He took a seat and watched the day's other winners take their turns on the podium. A white jersey was awarded to the best young rider. A big, strong cyclist retained the green jersey for being top sprinter. It was an honor he had earned on the flatlands. Now he must haul himself over the mountains to seal his sprinting supremacy when the racers returned to level roads during the last few days before they reached Paris. Many had expected Rikard from Banque Fédérale to be competitive in that category, but it hadn't happened.

Wiry little Luigi collected the red polka-dot jersey for having gathered the greatest number of climbing points. The announcer proclaimed him "King of the Mountains." Ben gave his Italian friend a thumbs up as he exited the stage.

Interesting to see what different body types the leaders in those two specialists' categories had. The final award would be the yellow jersey. While all sorts of cyclists might lay temporary claim to the maillot jaune over the course of the race, the man who retained it at the end of the race was most often defined by the size of his heart—both literally and figuratively. He must excel in every cycling discipline, his margin of victory built in the most demanding stages—time trials and mountaintop finishes. Thierry had always fit that description. Now Ben believed he did, too.

The announcer built up the presentation with all sorts of superlatives as the crowd roared in anticipation. Then he said into the microphone, "Ben Barnes of Banque Fédérale!"

Luigi slapped him on the back. "Go get your jersey."

Ben fought his way up the steps.

He held out his arms as the two beautiful podium girls, clad for this portion of the ceremony in yellow dresses, held the golden jersey in front of him. The moment felt surreal. There, within arms length was the most prized possession in cycling, and this version belonged to him. He extended his hands and the girls started to slide the garment onto his body. Superman couldn't feel more powerful when he pulled on his cape.

Ben straightened, his vision seemed to clear, and his strength returned as the Golden Fleece enveloped his body.

Suddenly, he confronted a terrible thought. He looked toward the announcer, wanting to ask advice, but the idea jammed in his throat like an unshelled nut.

How could he have overlooked something so important? It was as if his mind wasn't big enough to contain the emotions and facts all at once. With great effort Ben stepped back and pulled his arms out of the jersey. The crowd watched in silent shock. The podium girls held the shirt, staring at Ben with mouths agape.

"What are you doing?" asked the emcee, his voice echoing over the crowd.

"I ... I forgot myself. I can't wear this jersey."

A rumble passed through the crowd.

"What do you mean?" The words reverberated from the loudspeakers.

Sweat dampened Ben's brow. The prize he had dreamed of for all these years was within his grasp, it belonged to him, he had touched it; but now his conscience would not allow him to accept it.

"I inherited the race lead today due to the misfortune of my friend, Thierry. I wouldn't be standing here if not for his bad luck. Out of respect for my team leader I will wear Banque Fédérale colors tomorrow."

On several occasions in Tour history a rider who took over the yellow jersey as the result of another's misfortune voluntarily waited a day to put it on. Such was the respect for the storied garment. Now, when a cyclist inherited it from a fallen teammate, no matter how well earned, how could the new man wear the jersey?

Nevertheless, the mere experience of donning yellow, if only for a moment, had transformed him. He felt like a different man. Tomorrow would be an exceedingly difficult day. He would be attacked relentlessly, even without the trappings of the leader. Still, he sensed he'd done the right thing.

The crowd cheered louder and louder. He gazed at the throng, but he didn't exactly feel like the object of their affection. In some respects, it felt like an out of body experience.

One podium girl handed him a stuffed animal, the mascot of a major sponsor. She kissed him on each cheek.

The second woman handed him another bouquet of roses. She kissed him gently. "You did right."

Ben nodded. "Thanks."

He stepped to the front of the stage and flung first the flowers and then the toy into the crowd. The partisans roared their approval of the American's good etiquette. A comfortable feeling, like hot cider going down on a chilly day, descended through his body. Could this sensation make up for the prize he'd forced himself to walk away from?

His conclusion came easily. It could not, but he had no alternative. Thierry meant a great deal to both Ben and the fans of cycling. He deserved respect.

Ben blew kisses to the partisans, then turned his back and exited the stage. He felt as if he were leaving a body part behind.

Kyle leered at him from the bottom of the stage riser. "You just made a huge mistake Barnes. Kiss your only chance to wear yellow goodbye."

"I'd rather say goodbye to you."

"I'll grant that wish. I'm going to leave you in my dust tomorrow." Kyle stepped closer, his face reddening.

Ben reached the bottom step. "Terrific! That's what I hoped you'd say."

"What's that supposed to mean?"

Ben turned and walked away. "It means I've known you long enough to learn you never keep your word."

Kyle grabbed Ben's jersey from behind and twisted his rival around. "Oh yeah? Well that's about to change."

Chapter Twenty-Four

Ben couldn't get out of Kyle's presence quickly enough. The feeling of repulsion was familiar, but today the hunger in Kyle's eyes worried Ben as well. He had less than half an hour until his massage. He looped his arm around Bridgette's waist and walked. "I don't have much time before I have to report for meetings, and your Uncle Pierre has his team-members-only policy."

"I understand."

"You do? I don't. I want to hold onto you forever, but I can't even spend the evening with you."

Bridgette nodded. "I'm willing to forgive … if you win."

Ben chuckled. "And if I lose?"

"I have a punishment in mind, but it's too terrible to burden you with. Just win so we can avoid such messiness."

Ben faked an exaggerated shudder.

They reached the race support vehicles. Various team motor homes were parked tightly among dozens of large campers, semi-trucks, and other sponsor vehicles.

Bridgette grabbed Ben's hand. "I'm guessing you don't have the strength to walk to the city outskirts and lie in the wildflowers with me, do you?"

Ben shook his head. "I wish."

She dragged him down a makeshift alleyway between two huge trailers. "Then give me a kiss I'll never forget."

Ben glanced to each side. "I think you've discovered the least romantic spot in the French Alps."

"You can do better?"

He shook his head. "No. This is perfect." He gazed into her eyes and quickly forgot the surroundings. He slid an arm around her waist and put his other hand behind her head. He eased her against the trailer.

"I never dreamed I would have such an intelligent, witty, thoughtful, caring, and gorgeous wife. I love you so much that I can't even think straight."

"I love you, too. Even more than that."

They kissed. Time stopped.

Bridgette pressed against Ben, enveloping him with gentle arms and legs, caressing him with silken hands, seducing him with lips that begged for more. Behind Ben's closed eyelids a kaleidoscope of emotions, dreams, and goals formed and transformed. He found himself imagining possibilities previously too remote to contemplate. With this woman at his side he could do anything.

They separated, and Ben opened his eyes.

Bridgette stared at him, as if trying to memorize every feature. "Now, go out and defend that lead tomorrow or I'll be extremely annoyed. I warn you, my wrath is best avoided."

Ben grinned though his muscles ached. "I'll do everything in my power."

"You'd better, because I have more news for you. The sight of a man wearing yellow drives me insane."

"Insane is good?"

"I hope you get to find out. I'll be waiting for you at the finish line."

"I have the sudden urge to get on my bike and head there now."

Bridgette laughed.

Ben tapped his watch. "It's time."

They strolled to the hotel, kissed one last time, and said goodbye.

Ben showered, had his massage, then headed downstairs to the hotel conference room Banque Fédérale had converted into their private team dining room. Since the soigneur had granted him an extra fifteen minutes, the room was already alive with the din of conversation and clanking utensils.

Ben figured being a bit late was good. He could busy himself eating rather than dealing with team politics for the moment. On this evening those issues were particularly complicated.

He grabbed a plate and heaped on pasta, pouring olive oil over the top and spooning on grated Parmesan. He leaned a grilled chicken breast on one side of the mound and slices of fresh bread on the other. Then he dished salad into a bowl and ladled on dressing. Finally he loaded another small plate with plain yogurt, apple and orange slices, grapes, and a banana.

He balanced the feast in his arms and carried it to the table. The last remaining seat on the athlete's table was beside Rikard, the team sprinter. The support staff table was completely occupied as well.

"*Voila*. Here is our new team leader," Rikard said.

Ben sat. "Thierry's still the leader. Like you, I'm waiting for him to tell me what to do."

"Not true. I take my orders from Pierre."

Ben considered his answer. He didn't like the flow of this conversation. He noticed the table contained no champagne as it traditionally would when there was reason to celebrate. Normally, a stage win meant smiles, but Thierry's crash had put a damper on everything. How many here would be willing to celebrate an American's victory, anyway?

He reached past the red wine for his traditional soda water and poured himself a glass.

Rikard continued. "Word is you're trying to run Le Directeur out of—"

"*Calmes toi!*" The voice was Albert. "Enough, Rikard. Let me eat in peace."

The conversation halted, but the tension continued to mount. Maybe the team ban on friends and family at dinners was a good thing. Today it saved Bridgette from a hostile environment.

Loud ringing silenced the group. Ben looked in the direction of the sound and saw Pierre tapping his butter knife against his wine glass. "*Attention*," Pierre said.

Le Directeur tilted his head toward the entrance and a soigneur hurried to shut the conference room doors. The many conversations quickly subsided.

"The tour has delivered yet another day I'll never forget. I would think after thirteen seasons on the circuit I would have seen it all, yet I'm consistently amazed. Today, not only did we lose a great champion to injury—"

"How is Thierry?" someone interrupted.

"I just got off the phone with his nurse. She said he's beat up, but full of fight. An hour ago he was ranting incoherently, so she had to sedate him. She says that's to be expected in trauma cases. Nothing they can't deal with. Now he's sleeping like a baby. Lord knows, he's earned the rest."

A sigh of relief swept through the room.

"Now, as I was saying, not only did we lose our leader, but we witnessed an unlikely performance in his absence."

Conversation rippled throughout the group. It ceased when Pierre continued.

"Listen. I have important things to say."

A deadly pall settled. Even the soft clanging of silverware on plates stopped as every eye settled on Le Directeur.

Pierre cleared his throat. "This team has been through a lot today. Too much." He paused and looked around. "Suddenly we are without clear direction. I've consulted with ownership in search of strategy. We came to a difficult conclusion. It won't please everyone, but order must be restored. For more than three years Albert has served Thierry as his most loyal lieutenant, working tirelessly to earn glory for his leader."

Scattered grunts and applause verified that others agreed.

Pierre held up his hand and attention returned to him. "That's as it should be. Now that Thierry has fallen, we'll align our support behind Albert."

Ben's mouth fell open. Was Albert even in contention? He was speechless. He caught Albert's eye and the two men looked at one another for a confused moment.

Ben's mind spun. For all Pierre's faults, he wasn't a liar. If he claimed Monsieur Robidoux had agreed on this strategy, then that must be the case. Either way, Ben wasn't about to phone the owner and check out the story.

He shook his head. Why had it surprised him for even a moment that the team owner would reassess things after the heat of battle? From Robidoux's perspective, Ben probably didn't look to be the likely winner of the overall tour despite his success today. In fact, Ben's overnight success might be ample reason to believe it couldn't continue. Even he wondered how his legs would respond tomorrow.

What's more, by switching his allegiances to Albert, a popular rider who was very French besides, the owner would probably win favor among those most likely to do business with him. That was one thing Ben couldn't doubt. Where Monsieur Robidoux was concerned, business was what mattered most.

Albert broke the silence. "After all the American accomplished today?"

Ben stared at Albert in amazement.

Albert continued. "Not one man here can look me in the eye and say Ben's performance didn't prove he's the strongest man in this race."

Eddies of conversation spun through the room. Pierre crossed his arms.

Albert's voice rose. "I hear what you men are saying. Yes, I'm as surprised as anyone. I had no idea Ben had this in him, but now that I do, I'm as determined to get him to the finish line first as I ever was Thierry."

"I joined this team to race for Thierry, not Ben," Rikard said.

Albert shook his head. "Then you joined for the wrong reason. Banque Fédérale's goal has always been to get our strongest rider to Paris first. Now we know who that is."

"But he took advantage of Thierry's bad luck," Rikard said.

"Nonsense. As Thierry often says, 'In the Tour, luck is minimized, the strongest always wins.' For three consecutive seasons he proved his supremacy. No doubt, he had bad luck today, but his misfortune revealed our team's true strength. Ben rode a race Thierry never could have. Not on his best day. I know Thierry well enough to be certain he'd agree."

Ben looked more closely at the man who until this moment

had been Thierry's heir apparent. It amazed him that Albert of all people would spring to his defense.

Rikard's voice rose. "I'm with Pierre. If Albert has no sense, then to hell with him. I won't ride for an upstart opportunist."

Another man said, "Me either."

Pierre looked oddly pleased. The team was disintegrating fast. First Thierry had been lost, and now two more. That left only five members willing or able to race for Ben. Of those only Albert was likely to be of real assistance in the mountains, and there were a dozen major summits still to come. In reality, even Albert could provide no useful support if Pierre chose to block him. For that matter, without the support of team leadership Ben sat high and dry.

His heart sank. Pierre hadn't been bluffing. Apparently he had more power than Ben had given him credit for. He was determined to undo all that Ben had accomplished today, just as he had done in earlier stages of the race. With ownership on Pierre's side, he would succeed.

Ben's voracious appetite disappeared.

Pierre walked to the space opposite Ben at the table. "Now, do you see why your behavior today can't be tolerated? Yesterday this team was a well-oiled machine. Today it's shambles!" For emphasis he tipped over a vase.

Water poured into Ben's lap.

"What the ..."

Ben's chair screeched on the tile floor as he slid back. He inadvertently shoved his plate and glass off the opposite edge of the table. Both shattered.

Pierre laughed. "So now that your scheming has failed you want to leave?"

"I'm not leaving. What are you accusing me of?"

"It's a long list. You forced your way into my niece's life and pressured her into compelling me to offer a contract. You deceived Thierry into including you on the Tour roster. You abandoned him with blatant disregard at the scene of his accident. You turned circumstances to your advantage and benefited from his misfortune. You repeatedly ignored my orders. You—"

Ben couldn't contain his anger. "Wrong! Wrong about everything. For starters, the only thing I did today more difficult than riding away from Thierry was keeping my promises to him in the process."

Pierre lit a cigarette and blew a cloud toward Ben. "What promises?" He seemed instantly calmer with a Gitane in his hand.

Ben waved to clear the air. "He made me promise if instinct begged me to attack but you said otherwise, I would follow my gut. Last night it was an easy promise to make. How could I have imagined this day unfolding as it has?"

"Why would Thierry ask that of you?" Rikard said.

Ben looked at Rikard. "He believed Le Directeur hated me for being American. He said he meant to break me for it. At the time it made sense. I ..."

"But now you know differently?" Pierre interrupted.

"Not differently, more. Now I see you also believe I've manipulated your niece. You ought to ask her what's gone on."

Pierre tapped an ash from his cigarette. "I won't ask her anything. Any fool can see what has happened."

"Then you are not just any fool."

Pierre's face reddened. "You're playing with words. Are you trying to confuse these people?"

Ben shook his head. "It's not confusing. I've poured my heart into this team."

Pierre pounded a fist on the table. "Must we listen to this?"

"I'm interested. What went on today?" asked Albert.

"Pierre and I had some disagreements. He was criticizing me, trying to wear me down. I couldn't put up with it anymore, so I dumped the earpiece and concentrated on what Thierry asked me to do. And now I know, Thierry was right, not Pierre."

"Pulling the radio was insubordinate!" Pierre yelled.

"What you were trying to do was worse, for me and for the team."

"You're a fool. I gave you many chances, and you blew them!"

"I won't get into a shouting match, Pierre. You have the power to force me to leave, but I'll do so with my dignity intact. I know you can make life difficult for me, but I've overcome challenges before and I will again." He rose from his chair.

"Stop!" Albert walked toward him with a resolute expression. "I'm with you, Ben. This team has an opportunity to win the overall, but not in support of me."

"Why are you doing this?" Ben asked.

"Because I may be a good cyclist, maybe even great by some measures, but I can only compete at the highest level by lending my services to those who can soar."

Le Directeur looked like smoke might billow from his ears.

"Even mechanics have to take sides sometimes," Fritz said, walking toward Ben.

Ben nodded, swallowed hard, then kissed Fritz once on each cheek. As he pulled away the Frenchman smacked him on the lips.

"Not so bad, eh?"

Ben grinned as he wiped his mouth on his sleeve. "Yeah. It was."

"So, what do we do now?" Rikard asked.

A wave of exhaustion swept over Ben. "We need to fix this mess quickly or there won't be anything to fix. If we don't finish eating and get to bed, we may as well skip the race tomorrow."

Pierre rubbed his goatee. "Do you propose a solution?"

"No. You're the only one here with the authority to solve this, Pierre. But please remember that Albert, the man you support, is standing in support of me. Ignoring that creates a confusing situation."

Pierre worked his clenched jaw side to side. He paced across the room and back.

Albert spoke. "Ben says Thierry advised him. We all heard Thierry today; he said Ben was like his brother. Hasn't Thierry passed the baton to Ben? Isn't this what we should respect?"

Murmurs rippled through the team. Heads nodded.

Pierre's eyes darted throughout the room. He puffed furiously on his cigarette. "Thierry isn't the directeur of this team."

The murmuring ceased as Pierre's words echoed in the room.

"And none of you are the directeur of this team. I am. I've made a decision. What's more, Monsieur Laurent Robidoux agrees. Would any of you like to argue with him?"

He glanced quickly about. "No? But I am a fair man, no matter what Ben wants you to believe. I will take up the matter again with Monsieur Robidoux. I'll pass on your thoughts, Albert. If there's a change as a result, I'll inform you all tomorrow morning before the race."

"Good," Ben said. "I can't worry about this any longer, so I won't. Let's resume our routines, get our rest, and see what Pierre has to say in the morning. I'll follow his orders, whether I like them or not."

Le Directeur scowled. "Really? If you had done that today we wouldn't be in this situation, would we?"

Chapter Twenty-Five

Ben couldn't miss the morning headlines as he made his way toward the Stage Eleven starting area. Newspapers were everywhere. Emblazoned across the top were statements like: *Barnes Dedicates Victory to Depardieu Brothers, American Rises Like Phoenix, Fans Embrace Former Outcast.*

Loads of great publicity. No sign of the tempest brewing in the Banque Fédérale camp.

Ben pushed images of what might have been from his mind. In the morning strategy session, as expected, Le Directeur had jammed a wrench into Ben's spokes. Nevertheless, Ben would honor his promise to execute the team plan. The upshot would be that his foray to the top of the General Classification was going to be short. Given the circumstances, what choice did Ben have but to complete this Tour with dignity?

Thinking about it he realized there were other routes. Fritz had taken one. He had mysteriously abandoned the team in the night, running off with one of the team cars. That made no sense. At least there were competent apprentice mechanics left.

Luigi came by. "I'm told Pierre went around last night drumming up support for a break in today's peloton."

"Really?"

The Italian nodded. "Do your best to stay out of the middle of the group. I hear there may be some French cooperation today."

"*Grazie.*"

Pierre wasn't taking any risks. After yesterday's experiences he must have decided he couldn't take Ben at his word, so this made sense. Find a way to detain the American in a slower group of riders while his rivals sprinted up the road taking serious time out of him. That would end Pierre's little problem.

As he made prerace preparations Ben tried to hide in the middle of his team, but a journalist approached and singled him out.

"Strange rumors are swirling."

"They always are," Ben answered.

"One claims Banque Fédérale negotiated some back room deals last night."

Ben shrugged. "Isn't that how The Tour works? Alliances are part of the game."

"So is it true that Banque Fédérale cyclists will allow Gunter von Reinholdt to go up the road, even encourage him to take the overall lead from you?"

Ben drew silent satisfaction from the realization that the story was bound to get out. "No comment."

He looked at the time display on his cyclometer. The starter's flag would drop in five minutes. After that he could concentrate on cycling. Once he got his legs moving he figured he could work through this discomfort, but for the moment it felt like walking in mud.

From twenty yards away Kyle glared.

Ben averted his gaze. Out of the corner of his eye he saw a bevy of reporters excitedly surrounding someone. The journalist who had questioned him saw the melee too and, sensing a better story, hurried toward the crowd.

Ben looked at the ground, trying to relax and concentrate. Working so hard to come so close and having it swiped away over politics was more than he could stand thinking about. He had to shove the circumstances from his mind.

Funny how his goals had changed. Yesterday morning finishing the race in Paris had been enough to fulfill him. Now he might well accomplish that but leave disappointed, knowing he could have won. At least he'd see Bridgette again at the end of this stage. She was probably already waiting for him in the next finishing town.

He wished there was a way to call and tell her what Uncle Pierre was up to. Oh well. A stage win on Alpe d' Huez far exceeded his expectations coming into this race. He'd focus on the good and look forward to watching for Bridgette on the last climb.

The noisy nexus of people approached. He looked back toward the commotion. In the center was Thierry, ignoring the barrage of questions and hopping toward him, a large cast on his raised lower left leg.

Ben dismounted his bicycle and handed it to a teammate. He hurried toward the team leader. "What are you doing here?"

"I came to give you a piece of my mind, but it's turned into much more than that."

"Huh?"

"Last night I heard you announce you were not wearing yellow today. I got so furious I told the nurse she'd better bring me to your hotel immediately so I could talk sense into you."

"A nurse brought you here?"

"No. She stuck a needle in my butt, and I fell asleep for eight hours. When I woke I decided I'd better keep my plans to myself. I sneaked out of the hospital, liberated a motorcycle, and headed here."

"Liberated?"

Thierry lowered his voice. "Okay, stole."

"You can't be serious."

Thierry smiled.

"You rode wearing that cast?"

Thierry looked down at the plaster boot encasing his lower left leg. "I reached down and shifted with my hand."

Ben laughed. "I can't believe you."

"I haven't reached the unbelievable part. Halfway here I ran out of gas and couldn't unlock the tank. At three in the morning I hopped two kilometers to a pay phone, then called the team hotel. I couldn't bother cyclists, so I rang Fritz."

"Good ole Fritzy. Why should he get any sleep?"

Thierry smiled. "My thoughts exactly. On the way here he told me about last night's meeting."

Ben frowned. "We've had all sorts of fun without you. There was another meeting this morning, sort of a confirmation of strategy."

"I'm aware, but I bet you can't guess who wasn't."

"How about a hint."

"Monsieur Laurent Robidoux."

Ben stared. "Good hint. You called him? But Pierre said ... "

"Pierre no longer works for Banque Fédérale. As of this morning, I'm Directeur Sportif."

Ben raked his fingers through his stubbly hair. "Wow."

"*Oui*, but there is no time to dwell on it. We must devise a strategy for today."

Ben glanced at the journalists, busy scribbling notes as they tried to piece everything together.

"No time. The race is about to start."

Thierry looked around. "Yes. This will be difficult." He clapped one time. "All right. We'll go over it on headsets once the race is underway. Where is Bridgette today? I hear you find her motivating."

"She should be at the end of the stage. I don't know how you'd find her."

Thierry scratched his head as he turned for the team car, then spun back. "Oh, one more thing."

"Okay?"

Thierry reached behind his back, untucked his shirt and pulled something out. "I refuse to direct this team if you don't wear yellow." He tossed a crumpled jersey toward Ben.

Watching the yellow cloth arc toward him, Ben became intensely aware of cameras clicking, high-speed winders advancing frames, a well preserved moment.

He plucked the maillot jaune from the sky. "I promised the fans I wouldn't. Not today."

Thierry opened a palm indicating all the members of the press. "These folks can explain the change in plans. Put it on now. It's nonnegotiable."

Ben had no desire to negotiate. He shed his purple and green jersey and put on Thierry's present.

As the material settled against his skin he felt an aura of

invincibility. He glanced around. People regarded him differently than they ever had before. The yellow garment carried prestige. Both cyclists and fans were well conditioned to react with respect.

Ben winked at Thierry. "*Merci.*"

"You're welcome. Now go win your own so I can have mine back."

A soigneur wheeled Ben's bicycle to him.

Ben swung his leg over the top tube. "You sound pretty confident, Thierry. What makes you so optimistic?"

Thierry shook his head. "I'm not optimistic, I'm realistic."

All rigidity seemed vacuumed from Ben's upper body. He sagged onto the handlebars. "Wha ... What did you say?"

Thierry shrugged. "Nothing. What's gotten into you?"

Ben felt like a fifteen-year-old boy learning at his father's knee, only this time the opposite argument led to the exact same conclusion. Dad's words came back to him with perfect clarity. "I'm not pessimistic, I'm realistic."

Both Thierry and Ben's father had had their dreams ripped from their grasps, their futures stolen by circumstance. Dad had reacted by avoiding dreams and trying to teach his son to do the same, attempting to protect his only descendant from experiencing the excruciating pain he'd gone through.

Thierry's loss wasn't as drastic, but it was fresh. His reaction was diametrically opposite Dad's, yet they both saw themselves as realistic. How could two men have such conflicting views of reality? It struck Ben that maybe reality is more than where you stand or even how you interpret your surroundings. Reality includes the path traveled to get there—and how you view the trip.

Suddenly Ben knew why his own reality often seemed fuzzy. He knew where he stood. He couldn't change the path that had gotten him here, but thanks to Bridgette and Thierry, Thelma and Bill, even Fritz, his view of the road traveled—and the road ahead—had slowly changed from what his father had wanted him to see. Sometimes things went out of focus when his father's influence surged, but his friends were always there to help him clear his vision again.

Realizing how he viewed experiences, everything from the highs to the lows, were his brain's best effort to make sense of life events, Ben saw how each episode colored the one to come. It was the same for his father. Dad's pessimism was simply a wounded man's way of coping with a world that had stripped him of his most valued possessions.

Ben thought the pessimism was directed at him, and he came to resent his father for it. But Dad wasn't trying to hold him back. He'd been trying to do him the greatest favor he knew how. He'd simply meant to protect Ben from the harsh treatment that had so devastated him.

Ben's vision clouded behind a wall of unreleased tears. He whispered, "I'm sorry, Dad. I know you meant well. Thanks."

"What?" Thierry asked.

Ben laughed self-consciously. He gathered his tears with a swipe of his hand. All these years he'd driven himself to prove his dad wrong, pushing himself because he didn't think the man believed in him. Understanding at last what the world looked like to Dad, Ben realized his father had been his biggest fan.

"Are you okay?" Thierry's eyebrows knotted.

"You just said something that means more to me than you could ever imagine."

Thierry's expression relaxed. "Hmmm. I must be a natural at this directeur job. You ready to roll?"

Ben gave him the thumbs up. Thierry returned the gesture and hobbled away.

Albert wheeled beside Ben. The first lieutenant grabbed the old jersey, removed the racing bib, and attached the numbered cloth to the yellow jersey. "You look awesome, Boss. Now let's go kick some bootie."

Chapter Twenty-Six

Ben looked up at the big screen. A man in a yellow jersey stood straddling a razor-like racing bicycle ... the same jersey Ben had dreamed of every night for years. The man wearing it exuded confidence, competence, and strength. It was Ben's father. Ben studied the mature face. He smiled, and a moment later his father grinned in his characteristic way.

"It's so good to have you back, Dad."

The man on the screen mouthed some words in response. They appeared thoughtful and kind.

The image changed to a yellow jersey sailing through the sky, then a hand yanking it from the air. In the background Thierry smiled.

A hand slapped Ben's shoulder.

Ben turned from the screen to find himself facing Albert.

"Ready?"

"Yeah. I am now."

Standing through the sunroof of a red sedan, the race director swung his white starter's flag, conjuring the peloton to life. Ben's teammates surrounded him like bodyguards about a dignitary. Competitors rolled by, gazing at Ben with respectful expressions. The whole experience felt out-of-body.

Kyle passed by, glaring.

For a moment Ben wanted to glare back, but a newly acquired sense told him such posturing would play right into Kyle's warped reality. Jolting him would be better.

"Good luck, man," Ben said.

Kyle's confident smile sluffed in confusion. With effort he composed himself enough to say, "Unlike you, I don't need luck."

"Suit yourself."

Today, Ben didn't really care what Kyle needed. As long as Ben didn't allow his rival to poison his thoughts, he would possess the victory that mattered most. He controlled reality.

The kinks started coming out of the muscles. The soigneur had worked magic on the massage table the night before. Despite residual soreness and healing scabs he didn't feel too bad for a cyclist halfway through The Tour.

Thierry's voice came over the headset. "Start with a show of muscle. Control the pack from the front. Don't allow anybody to get away until we decide the racing should begin. Is everyone okay with that?"

"Let's do it," Ben answered.

Instantly, purple and green Banque Fédérale riders streamed toward the front of the peloton. Ben fell in behind his last teammate.

"*Bon.* You men look strong. Crank it up to forty K for now," Thierry said. "We'll assess the threat of each attack as it comes. We may let early glory hogs go, but no breathing room for Kyle or Gunter. I'll study maps and forward instructions as the conditions warrant. Any objections?"

Team members exchanged confident glances but no one spoke.

Ben keyed his mike. "We're good."

The tour streamed from the crowded city streets of Bourg d' Oisans and up the river valley. Banque Fédérale controlled the peloton easily as no one seemed inclined to launch an early breakaway. Yesterday's stage had obviously deadened many legs.

Ben was daydreaming, looking forward to talking with Bridgette, as he rounded a tight corner. For some reason, his eyes locked onto a pair of spectators at the opposite side of the road, a hundred yards distant. The two fans looked straight back. The big graying woman jumped joyously, clenched fist above her head. The man, wiry and calm, surveyed the peloton with a more discriminating eye.

Ben felt a magnetic connection between his eyes and theirs. Impossible!

"Go, Ben go! Fly!"

"Thelma? Coach Bill?"

Ben whizzed past, then glanced back. A tear ran down the familiar-looking man's cheek. Ben had to return his eyes to the road ahead.

He keyed his mike. "You there, Thierry?"

"I am. Just studying ... "

"Can you check someone out for me?"

"Depends. Will your fiancé approve?"

"In front of the traveler's rest on the right-hand side. A large enthusiastic woman in a plaid dress, you can't miss her, plus the man she's with."

Thierry chuckled. "Interesting request. I see them now. I'm pulling over."

Ben puzzled through possibilities. Could it have been an amazing likeness? A bizarre coincidence? What had caused him to lock on to them from such a distance?

The headset crackled. "You that kid from Hanksville everyone talks about?" The familiar musical voice sang in Ben's ears.

"It was you! What the ..."

Thelma sounded giddy. "Yesterday morning, the second the race ended, Bill calls and asks, 'Got a passport?' 'Yep.' 'Got scissors?' 'Of course.' 'Then here's the plan. Ben needs someone to fix his haircut. I've booked a flight that just might get us there on time. Meet me at Salt Lake International in four hours ... ' I cut him off right there. 'Four hours! I'll grab my piggy bank and I'm out the door.' I hung up the phone before giving it a second thought. Imagine. France on the spur of the moment! You should'a seen me drive. Pedal to the metal all the way up I-15. I think I left my curling iron on, but ..."

"Geez, you're a talker, Thelma! I'm so happy you're here, though! What a surprise."

"Let me finish, will you? Well, we make the connection at Kennedy just fine and the Paris connection too, but the flight into Lyon still arrived a bit late and Bill says, 'It'll be a miracle if we intercept them but I know a road I'll bet won't be too clogged,' and do you know what? He was right! We zoomed right up, parked, hopped out of the rental, scrambled to the intersection and half a minute later there you come barreling round the corner, all decked out in yellow. Purtiest sight I ever saw!"

Albert slapped Ben on the back. "Who is this crazy lady? I love her!"

Ben couldn't wipe the grin off his face. He winked at other confused teammates as they glanced back, obviously wondering about the message flooding their headsets.

"Thelma. Put Coach Bill on for a second," Ben said.

"Can I spot potential or what?" Bill asked. "I'll tell you, Ben, I've never lived a prouder day in my life. I could burst! Thelma could too. In fact, she nearly did already."

Ben laughed. "This is too much!"

A motorcycle cameraman pulled even and still Ben couldn't erase his smile. He must look silly to the world, grinning like a desert toad in a downpour, but he felt so joyous and confident he couldn't contain it.

"You were right, Ben. I'll never find Bridgette in time, but I think we can squeeze these two into the team car for the day. They seem to motivate you. Besides, they're too entertaining to leave behind." Thierry's words were laced with laughter.

Moments later, Thelma explained the arrangements. She sat in the passenger seat. She couldn't believe they allowed televisions mounted to the dashboard. Watching was fun. She was thinking of doing the same at home. Thierry drove. Good thing that big hunk of plaster was on his left foot rather than his right. Fritz and Coach Bill were already fast friends in the back seat, talking in English about the best chain oils. Nobody knew how they would get back to the rental car.

"Ben, you should have been at my café yesterday. Everybody in the county was crammed in there watching you on satellite TV. They cheered loud enough to trigger a rockslide. Southern Utah will never be the same."

"Sorry I couldn't have been there. How can I ever thank you for coming here instead?"

"Well, truth is I've been thinking on that."

"You have? Out with it."

"How about," Thelma swallowed so hard it could be heard over the headset, "you win one for me today?"

Recollections of requested victories crowded Ben's mind. With them came the memory of simpler times.

He felt a tear in the corner of his eye. "Just like the old days, huh?"

"Yeah. Win one like that," Thelma confirmed.

How simple the task sounded when suggested in such a naïve way—so full of optimism. It also struck Ben as a pretty good idea.

He looked at Albert.

His first lieutenant nodded. "I think we can."

In that moment Ben realized nothing could hold him back. Not anymore. "Okay Thelma, my love. Today the boys and I shall make your wish come true."

The End

Acknowledgment

I owe a huge debt of gratitude to my family. Without their assistance and encouragement I could never have completed this project. They have paid for my obsessions in more ways than I can recount.

Additionally I want to thank Noveldoc.com, the incredible online critique group whose members have taught me so much about the craft of writing. I specifically must mention J. R. (Jilla) Lankford (Noveldoc founder), Alan Jackson, Doug Osborne, Pat Brown, and Kate Jackson. Each one shared detailed observations to assist me in making the final version of this manuscript a far better tale than I ever could have written on my own. I'm also indebted to Noveldoc member Joylene Butler who took me under her wing from the first day I joined the group. She taught me how to turn an idea into a story.

More thanks go to Anne Lemon who did a stellar job of line editing. This book presented many special challenges, and I appreciated her patience in helping me work through them.

I owe Steve Horton, big time. He put up with my many demands as we bicycled together through the Alps, gathering atmosphere and anecdotes for this novel. His translation skills got me out of many a jam, and also resulted in some unforgettable experiences with the wonderful French people. J. P. Seguin Du Haime assistance with French saved me too. In one case he alerted me that my dialogue had a reporter asking Ben, "Are you glad to be dead?"

Finally, I must give special recognition to Keith Pyeatt, the best sort of friend an author could ever have (and I'm saying that about a guy I've never met face-to-face). He learned about this manuscript and volunteered a hand. I'm in awe of his incredible insight. Time and again Keith transformed my struggling ideas into concepts with wings.

There are so many others I wish I had space to mention, but if I did everyone justice this acknowledgment would fill its own book. Thank you all for your various contributions. I'm honored to have such wonderful friends.